FALLEN HEIRS

WINDSOR ACADEMY BOOK THREE

LAURA LEE

∾

Editing: Ellie McLove of My Brother's Editor

Special Edition Cover Design: Books and Moods

a note from the author

FALLEN HEIRS is book three of the Windsor Academy series. This is the conclusion to Jazz and Kingston's story. You <u>must</u> read book one, WICKED LIARS, and book two, RUTHLESS KINGS, prior to this installment to follow the story properly.

This is a dark high school bully romance that may contain triggers for sensitive readers. Due to mature content, it is recommended for readers 17+ only.

chapter one

JAZZ

"Ladies, you look stunning," Charles says as I join them in the foyer.

My sperm donor's words may be kind, but his body language and the accusatory glare he's flashing his wife are anything but. I wonder if he knows about Madeline's affair with Kingston's dad. It would certainly explain his sudden shift in attitude toward her.

Madeline looks nervous, but Peyton seems oblivious as she beams at the compliment.

Meanwhile, I'm fighting nausea as I mutter, "Thanks."

After spending four nights at Kingston's house, Charles sent his driver, Frank, to collect me. Despite my boyfriend's vehement protests—I'm still getting used to calling him that—I got into the car. Knowing Peyton is scheming against me simultaneously freaks me out and pisses me off, but after watching Mr. Davenport's not-so-subtle threat, warning her to stay away from me, I feel slightly appeased, as messed up as that sounds. Peyton may be a conniving bitch, but I do think she has enough self-preservation to hold off on fucking with me for the time being.

Kingston was right about my father's expectations regarding Thanksgiving. When I returned to the mansion, I was promptly given a lecture about propriety and playing nice. He informed me that although I'm eighteen now, I'm still living under his roof, and he's paying my tuition; therefore, I follow his rules.

When I asked him to be more specific, he said, "Quite frankly, I don't care where you sleep at night, or if you're fucking the entire polo team, as long as you're doing it behind closed doors and they come from good stock. But certain obligations come with being a Callahan. There will be times when you will be required to attend a gathering as a member of this family. And when that happens, you will *look* like a Callahan lady and *act* like a Callahan lady. In layman's terms, whatever you would normally do, do the opposite."

As I was mentally flipping him off, I made a note to legally change my name back as soon as possible.

You'd think my own father would make an effort to get to know me, but that clearly isn't a priority for this man. Like I'd *ever* sleep with some douche who played polo. It was no surprise Madeline had a cocktail dress and a team of stylists waiting to get their hands on me to fulfill that whole *look-like-a-Callahan* part. What was unexpected, however, is how sexy the dress is.

Madeline chose a form-fitting sleeveless mermaid-cut gown with a plunging back. Strategically placed black lace appliques set over a nude liner make it look like I could expose the goods at any given point in time. The dress is *gorgeous* and, based on the designer, likely expensive. Still, I would assume it's far too provocative for a holiday dinner. Given my father's reaction when he first saw me, I'd wager he hadn't seen it before now, and he's less than pleased with Madeline for selecting it.

Considering both Peyton and Madeline's dresses are *much* more conservative, I can't help but question my stepmonster's motives, given Kingston's suspicions about some of the guests. I can't lie, though, and say the thought of Kingston seeing me in this dress isn't thrilling. It's a double-edged sword, really; I'd love to have my boyfriend's eyes on me, but not any of the sick bastards who may be in attendance tonight. The other major downfall is there's no way I'll be able to gorge on mashed potatoes in this thing, and I really fucking love mashed potatoes.

Charles looks at his diamond-encrusted watch. "We should get going. Frank is waiting out front." His blue eyes turn toward me. "Jasmine, I trust your date will be here at any moment?"

I don't miss Madeline or Peyton's scowls when he refers to Kingston as my date.

"He texted me right before I came downstairs. He should be here in just a few."

He nods. "Very well. We'll see you there."

Peyton flashes a wicked glare in my direction as she walks away. I'm trying really hard not to look at her differently, but that's easier said than done after seeing the video of her with Mr. Davenport. The way he slapped her across the face, how he forcefully shoved his dick down her throat, the fact that it clearly wasn't the first time either of those things had happened, I'm seeing her in a different light. Dare I say I actually feel sorry for her?

Don't get me wrong; I still think she's a massive cunt who should take the fall for her actions. But *no* woman should be beaten or violated, no matter the circumstances. I have to keep reminding myself that Peyton doesn't live by the same code, and she doesn't deserve my empathy. After all, she sent some guy to beat and violate *me*, not once, but *twice*, without any qualms.

I wonder if Madeline knows about the deal her

daughter made with Satan to split her inheritance, or the fact that Preston is fucking both mother and daughter. For some reason, I can't see Madeline being okay with the latter. Not because she has some sort of moral aversion to an almost sixty-year-old man screwing a girl who just turned eighteen. Considering the massive age gap between Madeline and Peyton's birth father, it's par for the gold digger's course. But Madeline seems like a woman who does *not* like competition, and Peyton is the younger, hotter version of her mother.

I step outside as I hear Kingston's sex-on-wheels car pulling up the driveway. The tint on its windows is so dark, I can't see him, but I can feel his eyes on me as he brings the vehicle to a stop right in front of the wooden double doors. Kingston's big body practically leaps out of the car once he kills the ignition.

Goddamn, he looks good in a tux.

Kingston scrubs a hand over his slightly stubbled jaw and mumbles a curse. His golden-flecked eyes eat me up, probably the same way mine are doing to him, as he closes the distance between us. Once I'm within reach, his fingers bite into my hips as he pulls me into him until our bodies are flush.

"I changed my mind; fuck the dinner. The only place you're going in this dress is my bed." His eyes travel down my body and back up again. "Christ, Jazz."

"You're not so bad yourself." I smooth down the

lapel of his jacket. "But the bed will have to wait until after our fathers' fabulous Thanksgiving feast."

He frowns, probably because he can sense my apprehension beneath the sarcasm. "It'll be okay, Jazz. I'll be right by your side, and if I have to leave for any reason, Bentley or Reed will take my place."

"I know," I assure him. "But it won't change the fact that we'll be in the same room as a bunch of revolting predators. Not to mention the fact that this will be the first time we're seeing your dad after watching that video. I honestly don't know if I can hide my disgust, which would reveal the fact that we're on to him."

Talking Kingston off the ledge after watching that video was no easy task. He was ready to go after his dad and ex-girlfriend, full-throttle, without any concern for consequences. Thankfully, my boyfriend is one of the most logical people I know, and I could leverage that. I reminded him that Peyton and Preston may not be the only threats, and Kingston can't be with me—nor protect me—from prison. The feminist in me hates admitting that I need a man's help, but facts are facts. I'm in way over my head here. Kingston has the information and resources we need to take down these bastards, which takes priority over my pride.

"I know you can do this, Jazz, but if you need a break at any time, just say the word. We'll step out until you can regroup." He bends his knees until our eyes are at the same level. "Okay?"

I gaze into his golden-green orbs and nod. "Okay."

Kingston pulls me into a quick hug, kissing the top of my head, before opening the car's passenger door and helping me in. We keep our conversation to a minimum as we drive, probably because I'm too busy focusing on my breathing to avert a panic attack. As we pull in front of the fancy hotel and Kingston bypasses the valet in favor of parking the car himself, I laugh, grateful for the sudden levity.

"I'm not giving those fuckers the keys to my baby," he explains. "It's one of the rarest cars in the world."

I laugh again. "Of course not. No one drives your *precious* but you."

"Damn straight," he mutters, totally ignoring my awesome Gollum impression.

I raise a brow. "Well, now that you've said that, it's the first thing I'm going to do when I get my license."

Kingston scoffs as he slides the Agera into a parking spot and kills the engine. "Yeah, right. If I won't let someone who parks cars professionally touch it, why would I hand the keys over to a brand new driver?"

I cross my arms over my chest, not missing the way his eyes travel to my cleavage as it's pushed up.

"I bet you'd change your tune if I threatened to withhold sex."

He gives me a good once over, making no attempt to disguise his desire. "Yeah, right. You'd be begging for my dick within hours."

I tell my vag to slow her roll because the bitch *really* likes the visual Kingston's words just conjured.

"You think so, huh? How about we test that theory now?"

The conviction in my tone is lacking, and with the way Kingston is smiling right now, I'd say he damn well knows I'm full of shit.

"Sure, Jazz. Let's see who can hold out the longest. What do you say we make this interesting and add a little wager?"

I eye him skeptically. "What *kind* of wager?"

He thinks about it for a moment. "If I win—which we both know is going to happen—you owe me a blow job every day for a week straight."

My lips turn up in the corners. "And what do I get *when I win?*"

"I eat your pussy until you've come at least three times for a week straight."

I squirm in my seat. "You do realize neither one of those things is an actual punishment, right?"

Kingston's a *big fan* of going downtown, and I don't exactly mind returning the favor.

His shoulders lift. "Bragging rights."

I shake my head, fighting a smile. "You're an idiot."

"Maybe." He grins. "But I'd bet this two-point-five-million dollar car that your pussy is soaked right now just thinking about it. Shall I check?"

I flip him off in reply, but what I really want to do is pull my panties down and shove his face between my legs.

Kingston unfastens his seat belt and leans over the center console to lift my chin. "You feel better?"

My eyes drift shut when he pulls my lower lip between his teeth. "Yeah."

I don't know how this man can always sense what I need. He *sees* me like no one else can. Whether it's tempting me with his body because he knows I need a physical release, or picking a stupid fight because it allows me to vent the frustrations running through my head, or playfully teasing me because I could use a good laugh, Kingston just *knows*. The funny thing is, I don't think he even *tries*. He's so attuned to me, it's pure instinct.

Lately, it seems as if my soul is colored in every shade of gray. Kingston understands that better than anyone because the same war is waging inside of him. If I believed in fairy tales, I'd say we were fated for one another. Like, maybe everything has happened for a reason, and we were meant to fall back into each other's lives at precisely the same moment in time. But then again, I'm not exactly a rescue-me-from-a-tower kind of girl, and Kingston Davenport is certainly no prince.

"You ready to do this?"

I take a fortifying breath. "Let's get this shitshow on the road."

chapter two

JAZZ

Hundreds of eyes track us as Kingston and I walk into the lavishly decorated ballroom. Geez, I feel like I just stepped into a wedding reception, not a holiday dinner. The entire space is filled with round tables dressed in crisp white tablecloths, although most guests are standing around, mingling. Like Kingston promised, there's a decent amount of guests in our age bracket, and every single one of them looks bored out of their minds. Can't say I blame them.

A long, rectangular table sits toward the back of the room—I'm guessing it's reserved for the Davenports and Callahans—complete with a few tall floral arrangements. Crystal chandeliers are glinting off the crystal goblets below while waitstaff are making their rounds, offering hors d'oeuvres and flutes of champagne. I grab a glass of bubbly from a nearby waiter and down half of it in one go. I'm not stupid enough to get drunk at this thing, but I need something to take the edge off. It's either this, or sex in a coat closet, and I don't think Kingston and I could get away with option número dos.

"Why are they all staring at us?" I whisper, stifling the urge to lift my middle finger in the air.

Kingston's fingertips press into my spine as he guides me to the right. "They're all staring at *you*, princess. You're the sexiest belle of the ball."

"It's the dress."

I surreptitiously scan the room, seeing if anyone triggers my perv-o-meter.

Kingston chuckles. "It's not the dress, Jazz, although it is hot as fuck."

My eyes narrow when I spot some politician-looking dude eyeing me like I'm a big, juicy ribeye. "Regardless, this is the last place I want to draw attention to myself."

He laces our fingers together. "I know, but it would've happened no matter how you were dressed. Charles Callahan's long-lost daughter is big news in this circle."

"If that's true, these people need to get a life."

"I won't argue with you there." Kingston points his finger. "There's Ains."

My eyes follow Kingston's finger to find his twin standing next to Reed. Ainsley looks absolutely

14

gorgeous in her dark green one-shoulder gown. Its layered chiffon falls to the floor, and the color brings out the green in her eyes, really making them pop. For a little extra flair, there's a dramatic slit up the front, showcasing her toned dancer's legs. It's sexy, yet classy, which suits her perfectly.

"Wow. You look incredible, Ains."

Ainsley smiles as Reed wraps his arm around her. "Thanks, Jazz. You, too. That dress is... *wow.*"

A low whistle sounds from behind me right before I hear the familiar voice.

"Damn, ladies, you're looking mighty fuckable tonight."

Bentley sidles up to us while Kingston glares at him. I know Bent's comment was absolutely harmless—especially because Ainsley was also included in that statement—but it still pushes my boyfriend's buttons. It's not like that's a hard thing to do, though. Kingston has become even more in touch with his inner Neanderthal lately. Come to think of it, Bentley probably needles his bestie *because* it irritates him.

I playfully jab my elbow into Bentley's stomach. "Yeah? Well, I suppose you look a'ight, too."

Bentley scoffs. "Please, woman. I look fly as hell, and you know it."

He really does. Kingston, Bentley, and Reed have panty-melting features on any given day, but in a tux, we're talking volcanic-explosion-in-your-pants good-looking. I thought they couldn't get any hotter than when they wore their finely tailored suits for homecoming, but clearly, I was wrong. This is upper echelon shit right here.

I glance around, raising my brows as I spot several recognizable faces. Man, Kingston wasn't kidding when he said there'd be some famous people in attendance. It's not like a celebrity sighting is a rare occurrence in LA, but I can't say I ever thought I'd be in the same room as one of Hollywood's hottest leading men.

I point to the actor and whisper, "Please don't ruin it for me and tell me he's on your list of suspected perverts."

Kingston's low growl rumbles in my ear. "I'm half tempted to lie to you, to wipe that thirsty look off your face."

"Oh, stop. You'd have to be blind to miss how pretty that man is." I lift up on my toes to nip Kingston's jaw. "Don't worry, big guy, I'm not going anywhere."

His fingers flex around the side of my waist. "If you tried, you'd best believe I'd hunt your ass down."

I ignore the sudden throbbing between my thighs and, instead, give him a wry look. "I have no doubt, Caveman."

I continue scanning the ballroom until I stumble upon Charles and Preston, chatting with a couple of people. Mr. Davenport's attention wanders as if he can sense someone watching him. My skin crawls when our gazes collide, and his eyes take a leisurely stroll down my body and back up again. Preston smirks when he comes back to my face and sees the shade I'm throwing. If I didn't already know he prefers submissive women, I'd swear the bastard actually *likes* my attitude. Like, legit gets off on it. Thankfully, only a moment passes before his notice returns to the people in front of him.

Kingston's hand tightens around mine when he sees what's snagged my attention. Or *who*, rather.

"Relax, Jazz. He can't touch you."

"Cool as a cucumber over here," I bluff.

"What are we talking about?" Ainsley asks, her confused gaze flicking between her father and us. "*Who* can't touch you?"

Fuck. I forget there's one person in our party of five who has no idea what's going on.

Kingston answers before I get the chance. "There's a good chance the guy who attacked Jazz is here tonight. I was reminding her that he won't have a chance to get to her because one of us will be with her at all times."

Shit. Is that true? I don't know why I didn't think about it before, but it's absolutely possible. We already know he's a student at Windsor, and he knows Peyton, which means he's part of a wealthy family who runs in the same circles. Why did I agree to come to this thing again? Oh yeah, nailing sick fucks to the ground. That thought helps strengthen my resolve.

I straighten my spine, jerking my head to the patriarchs. "Any idea who they're talking to?"

"My parents." Bentley inclines his head toward the couple.

I startle, not expecting that answer, although now that I'm really looking at them, I can see the resemblance. Bentley's dad is a light-skinned African American man, and his mom looks kinda like a Polynesian Heidi Klum. Both are absolutely stunning, which is no surprise considering how attractive their son is.

"Well, that solves the race equation. Sort of."

"What?" Bentley laughs.

"You're racially ambiguous, like Dwayne Johnson," I explain. "Surely that's not the first time you've heard that."

"Never in those exact words," Bentley says. "If people want to know, they usually just ask."

"Eh." I shrug. "It doesn't really matter—I was just curious. I've always known I was biracial, but I think never meeting my father until recently made me naturally inquisitive about other mixed-race people. I know how annoying that question can be, though, so I would've never asked."

Bentley swings his arm over my shoulder, much to Kingston's annoyance. "Well, to satisfy your curiosity, my little kitty cat, my dad's half Irish—

hence, the Fitzgerald—and half Black, and my mom's half German, half Hawaiian."

All four parents look like they're discussing something serious. "What do you think they're talking about?"

Bent shrugs. "Probably VC stuff. My dad owns a firm."

"What the hell is a VC?" I scrunch my nose.

"Venture capitalist," he explains.

"Ah." I nod my head in understanding.

"Should we take our seats?" Ainsley asks. "They should be serving the first course anytime now."

Kingston knocks Bentley's arm off my shoulder and takes my hand, leading me to the head table. However, before we can get there, Charles calls my name, motioning to join him.

"Fuck," I mutter. "Looks like it's showtime."

"You guys go ahead. We'll be right there." Kingston's fingers tighten around mine. "I'm right here, Jazz."

Bentley, Reed, and Ainsley continue their trek across the ballroom, while Kingston and I veer left to meet with the sperm donor.

"Ah, there's my beautiful daughter now," Charles boasts. "Jasmine, I'd like you to meet some people."

I stiffen when Charles wraps his hand around my shoulder, and his grip tightens in warning. "William and Lani Fitzgerald, I'd like you to meet Jasmine."

I pretend not to notice the tension between

Kingston and his father as I exchange pleasantries with Bentley's parents. Mr. and Mrs. Fitzgerald seem like genuinely good people, but it's difficult to relax considering Kingston and I are currently book-ended by his father and mine. Preston is standing slightly behind the Fitzgeralds, so they're oblivious as he pins me with a blatantly lascivious stare.

I know Kingston's trying to ignore the bait, but the rigid set of his jaw and the slight shift of his body to shield me from his father's gaze gives him away. Preston's lips curve into a smile as if he's pleased by his son's actions. Or, more likely, he's pleased with *himself* for getting that reaction. Kingston's dad looks positively gleeful when Charles pulls me back, nearly causing me to stumble. What the hell? It's as if Sperm Donor is trying to widen the space between Mr. Davenport and me. Kingston and I exchange a quick glance, and it's obvious he's just as surprised by that move as I am. You know who's not surprised?

Preston Davenport.

I think he's intentionally goading Charles *and* Kingston right now. But *why?* It's not like Charles has any actual parental instincts that would demand he protect me at all costs. I'm sure that thing he did a few seconds ago was a one-off. This has to be about control. I'm pretty sure I'm standing smack dab in the middle of a power struggle between Kingston's father and mine. Awesome.

Not.

When Bentley's parents excuse themselves to find their seats, Preston turns to me.

"Jasmine, you're an absolute vision in that dress," he practically purrs. "Remind me to thank whoever picked it out later."

"Preston..." Charles says in warning.

"Dad," Kingston grits out at the same time, shifting his body again so he's blocking me even more.

"Relax. It was a compliment—I meant no harm. Although, it seems my son hasn't gotten the memo. He's practically pissing circles around her right now, isn't he?" Preston's greedy eyes are fixed on me the entire time, and I have to put some serious effort into not gagging.

Screw it, if Preston really wants to do this in front of all these people, *game on, motherfucker.*

I straighten my spine and step forward so my shoulders are flush with Kingston's. "Why would he need to do that? It's not like there's anyone here who poses a threat. I mean, I share DNA with this one"—I jerk my head back toward Charles—"and the only one left is *you.*" I take a moment to look Preston up and down, my disinterest clear.

Kingston's fingers tighten around mine so hard, I wince. He immediately loosens his grip, but the warning is clear. I'm not stupid; I know Preston Davenport is a lot more dangerous than he looks on the surface. But guess what? He's not the only one.

Mr. Davenport's cheeks redden. "You certainly are spirited, aren't you?"

I pop a brow. "Your point?"

He pastes a fake smile on his face. "No point. Just an observation." Preston slaps Kingston on the back. "Wouldn't you agree, son?"

Kingston is practically vibrating with rage as he shrugs out of his father's hold. "It's one of the many things I appreciate about her."

"I bet." Preston laughs. "I'm sure she keeps things... interesting."

"Can you not talk about me like I'm not standing right in front of you?"

Preston's eyes narrow, but before he can say anything else, Charles speaks up.

"Enough," Charles commands. We're all careful to keep the volume of this discussion down, but I don't miss the anger in his tone. I thought his ire was due to my insolence, but my father's glare is fixed on Kingston's father when I look up. "Preston, didn't you mention you wanted to speak with a certain *supplier* before dinner? They're about to start serving, so you should probably go do that now."

Preston brushes imaginary lint off his sleeve. "Yes, of course. Thank you for reminding me."

Charles nods.

When his father walks away, Kingston clears his

throat. "We're going to get some fresh air before dinner."

We don't bother waiting for Charles' response; we just walk away. Once we're outside on the balcony, Kingston yanks me into a darkened corner and wraps me in a bear hug.

"Fuck." He takes a few deep breaths before pulling back to frame my face with his hands. "Are you okay?"

"Are *you?*"

He shakes his head. "Doesn't matter."

"Like hell, it doesn't!" I argue. "It looked like you were two seconds away from knocking your father out cold."

Kingston presses his forehead against mine. "That's because I was."

I sigh. "Kingston."

"I couldn't stop thinking about the video." He pulls back to look me in the eye. "I can't unsee that shit."

He turns his face into me as I run my finger along the length of his eyebrow. "Me, either."

Kingston looks around to ensure we don't have any possible eavesdroppers. "I thought I could handle it; that it'd be just like any other day I had to put on the front. But when I saw the way he was looking at you, I wanted to fucking *kill him*, Jazz. Right on the spot, no concern for witnesses. I was envisioning bashing his head into the floor until brain matter was seeping out of his skull."

I cringe from that disturbing—yet, also strangely satisfying—visual. "We can't let your dad get to us, Kingston. He'd win, and that's *not* an option."

"Agreed, but it's not going to be easy. Suspecting my father wanted you was one thing. *Knowing* he's fantasizing about you while fucking someone else? That he sees you as a barrier between him and ten billion dollars? It's an entirely different ballgame, especially when you're within his reach. I don't want you anywhere near him, Jazz." Kingston blows out a breath. "Logically, I know he wouldn't have actually touched you in front of all those witnesses, but it's like my brain short-circuited. That crap he just pulled? He wouldn't be so brazen if he wasn't confident in his ability to win whatever game he's playing."

"Speaking of games… is it just me, or did it seem like he was goading my sperm donor? Do you think he knows your dad is sleeping with Madeline?"

"Maybe." He shrugs. "Shit's definitely going down between them, but my gut is telling me it's bigger than an affair."

"Like what?"

Kingston shakes his head. "Add it to the list of things I don't know."

"So, what do we do now?"

He leans down and pulls my lower lip between

his teeth. "We go in there and play nice. Completely act like that entire encounter never happened. After we eat, I make my rounds, then we can ghost this place."

"Pretending that didn't happen is easier said than done when we have to sit at the same table. Just thinking about that look your dad gave me makes me want to vomit."

Kingston tilts my chin up. "Don't give him the satisfaction of knowing he rattled us. You're the strongest person I know, Jazz, and my near freak-out back there was just a blip. I wasn't prepared for his aberrant behavior, but I am now. We just have to remember nothing's off the table when it comes to Preston Davenport. And you and me? We're a team. If anyone can do this, it's us. Don't let him fucking win this round, Jazz."

"I won't." I throw my shoulders back, steeling my resolve. "*We* won't. If your dad wants to fight dirty, let him. We'll just have to show him what badasses we can be."

Kingston smiles. "There's my girl."

chapter three

KINGSTON

The head table is one of those rectangular ones that's set apart from the other guests. I frown when I see place cards, indicating where each person should sit. There's a total of eight place settings, with—surprise, surprise—our fathers in the middle, lording over everyone. Madeline and Peyton are seated to Charles' left, and my sister and Reed are to my father's right.

Ainsley must've specifically requested Reed's spot because neither my dad nor Charles are considerate enough to think of something like that. The place card bearing my name is directly next to my dad's, so this should be interesting, to say the least. Since Jazz and I are the last two to arrive, we don't really have the option of rearranging the cards. Switching to another table defeats our objective.

"Assigned seating?" Jazz whispers. "Seriously?"

I lean into her ear. "It's bullshit, but the one good thing is you're three people removed from my father."

"I'm not sure Peyton's much better," she mumbles. "They'd better be serving mashed potatoes, or I'm staging a goddamned riot."

I laugh and lean into Jazz to kiss her cheek before she takes a seat.

"Whore," Peyton mutters under her breath.

I glare at my ex-girlfriend, but Jazz doesn't let it get to her. She simply raises an eyebrow and says, "Aw, what's the matter, Peyton? Jealous much?"

Peyton huffs and turns to Madeline while Jazz averts her attention back to me.

"Behave." I wink. "I'm right on the other side of the table if you need me."

She makes a shooing gesture. "Yeah, yeah. Go sit down. I got this."

Neither one of us misses the attention we're garnering from all three parents—and I use that term loosely. Jazz and I share a knowing look, silently acknowledging that we're on display. The second I sit down next to my father, he starts interrogating me.

"Son." He eyes me as he slowly takes a sip from his wine glass. "I was beginning to think you weren't going to join us."

"Why would you think that?"

A waiter swoops in, so I watch as he fills my glass with some kind of merlot. Once he leaves, I take a leisurely sip from my glass—even though I can't stand this stuff—before turning my gaze to the left, waiting for a reply.

"You and Jasmine seemed rather... upset earlier."

I lean over and lower my voice so only my father can hear me. "You'd have to work a lot harder than that to upset Jasmine, old man. She's a tough nut to crack, remember? As for me, it's all part of the job Charles tasked me with, which you made *quite* difficult earlier."

When I pull back, my father's gaze is shrewd. Assessing. I can tell he's weighing the truth of my words. I think back to what he said to Peyton in that video—how he knows I'm in love with Jazz, how he *expected* it to happen. Shit, I don't even know how to explain what I feel for her, but he seems convinced, which means I need to persuade him that he's mistaken. That it's all part of the act.

"Is that so?"

I lift an eyebrow in challenge. "Have I given you any reason to think otherwise?"

My dad's eyes shift down the table in Jazz's direction before coming back to me. "I—"

"Dude." Ainsley nudges my shoulder with hers. "When are they going to serve up the food? I'm starving."

"Me too," I tell her.

Putting up with this dinner every year is only tolerable because the feast is spectacular. I smile to myself when I think about the mashed potatoes, more specifically, how much Jazz will love them.

My father is irritated by the interruption, but I'm grateful to my twin. "We'll continue this conversation another time."

"Sure thing." My tone is dismissive, which aggravates him further, but I pretend not to notice. I simply turn back to my sister and engage her and Reed in conversation.

After the final plates are cleared, people resume socializing, which I take as my cue to work the crowd. Charles is making his rounds with Jazz, treating her like a prized possession as he introduces her to several business partners or acquaintances. My girl looks miserable, but I don't think anyone else can tell. She knows I need time to gather information, so she's taking one for the team. I ensure Bentley has an eye on Jazz before I seek out the man I'm looking for. Unsurprisingly, Alexander Ivanov— one of my father's suspected associates—is standing next to my dad off to the side, deep in conversation.

Both men straighten as I approach.

"Kingston! It's good to see you again." Alexander extends his hand. "Preston and I were just talking about you."

My grip is probably tighter than it should be as I shake his hand. "All good things, I hope."

Alexander chuckles. "Of course, of course."

"Alexander was just telling me about a holiday party he's hosting in his home," my dad says. "He was encouraging me to invite you and Jasmine to the festivities."

"You don't say. That's awfully kind of you to think of us."

Fuck, I hate this schmoozing shit, especially with pompous assholes like this.

"Of course I'd think about you," Alexander assures me. "You are the heir to Davenport empire, after all. So, what do you say? It's next Saturday."

"I'll have to check with Jasmine and get back to you."

Going to this dickhead's house is probably one of the last things I want to do, but it could be fruitful, even I have to admit. That doesn't mean I want Jazz anywhere near him, though.

Alexander flashes a confused look in my father's direction.

"I'm afraid my boy here has his hands full with the Callahan girl. She's not exactly keen on taking orders. *Yet.*" My dad laughs conspiratorially. "I doubt she'd be... receptive if Kingston accepted an invite on her behalf without consulting her first."

My father's not wrong, and I fucking hate it that he knows that about her. Hell, I hate it that he knows *anything* about her.

Deep lines form around Alexander's beady eyes

as he grins knowingly. "Ah, she's a bit of a wild mustang, huh? They're a bitch to tame, but that makes owning them that much sweeter, right?"

I smirk as I imagine clocking this guy in the jaw. "Right."

"What about the blonde with the big tits? The Devereaux heiress? Weren't you two discussing marriage? You still keeping her on the line for some variety?" He holds his hands out in front of his chest like he's grabbing a pair of breasts and wags his eyebrows.

Douchebag.

Neither he nor my dad sees how wrong their misogyny is, nor do they understand why objectifying someone who's barely eighteen is not okay. Ivanov is in his early forties, so the age gap isn't nearly as significant as it is with my father, but still. There's something fucking wrong when a middle-aged man is lusting after a teenager.

"Nope. Peyton has a problem sticking too many dicks in her mouth. And other places, I'm sure." I briefly glance at my father. "She's rather indiscriminate in that regard. You never know who she's going to give it up to next."

My father's eyes narrow, but I'm not sure if it's because I'm putting Peyton's inheritance at risk or because he suspects I know he's fucking her. Probably both. Oh, the tangled webs we weave when we conspire to deceive.

Alexander blinks a few times before he figures out how to respond to that. "Well, if you ask me, you traded up."

Look at that: a kernel of truth amongst all the bullshit.

"I'm not going to argue with you on that."

I scan the room, relaxing marginally when I find Jazz. As our eyes meet, a genuine smile stretches across her face that I can't help but return. Charles pulls her into his side, introducing her to yet another rich prick, causing her to frown. My brows draw together as I mimic the gesture. I hate how uncomfortable she is, being so close to Charles, acting like the perfect daughter he'd like her to be.

I turn back around and find both my dad and Alexander staring at me. Ivanov is giving me a *good for you, son* wink, but my father's gaze is suspicious with a healthy dose of jealousy. It's odd seeing this man be anything but cold and robotic. He's been so closed off my entire life, yet lately, he's practically hemorrhaging emotion. It's fascinating how Jazz's arrival has lifted the veil we all worked hard to maintain over the years. Charles, Madeline, Peyton, my dad, Bentley, *me*—no one's immune. Jazz just has that effect on you. Fighting it is futile.

"If you'll excuse me, I'd like to speak with a few more people before I need to leave." My eyes flick to Alexander. "I'll get back to you about the party as soon as possible."

He nods. "Please do. If it helps convince your lady friend, your sister will be there."

That gives me pause. "Why's that?"

The question was directed at Ivanov, but my dad answers instead. "Alexander's good friend is the dean of the Los Angeles School of Performing Arts. Alex was kind enough to arrange an introduction. I know your sister has her heart set on Juilliard, but it doesn't hurt to have other options, especially one so close to home."

Fuck. Now I have to go, regardless. There's no way in hell I'm leaving Ainsley exposed like that. Who the hell knows what the guest list will look like?

I take a deep breath, reminding myself to stay calm. "We'll talk soon. It was nice seeing you."

On a mission to get to Jazz, I cross the room, but I'm stopped about halfway there when a thirty-something dark-haired man steps in my path.

"Mr. Davenport."

I try to place this guy, but I'm coming up empty. "Do I know you?"

He shakes his head. "No, but we have a friend in common." The man reaches into the breast pocket of his tuxedo jacket and produces a business card.

Rafe Garcia, Financial Analyst

"Oh, yeah? And who's that?"

"John Peterson."

My eyes instinctively scan the room, looking for anyone who might be listening to this conversation. What is this guy playing at? Did my dad somehow find out about John? Did he hire this guy to get information out of me?

"I'm sorry, but I don't think I know anyone named John Peterson."

Rafe smiles softly. "I understand your hesitancy. I wanted to introduce myself so you could put a face to a name. The number on that card leads to an untraceable cell. Talk to John; he'll vouch for me. Afterward, give me a call, and we'll arrange a time to meet."

I don't like being caught off guard like this one bit. Tucking the card into my jacket pocket, I say, "Like I said, Mr. Garcia, I don't know anyone named John Peterson. If you'll excuse me, I was on my way to speak with someone. Enjoy your evening."

He nods. "You as well."

I reach Jazz and Charles right as a senator and his wife are walking away. "Charles, do you mind if I steal my girlfriend away?"

He looks irritated, but he's not going to make a scene. "Of course not. You kids have fun."

I wait until we're out of earshot before speaking. "You ready to get out of here?"

"*So* ready."

Neither one of us says a word until we're inside

my car, away from any prying ears. I didn't get to speak with nearly enough people tonight, but my instincts were screaming at me to get Jazz away from my dad. He's in a mood, and my gut has never led me astray before, so I wasn't about to ignore it now. Besides, since attending Ivanov's party is no longer optional, I'm confident I'll have another chance. He and my father have multiple *friends* or business associates in common.

Jazz sighs as she buckles her seat belt. "I swear, if I had to meet one more congressman, or judge, or whatever, I was going to scream. You should've heard some of the sickeningly sweet things my sperm donor said about me. He had them all eating out of his hand."

"I'm sure. To Charles, it's all about the show and how many people he can stuff in his pocket."

"Ugh. I don't know how someone lives their life being so fake. They all had the same shiny veneer."

I shrug. "When you grow up in a world where material possessions or power determine your worth, you get used to performing. It's all most of us have ever known."

"Well, if you ask me, that's a shitty way to live. I don't know how anyone could do that long term. I could barely handle it for what? Half an hour, maybe? I had to physically bite my tongue as Charles paraded me around like a goddamn trophy. Every time he touched me for whatever reason, even though it was only my shoulder or arm, I was fighting the urge to recoil or cuss him out. I couldn't stop wondering about my mom. If she ever had to work a crowd like that and how she handled it. Or if she ever looked at me growing up and was reminded of him somehow."

"I highly doubt *anything* about you reminded your mom of *him*."

"Yeah, but you don't know that *for sure*," Jazz challenges. "He's half the reason I exist, and considering what you suspect about how I came into this world, how could she *never* look at me and be reminded of that time in her life?"

She has a point, but I'm not about to let her think she shares any traits with that man. I've known Charles Callahan my entire life, and he and Jazz couldn't be more opposite.

"Well, I made it out of there without throwing any punches, so I think we should consider the evening a win. I've no doubt my dad would've somehow used a distraction like that to his advantage, which was the main thing holding me back."

"The fact that *I* didn't throw any punches in Peyton's direction after all the snide comments she made makes this evening a win."

I laugh. "But it would've been fun seeing the look on Peyton's face if you did."

Jazz's full lips curve. "Yes. Yes, it would have." After a moment of silence, her smile morphs into a frown. "There is an end in sight, isn't there? We won't always be chasing monsters, right?"

I grab her hand over the console and press my lips to her knuckles. "Not if I have anything to say about it."

chapter four

JAZZ

"What about this one?" Ainsley holds a red lacy bra in front of her. "It's hot, right?"

"It is," I agree, thumbing the price tag. "But are you really going to spend four hundred dollars on a bra?"

She holds the lace to her chest, looking at herself in the gilded mirror. "Why wouldn't I?"

I pinch the bridge of my nose. "Because you could probably get almost the exact same thing at Victoria's Secret for ten percent of that?"

Or Walmart for about three percent of the cost, but I leave that thought to myself.

Her delicate chestnut brows furrow. "But... this is *La Perla*. Handcrafted Italian lingerie. And it's a Black Friday deal, so it's really only like three-hundred and twenty."

I love Ainsley to death, but she really has lived a sheltered life when it comes to things like money. I legit almost turned around and walked out the door as soon as I saw the first price tag in this store. I mean, we're in Beverly Hills—on Rodeo, no less—so I knew stuff would be well out of my pay grade, but I had no idea the designer markup was *this* ridiculous. It makes me a little sick knowing my own dresser is filled with equally expensive lingerie, no doubt, thanks to Madeline. That scrap of lace in Ainsley's hands could be almost a month's worth of groceries for some families.

"Never mind." I shake my head. "It's pretty. You should get it."

"I don't want pretty. I'm looking more for *I-want-to-rip-that-off-with-my-teeth* sexy. This is part of Reed's Christmas present, after all."

"That it is." I wag my eyebrows. "Grab some matching panties with cutouts in the back, and you're golden."

"Jazz!"

My lips kick up in the corner. "What? You're the one who decided to give the gift of anal for Christmas."

My voice was quiet enough that no one else could've possibly heard us, but Ainsley's cheeks turn crimson anyway. God, she makes it so easy to give her a hard time about Reed's inner freak.

"That reminds me... I need to buy some things online when I get home."

"Like what? Lube?"

A snooty blonde picks that moment to walk by and scoffs in disgust, making me laugh.

Ainsley covers her face with her hands. "Oh, my God."

"C'mon, Ains. You know I'm just giving you shit." I pull her hands away. "See what I did there?"

She shakes her head with a smirk. "You're ridiculous."

"Maybe." I shrug. "But you love me anyway."

"I do, Jazz. I really, really do."

"Likewise, babe." I give her a soft smile. "Hey, what do you know about this party next weekend?"

When Kingston told me about this holiday party, my first instinct was, *hell no*, but when he mentioned Ainsley would be there, I had to consider it.

She picks up a yellow balconette bra and holds the satin garment out before deciding against it. "Not much. Just that some guy my dad works with on occasion is throwing it. But apparently, he's connected to some other guy at the Los Angeles School of Performing Arts. There might even be a few instructors in attendance. I thought it would be good to make that connection, and my dad agrees, which is why he invited me to come along."

"So, you're going to the party *with* your dad?"

"No. Reed's coming with me, but my dad will be there."

"I thought you were dead-set on Juilliard?"

"I was." Ainsley grabs a few pairs of panties. I have to remind myself not to mentally add up how much money she's spending.

"But?"

"But... I don't know if I want to move across the country anymore."

"Because of Reed?" I guess.

She sighs. "I don't want to be the girl that skips out on her top choice for a boy, but it's not just Reed that I'd miss. It's my brother, Bent, *you*. You all plan on staying in Southern Cali, and I don't want to be that far away from you. I know we could visit, but it's not the same. Besides, it's not like the LASPA is a crap school. They have one of the highest post-graduation placement rates in the country. They're constantly funneling graduates into the Los Angeles Ballet."

"Why are you at Windsor anyway?" I quirk my head to the side, surprised I haven't thought of this before. "You've known you wanted to dance professionally since you were little. It's not like there aren't several performing arts high schools in the area."

"I actually got into one of the best, but my dad guilted me into attending his alma mater. 'Davenports graduate from Windsor, and you are a Davenport, Ainsley.'" Her voice drops a few octaves on the last sentence. "That's why I take so many classes. They even offered me a teaching job after winter break, which would look great on paper, so I think I'm gonna do it. I don't think many people realize how many hours dancers need to practice each week to go pro."

"So, you can't hone your skills during the day—even though that *was* an option—and you have to maintain a full academic course load? Then, not only keep up with homework but attend dance classes for hours after school, leaving very little time to just be a normal teenager." I shake my head. "What a selfish ass."

"I'm used to it." She shrugs. "He's been that way for as long as I can remember. That's why I'm always trying to do stuff on the weekends. I want to have a normal teenage experience, like boyfriends, and parties, and hanging out with my friends. As much as possible anyway."

"You really think you'll stay in LA?"

"I guess it depends on where I'm accepted."

"Well, I'm not going to complain if you do because I can't leave Belle." I point a stern finger at her. "But only if you stay for the right reasons, *not* for a boy."

Ainsley smiles. "Reed actually offered to go wherever I go. He's been applying to schools in New York just in case."

I raise my brows. "Things between you two are

that serious already, huh? Damn, when you commit, you *commit*."

She chuckles. "A, Reed and I have known each other almost our entire lives. This thing between us has been brewing for *years*. And B, you're one to talk, lady. You do realize I see the way you and my brother look at each other, right? How different he is since you've been around? I was really worried about Kingston for a while, but you make him *happy*, Jazz. I think it's the first time I've seen him *genuinely happy* in over ten years."

Since before their mom died.

I can't imagine how awful it must've been for Kingston and Ainsley growing up with their cold-hearted, absentee father after losing their mom. I may not have had much during my childhood, but I was loved. Belle and I never wanted for affection, even with as often as our mom worked. We knew she did that because she was trying to make a better life for us.

And when the three of us *were* together? My mom would always ensure it was pure quality time. Whatever we chose to do—whether it was playing games, going to the beach, or having movie nights— all three of us were involved and actively engaged. I'd give anything for another chance to snuggle with her and Belle while we watched Disney movies.

Will I ever stop missing her so much?

My phone buzzes in my pocket, making me

jump. I smile when I pull it out and see a text notification from Kingston.

Kingston: Are you two done yet??? How long does it take to buy shit?

Me: Impatient much?

Kingston: When I'm waiting to see you? Always.

"See!" Ainsley points at me. "That look on your face. A minute ago, you looked sad, but now you're practically *glowing*."

I roll my eyes. "I am *not*."

"Sure, Jazz. Whatever you say."

I give her the finger before typing a reply to her twin.

Me: We're at La Perla, but I think this is our last stop.

Kingston: Tell me more... Better yet, send me a pic from the fitting room. *prayer hand emoji *prayer hand emoji

I chuckle, still getting used to the fact that this broody boy likes to use emojis. I would've pegged him as more of an *only-type-in-complete-sentences-using-proper-grammar-all-serious-all-the-time* kind of texter.

Me: Sorry, but I'm not the one doing the shopping. Your sister is picking out skimpy lingerie to wear for Reed right before they get it on. Or maybe WHEN they're getting it on.

I can just imagine the horrified look on his face

right now. As dirty as Kingston can be, he wants no part of sex talk when his sister is involved.

Kingston: You are the *devil emoji

"What's so funny?" Ainsley asks as she sees my amused expression.

I hand her my phone so she can scroll through my convo with Kingston.

"Oh, man, you're so awesome. I bet he's literally gagging right now."

"Probably." My thumbs fly over the screen as I type my reply.

Me: I'll make it up to you with a *kiss emoji *tongue emoji *eggplant emoji *OK hand emoji

Kingston: You're forgiven. And I'll GLADLY return the favor *tongue emoji *peach emoji

I snort-laugh as I shove the phone back in my pocket.

"Now what?"

My lips twitch. "You don't want to know."

Ainsley has the same *no-go zone* rule when it comes to talking about her sibling's sex life.

"Ugh." Ainsley's face is scrunched like she's sucking on a yellow Sour Patch Kid. "New subject. Have you decided what you're doing for your sister's birthday?"

Belle is turning eight soon. This will be her first birthday without our mom, so I want to make sure it's extra special.

"Kingston said he's working on something, but

he won't give me details until he gets confirmation because he doesn't want to get my hopes up."

"What kind of confirmation?"

I shrug. "Dunno. I told him I wanted to be involved in the planning because she's *my* responsibility, but he said it's a surprise for me, too. He promised I would be happy with the outcome if he could make it work. He's never failed to deliver a good time when he makes Sunday plans, so I'm sucking it up. Making the day great for Belle is what's most important."

"He loves her, too, you know." Ainsley smiles.

"Huh?"

"Belle. Kingston loves Belle, too. I've never seen him so invested in a kid before. I think it's partly because she's an extension of you, but also because he enjoys being around her. His face lights up when he talks about her."

"He talks about my sister? When? What does he say?"

She nods. "Every time you take her out. If I'm not with you guys, he has to recap the entire day for me. Did you know she FaceTimes him sometimes?"

"What?!"

Ainsley chuckles. "Yep. I think he programmed his number into her iPad as a backup, or whatever if she couldn't reach you. But she called him one day, and they talked for over an hour. Then, they started making it a semi-regular thing."

"They did not."

She makes an X over her heart. "Bible. I was with him in the pool house the first time it happened."

I shake my head in confusion. "Why am I just now hearing about this? And no offense, but why am I hearing about it from *you* and not *him?*"

"Honestly? I think it's because he's afraid you'll think he's using her to get closer to you."

I blink a few times, not really knowing how to respond to that. I *have* thought that more than once, at least in the beginning. Belle doesn't keep secrets from me, but she obviously kept this to herself, which tells me she cherishes those private conversations with Kingston. She wants a special connection with him because she loves him, too.

"And you *don't* think that's the case?"

Ainsley's head slices to the left, then the right. "Not at all. I think he just really likes being around her. Maybe Belle reminds him of what life was like before he became so jaded."

I dab at the corner of my eye. "Is he ever going to stop surprising me? Kingston really is one of the good guys, isn't he?"

I already knew there was more to Kingston than he lets most people see, but being there for Belle like this, with no ulterior motive? That's something someone who plans to stick around would do.

"He is," Ainsley confirms. "Unless you threaten the people he loves. I don't know why, but I think we only got a glimpse of what my brother's capable of when he was beating that Lawson guy into a pulp, Jazz. I honestly couldn't tell you how far he'd be willing to go to hurt someone—and I probably don't *want* to know, to be honest—but *good* is the last word I'd use to describe his intentions. Kingston's a-hundred-percent alpha when it comes to his pack. If you fuck with his people, he'll rip you to shreds."

I don't doubt that for a second. The question is, why do I find that so hot? One of life's mysteries, I suppose.

chapter five

KINGSTON

"How was the dinner?" John asks. "Any progress?"

"Not as much as I would've liked," I admit. "But I had to get out of there. My dad was in rare form."

"How so?"

I rake my fingers through my hair. "He was much bolder than I would've liked with Jazz."

"I can't say I'm surprised after watching the footage from his office. Your father seems more... emotionally reactive than usual."

After we came across the video of Peyton and my dad in his office, I sent John a message with the time stamp so he could view it as well.

"He is, which is really starting to concern me. Preston Davenport doesn't *do* feelings, and he's too much of a control freak to allow others to outwardly affect him, yet that's changing more and more each day. I had to get Jazz out of there last night. I was worried either she would cause a scene, or I would. His behavior caught us off guard."

"I bet."

"Speaking of being caught off guard... a man introduced himself to me at the party. I've never seen him before, but he said he knew you."

"He mentioned me by name?" The surprise is evident in John's tone.

I nod before remembering he can't see me over the phone. "Yeah, which for obvious reasons didn't sit right with me. He gave me his business card and said you'd vouch for him. The guy's a financial analyst, I guess."

"What's this guy's name?"

I look down at the card. "Rafe Garcia. You know him?"

My PI doesn't say a word for a good thirty seconds. "Could you describe him for me?"

"Mid to late thirties, average build, brown hair, possibly Latino. His voice was pretty gravelly."

"It's from an on-the-job injury quite a few years back."

My brows lift. "So you *do* know him?"

"Yeah, I know him," John confirms.

"So what's his deal? And how does he know about our association?"

John clears his throat. "Well, one thing I can tell

you is Rafe's definitely not a financial analyst, and Garcia is an alias."

"Like Peterson," I surmise.

"Exactly." He chuckles.

"So, if he's not an analyst, why is he pretending to be one? What does he actually do?"

"He's an FBI agent—an old buddy of mine. If he told you I'd vouch for him, he wants you to know that."

John was an agent before he became a private investigator. I've always suspected Peterson wasn't his real last name, but he's never confirmed that until now. I don't know much about his past, other than the fact he worked deep undercover. It's likely why he's so damn good at his job. He left the bureau after some major shit went down, but couldn't shake feeling restless. Being a private investigator allows him to get his fix, I guess.

"So, this guy is an agent? You think he's undercover?"

"I'll have to make some calls to be sure."

I let out a heavy breath. "I don't like that he sought me out at that dinner. What if my dad saw us? What was he doing there in the first place?"

"Kingston, the one thing I do know is that Rafe wouldn't have approached you unless he felt it was safe. He's highly trained to assess risk, and he's damn good at his job."

I rub the back of my neck. "Do you think the FBI is watching my father or Callahan? Or both?"

"If they are, it's going to make my job a lot easier."

"Why's that?"

I swear I can hear John smiling. "Because the FBI likes to push boundaries when it comes to outside *contractors*, so to speak. They'll happily share their information and resources. If Rafe wants me to be their liaison—which I suspect he might, considering the way he approached you—I'd have a lot more manpower at my disposal."

"Why would the FBI do that? It seems risky."

"Because if shit goes south and an agent isn't directly involved, the government can deny any involvement. But if things *do* go the way they planned, you have the agency behind you to make arrests and protect your anonymity. If you ever see news breaking of a mob bust, that's a perfect example. They'll often use someone on the inside because crime outfits don't take well to newcomers. But you never hear about those people, do you?"

"Why do I feel like I just stepped onto the set of a mafia movie?" I mutter.

"Those are a lot more accurate than one might think." He laughs. "Rafe obviously knows I'm digging, and if he knows that, it's because he was looking *very* carefully. I know how to cover my ass, and only someone with a certain skill set could trace me."

I stretch my neck from side to side. "And this Rafe guy has that skill set?"

"He does."

"So, why not just approach you if you already know each other? Why come to me first?"

"What exactly did he say to you?"

"That we had a friend in common—*you*—and that he wanted me to put a face to a name. He told me to call him to arrange a meet after you vouched for him."

"Knowing Rafe, it's as simple as that. You were in the same place simultaneously, and he took the opportunity to meet you in person. He would've known I'd fill in the blanks as soon as you talked to me."

"So, I should call him?"

"Hold off on that for now. Let me make a few calls, and I'll get back to you with our next steps."

"You really think this guy could help us take down my father and Callahan?"

"I think it's worth a shot."

Well, shit. How can I say no to that?

∾

"Damn," Reed says. "This is a good thing, right?"

I just finished telling Reed and Bentley about John's FBI friend. They were hanging at Reed's house, so I came over as soon as I hung up the phone.

"John thinks it could be. He's going to dig into it a little before figuring out what our next course of action should be. Whatever that is, it needs to happen soon. I don't know how much more of this I can take."

Reed frowns. "What do you mean?"

"My dad... his fixation on Jazz. I've had no trouble focusing on the endgame for two years, yet it's a struggle every damn day now since I saw that video of him with Peyton. And with the shit he pulled yesterday? I wanted to kill him, dude. *I literally wanted to end his life* on the spot. I know he's planning to do something really messed up, and Jazz is at the center of those plans. It scares the shit out of me."

"How can you be so sure?" Bentley asks.

"Because I know him," I deadpan. "I've spent my life studying him. The man's a sociopath and completely fucked in the head. I've watched him treat women like shit for years, and I've never felt right about it, but that's not what this is. I've never seen him so obsessed over anything. It's like he wants more than just sex with Jazz. He wants to *own her*, mind, body, and soul. The craziest part of all... I honestly think he might have some warped idea in his head that she'd want to be with him."

Bent's lips thin. "That's insane."

58

"I never said he was sane." I shrug. "The thing is... I don't get it. *At all.* He barely knows her, has been around her less than a handful of times. I think that's why I feel so off-kilter. It just doesn't make any damn sense."

Reed clears his throat. "Could this have anything to do with her mom?"

My eyes swing to him. "What do you mean?"

"He knew her mom, right?"

"Yeah. And?"

"Do you think it's possible maybe he was obsessed with *her*, and he's transferring those feelings onto Jazz?"

My breath whooshes out of me. "Holy shit. Now, that *does* make sense."

Why the fuck didn't I think of that earlier?

Reed lifts a shoulder. "Maybe it's not so complicated after all."

"Fuck." I scrub a hand over my face. "That might make it worse. He would've had *years* to develop an obsession with Jazz's mom. Who knows what the hell happened between them back then? The only person I could've ever flat out asked is dead."

"Dude, maybe this FBI thing could be the breakthrough you've been waiting for." Bentley pulls the pool cue back and breaks, sinking two stripes. "Maybe you just need to keep him away from Jazz until they can make arrests. Go out of town for a while. You two could make arrangements to take online coursework."

I shake my head. "She would never leave her sister, and even if that weren't an issue, Jazz is too fucking stubborn to run. Plus, that would be suspicious as fuck. We can't afford to do anything that would tip my dad or Callahan off. Besides, we have no idea how long it'll take for the FBI to do their thing. John said they won't make a move without enough irrefutable evidence because they only have one shot at it."

"Well, shit," Bentley mutters while lining up his next shot.

I take a long pull from my water bottle. "Agreed."

Bent fiddles with his phone for a sec before Foo Fighters' "The Pretender" starts blasting through the Bluetooth speakers.

I raise my drink to him. "Nice song choice."

He smirks. "I thought it was appropriate."

Bentley finally misses, so Reed grabs a cue and sinks the three-ball. "Ains just texted to say they'll be here in a few."

Ainsley and Jazz decided to meet us here after their shopping excursion. Reed's parents went to their cabin in Tahoe for the long weekend, so we have the place to ourselves. Both of our fathers are home, so Jazz and I will probably crash in one of his guest bedrooms tonight.

"I got the trip all worked out," I say. "I'm going to tell Jazz tonight."

Bent gives me a fist bump. "Damn, son, somebody's gettin' some extra good lovin' tonight."

I roll my eyes at this fool. "That was happening regardless."

Jazz's little plan to withhold sex crashed and burned real fast. She lasted a whole ten minutes after we got back to my place last night before she was practically gagging for it.

"What are you so smiley about over there?" Reed asks.

Huh. I didn't realize I *was* smiling. "Just remembering something from last night."

Reed gives me a knowing look. "Ah. Got it."

These fuckers can read me too well sometimes.

"So, Jazz has *no* idea what you have planned?" Bentley's lighter flickers as he takes a hit from his pipe.

I shake my head. "None."

Belle's eighth birthday is coming up, and Jazz wanted to do something special to celebrate. Since I wanted to do something special for *both* of them, I made arrangements with Belle's dad to have her for the entire weekend. I can't wait to see the look on that adorable little girl's face when we pull through the gates at Disneyland.

"Belle's going to be pumped when she sees where we're going. Neither one of them has ever been to

Disney, so I got MaxPasses. I was going to do the whole VIP thing, but I think Jazz would prefer to roam the parks without a tour guide."

Bentley's eyebrows draw together. "How can you grow up in Southern Cali and never go to Disneyland?"

I give him a moment to think about it before I see the proverbial lightbulb flicker on. Disney theme parks aren't exactly cheap. Honestly, I don't know how the average middle-class family affords it, let alone someone who grew up in state housing.

Reed and Bent are wearing matching shit-eating grins.

"What's that look for?"

Reed's lips twitch. "Never thought I'd see the day, man."

I frown. "The day for *what?*"

"That you became a pussy-whipped motherfuck-er." Bentley makes a whip-cracking motion—complete with sound effects—to emphasize his statement.

I flip these assholes off as they laugh it up.

"What's so funny?"

Reed's eyes light up when Ainsley walks into the room. "Just giving your brother shit."

My lips twitch when Bent switches the song.

She makes some weird rolling hand gesture. "By all means, don't let me stop you."

My eyes narrow. "You can all fuck right off."

When Jazz walks into the room, I fist the hair at the nape of her neck and land a solid kiss on her mouth. Damn, she looks good today. She's fine as hell on any given day, but for some reason, even more so right now. I was inside this woman less than twelve hours ago, but I can never seem to get enough.

"Not you. You can fuck *me*, though." I wag my eyebrows suggestively as Cardi B raps about parking a Mack Truck inside a little garage.

Jazz's chocolate eyes twinkle in amusement. "I'm so sure."

I smack her ass as she walks past me to take a seat on the leather couch. "Just name the time and place, baby."

"How was shopping?" Reed asks my sister.

Ainsley smiles. "Let's just say I'm glad I borrowed Kingston's Rover."

"You should see the dress Ainsley bought for that holiday party. It makes her ass look *spectacular*. I mean, it was already great to begin with, but the dress is straight fire. I bet you can't wait to see it, huh, Reed?" Jazz flashes a toothy smile and makes a spanking motion in the air.

Sadly, that mind-reading thing between the guys and me works both ways, so I know *precisely* what Reed is thinking right now. The twin link is also in full effect, so I have a pretty good idea what's on my sister's mind as she widens her eyes at Jazz, although I try my damnedest to bleach all of it from my brain.

Reed's eyes flash briefly to me before working their way over to Jazz. He looks pensive as he considers her question, though I doubt he's trying to formulate a response. He's probably wondering exactly how much Jazz knows about his sexual proclivities. My eyes wander to her, wondering the same thing because it seems like she's purposely fucking with him.

Jazz and I have engaged in some light ass play, which she definitely enjoyed, but we've never actually had a discussion about full back door access. I don't *need* it like Reed does, but I can't say I wouldn't love to have Jazz's tight ass hugging my cock. I find myself curious about how open-minded she is on the subject.

Fuck.

I really need to think of something else because the last thing I want is to have a boner in front of my sister and these two jackasses.

My eyes narrow in Reed's direction as I join Jazz on the couch, pulling her back into me. "Don't answer that."

Reed holds his palms out. "Wasn't planning on it."

My sister scoffs. "Idiots."

Bent abandons their game of pool and takes the seat next to Jazz. He places a small bud in the bowl of his pipe and hands it to her. "Ladies first."

"Such a gentleman." Jazz wraps her lips around the mouthpiece, making me think about her wrapping her lips around my dick.

Shit. I'm doing it again. I squeeze Jazz, grinding my growing erection against her back to get some relief. She wiggles as she pushes into me before turning her head and winking.

I pinch her side and lower my mouth to her ear. "Don't push me, Jazz. I'm *this close* to dragging you out of here." I hold my index finger and thumb an inch apart to demonstrate.

"Put the club away, Caveman."

Jazz attempts to pass the pipe to me, but I decline. If she keeps teasing me like this, we won't be in this room much longer. If she wants to call me a caveman, I'll throw her over my goddamn shoulder and show her a caveman.

"You're going to pay for that later."

"Bring it, babe," she retorts.

I groan. This girl is always testing my patience and self-control. I've obviously become a masochist because I get off on the shit.

Big time.

chapter six

JAZZ

Thanksgiving break went by way too fast if you ask me. I spent most of it at Kingston's except for my shopping trip with Ainsley or my weekly date with Belle. I still can't get over what Kingston has planned for Belle's birthday. It was so hard not spilling the beans when I saw her yesterday. Kingston and I agreed to keep it a secret until we get there. I've never been to Anaheim, but he said there are Disney signs everywhere as soon as you get into town. Kingston thinks there's still a good possibility it won't register with her until we're pulling the car through the gates, though.

Belle's going to absolutely freak, and I can't wait to see her reaction. And if I'm honest, I'm crazy excited myself. I already have a list of princesses we need to see, and I'm sure my sister will want to hit up some fairies too. It's bittersweet in a way because I always thought if I did have a chance to go, it'd be with my mom and Belle, but I know our mom would want this for us. She loved Disney movies—hence, our names—so much so that she ensured Belle and I got to see as many as possible.

Whenever she saw a DVD at a yard sale, or if one was on clearance at Walmart, she'd add it to our collection. Every time we had a family movie night, odds were high we'd choose one of those. I'm glad Belle was able to take that collection with her to her dad's house. Maybe one day, she can pass on the tradition.

"You ready to do this?"

I blink rapidly, taking in my surroundings. I was so lost inside my head, I didn't even realize Kingston and I had pulled through the Windsor Academy gates.

I turn my gaze toward my boyfriend. "If I have to be."

"At least we only have a few weeks until winter break." Kingston's eyes twinkle in amusement. They're extra green today, with just tiny little flecks of gold. It always amazes me how drastically they change color. "Then, ten weeks until spring break and after that, just over two months before we're out of this hellhole for good."

I smile. "Not that you're keeping track or anything."

"Noooo. Not at all." He smirks before his expression turns somber. "You know, I honestly didn't mind school all that much before you came around."

I scoff, crossing my arms over my chest. "Gee. Thanks a lot."

He reaches over and untangles my limbs. "Not what I meant. It's just that things were easy for me. I could go through the motions with minimal effort beyond classwork. Nobody got in my way; one day bled into another. It was actually a nice reprieve from all the bullshit I had to face with our dads after school."

"What changed?"

"Since you've arrived... I'm hyper-alert all the damn time. At first, it was because you intrigued me, and I was trying to puzzle out what made you so different. Now, I'm constantly keeping an eye out for anyone who'd try fucking with you. And before you say it, I know you don't *need* me to do that, but I can't help it. That inner caveman of mine you love so much demands it. Plus, it's pretty obvious you hate this place, and that doesn't exactly give me the warm and fuzzies."

I pop a brow. "Does *anything* give you the warm and fuzzies?"

"I can think of something that keeps me *nice and warm*."

"I meant *besides* my vag," I say dryly.

His stupidly kissable lips twitch. "A couple of

other places come to mind, but I can't speak from experience on one of them. *Yet.*"

I shiver involuntarily as heat spreads between my thighs. "Are you really bringing up anal right now?"

Kingston shrugs unapologetically. "It's been on my mind."

I laugh. "Oh, really? What makes you think I'd be interested?"

"Oh, you'd be interested." His eyes burn a path down my body and back up again. "I can't stop wondering..."

"Wondering about *what?*"

"Whether Taco Truck Shawn took *both* of your virginities." Kingston places his hand on my bare thigh, giving it a little squeeze.

I slam my hand over his when he tries creeping under my plaid skirt. "First of all, it's still *just Shawn.*"

Now his eyebrows lift. "And secondly?"

"And secondly..." My eyes narrow when he shrugs out of my hold, and his hand starts climbing. My breath stutters when he reaches the lacy trim of my cotton panties. "Secondly..." My legs part involuntarily, giving Kingston better access. I grip the edge of the leather seat when he runs an index finger over the crotch of my panties.

"What's the matter, Jazz?" the asshole taunts. "You lose your train of thought?"

"Fuck off."

I gasp and throw my head back as he dips

beneath the material, sliding his finger through my wetness. I'm glad he took the Range Rover this morning so we're high enough off the ground where a passerby couldn't see what we're doing unless they come right up to the window because I *really* don't want him to stop. Kingston's tongue traces a line down the nape of my neck as he inserts two long fingers inside of me, all in one go. I'm so embarrassingly wet, there's no resistance whatsoever.

"Mmm... I'd rather fuck *you*. But I'll have to settle for this right now."

He pulls back, studying my face as he pumps his fingers in and out, carefully cataloging each one of my features. I'm sure my eyes are as wild as his, and I can feel the flush in my cheeks. Kingston's gaze lowers to my mouth as I nibble on my bottom lip, trying not to make any noise. It takes considerable effort because the boy is just as talented with his hands as he is with other parts.

The pad of his thumb is drawing lazy circles over my clit, bringing me closer and closer to the edge. I squirm as he curls his fingers inside of me, triggering the mother of all orgasms. It comes on so suddenly, I inhale sharply from the surprise as I ride the wave. Kingston removes his hand from under my skirt once it ebbs and begins the process of licking his fingers clean. It's utterly obscene and self-evident why he's doing it, but I'm too blissed out in my post-orgasmic haze to care.

He flashes a wicked grin. "You never answered my question."

"Yeah... well..." I gesture to my lap, where my panties are still askew. "You distracted me."

"Not going to apologize." Jesus, could he be any smugger?

I look out the window and see the parking lot is entirely devoid of people. When my eyes flicker to the clock on his dash, I curse.

"Fuck. We're late for first period."

"Totally worth it."

"Yep." I pop the P at the end.

"So? You gonna answer the damn question?"

I give Kingston a lazy smile. "I don't want to tell you because then you'll get all, *'Must be the first—and only, if I have anything to say about it—to conquer'* on me."

"All the answer I need, babe." He grabs the back of my neck and presses a hard kiss against my mouth. I can faintly taste my arousal on his lips. "And you can bet that sweet, *untouched* ass of yours that it won't be that way for long."

"So cocky." My eyes roll to emphasize my point.

Kingston's full lips quirk. "There's a reason for that."

Yes. Yes, there is.

I don't give him the satisfaction of saying that out loud, though. The last thing Kingston Davenport needs is for someone to feed his enormous ego.

Instead, I stick my tongue out—adding a middle finger for good measure—but that only makes the jackass laugh.

My eyes narrow. "You're lucky I like you."

"Oh, you do, do you?"

I hold my thumb and pointer finger half an inch apart. "Just a little bit."

His big body climbs over the center console and lands on the back seat.

I turn in my chair. "What are you doing?"

Kingston reaches over and unbuckles my seat belt. "Don't act surprised, Jazz. You're the one who threw out the gauntlet."

"And what are you going to do about it?" I'm pretty sure my tone couldn't have possibly been loaded with more sass.

"I'm going to remind you that you like me a *helluva lot more* than 'a little bit.'" He extends a hand. "Now, get your ass back here."

If anyone asked, I'd deny it until I was blue in the face, but I'm reasonably sure no one has *ever* hopped into a back seat faster.

~

"Has Ainsley said anything about me lately?"

I smile up at Reed. "She says lots of things about you."

While we're walking down the busy hall, I can see

him giving me the stink eye out of my peripheral. "Like what, specifically? Has she said anything about... 'cause it seems like maybe you know..."

I prop my foot against a locker that's adjacent to my last class of the day. I share the same class with Ainsley, so it's pretty ballsy of him to be asking me this right now. She should be here any second. "Know about *what?*"

"About me. About *being* with me."

I sigh. "Look, Reed. I'm not going to violate girl code, but let's just say Ainsley is a happy girl. You make her very happy *in all ways*. If there's anything else you want to know, you need to ask her."

Reed looks unsure. "You genuinely mean that? She's not weirded out?"

"Why would she be weirded out? Because you happened to think she has a *really* great ass? Anyone with eyes can see that."

His green orbs widen. God, I love fucking with him.

"You *do* know."

"Haven't the slightest clue what you're talking about, buddy." I pat him on the cheek condescendingly.

He scrubs a hand over his face. "Christ, I can see why Kingston's so frustrated all the damn time."

"Meh." I shrug. "He may act like he hates it, but you and I both know that's not true."

His lips twitch. "Touché."

"Hi, guys."

Speaking of the woman of the hour...

Reed's face brightens when his gaze finds my bestie. "Hey." He cups her jaw with both hands and plants a kiss right on her mouth.

My eyebrows lift. "So, you're doing this now, huh?"

"Guess so." Ainsley's still giving Reed starry-eyes when she answers me. "What was that for?"

"Missed you," he murmurs against her lips.

She briefly closes her eyes and smiles softly. "Missed you, too."

Ainsley and Reed have been pretty quiet about the fact that they're together during school. They said they didn't want to deal with the mean girls' cattiness while their relationship is so new, but I guess that's no longer a concern.

"Aw, you two are so cute, it makes me want to puke in my mouth."

Ainsley flips me off as she sneaks one more quick kiss. "You need to haul ass if you're going to get to math in time. I'll meet you by the car after class."

"Have fun." Reed gives her a discreet pat on the butt before walking away.

"Why are you blushing, Ains?"

"Shut up." She rolls her eyes as she leans against the wall.

We still have a few minutes before class, so we take advantage of that to continue our conversation.

"What were you and Reed talking about before I got here?"

"You."

"What *about* me?"

"He's still having doubts that you're not okay with his..." I lower my voice before adding, "kinks."

She pulls back, her delicate brows raised in surprise. "Reed said that?"

"Sort of. As much as he could without revealing what that thing of his is. He suspects I know, but I haven't confirmed anything."

Ainsley smirks. "Well, to be fair, you're not exactly subtle about it."

I shrug. "I respect the fact that Reed wants to be discreet, but you know damn well the guys know. And I hate bringing this up, but odds are, most girls he's been with know too, so it's not like it's a take-it-to-the-grave kind of secret. He has nothing to be ashamed of, but I don't think he believes that."

"I think I know the reason behind that." She sighs heavily. "His parents are *über* conservative. Judgy assholes, really. Reed's grown up listening to them preach about Christian values, which they like to fall back on to justify their bigotry. In reality, their behavior is very *anti*-Christian. He doesn't buy into their bullshit—especially after what they did to his sister—but I think he still fights a lot of deeply-rooted stuff in his head."

"Reed has a sister?"

"Yep." Ainsley nods. "She's four years older, but they're close. Reed usually spends most of the summer break at her place. He actually asked me if I wanted to fly up there for Christmas."

"Why haven't I heard about her before?"

Ainsley's shoulder lifts. "She moved to Oregon literally the day after graduation with nothing but the clothes on her back. Couldn't get away from their parents fast enough."

"Why? What happened?"

She frowns. "Regan—that's her name—is bisexual. She decided to finally come out to her parents toward the end of her senior year because she fell in love with a woman and didn't want to hide her feelings anymore. The 'rents were *not* okay with it in the least. Those jerks threatened to cut Regan out of their will unless she got that *'lesbian nonsense'* out of her head. In turn, she told them if they couldn't understand that love is love, regardless of what that looks like, they could take their money and go fuck themselves with it."

"That's sad."

"Very. Regan's girlfriend, Cass, had some family in Portland, so they packed up and left town as soon as they could. When Reed told his parents about Regan and Cassidy's engagement, they acted like they didn't even have a daughter. That pretty much the last straw for Reed—he wants nothing to do with them. He can't wait to get out of that house, either."

I sigh. "Poor guy. No wonder he's so serious all the time. I sorta feel bad for screwing with him now."

"Yeah." Ainsley blows a hair out of her face. "And don't feel bad, Jazz. You didn't know, and he could definitely use a little more humor in his life. He'd understand you meant no harm."

"Well, you should tell him you told me and that he'll get no judgment from me on the matter." I wag my eyebrows suggestively. "And you should *definitely* try convincing him that you're *more than okay* with it. *Whatever* you need to do to ensure he has no doubts, *do it*."

The flush in her cheeks deepens as we walk into class.

"*Buenas tardes, señorita Davenport y señorita Callahan.*"

"*Buenas tardes, señor Reyes,*" Ainsley and I reply in unison.

Before we split off to take our seats, Ainsley winks and says, "I'll see what I can do."

I chuckle. "I bet you will."

chapter seven

JAZZ

If I thought Thanksgiving break went by fast, it was nothing compared to our first week back at school. On Monday, I had a pop quiz in almost every one of my classes because the teachers at Windsor are clearly giant assholes, and it didn't get much better from there. The one nice thing is that Peyton and posse have been relatively quiet, save for a few whispered insults here and there. After school, the guys and I reviewed video footage while Ainsley was at dance class. However, the boys have taken over anything from Preston's offices because I can't stomach seeing the man for any length of time after recent events.

Nothing exciting has happened since we saw Preston abusing my stepsister on that video, although you can definitely sense the growing tension between my sperm donor and his wife. I won't lie and say watching Madeline squirm hasn't been entertaining. We've finally made it to Saturday, where we're just about to head to another fancy party. If you would've told me six months ago I would be attending gatherings like this wearing designer dresses, I would've laughed my ass off.

"There. I think I got it." Kingston finishes buttoning his dress shirt and begins the process of knotting his bright red tie.

"Do you need to test it out?" I straighten the corner of his collar.

"John and I did that earlier," my boyfriend says. "It was just a matter of getting it taped up properly without smothering the mic. All I need to do at this point is to hit the button to activate it once we're there."

It turns out, John Peterson's FBI friend is, in fact, investigating mine and Kingston's fathers. John wouldn't give us any real details because he doesn't want to compromise the case, but he seems to think this is a positive development. Kingston agreed to wear a wire to the party tonight since there's a possibility several vital players will be in attendance. He's also decided to hand over any incriminating video footage we have, though I don't know how Kingston's getting around the fact that he's technically engaging in illegal surveillance. John says he trusts this guy, and Kingston trusts John, so I'm going with it.

"Well, look at that. We clean up well, don't you think?" I gesture to our reflection in the mirror above Kingston's dresser.

His eyes darken as they take me in, lingering on my subtle cleavage for a few seconds. "You look incredible, but that's really no different from any other day."

I'm wearing an emerald green midi-length dress that's fitted through the bodice with a flowy skirt. It's simple and delicate but totally appropriate for my age. More importantly, unlike the last dress I wore to a stuffy event, this one lacks the sex kitten vibe. When I moved to the hills, my closet was filled with beautiful clothing, but there wasn't a single cocktail dress because Madeline says evening wear should only be worn once then promptly discarded. She didn't appreciate my scoff after that ridiculous statement, but it's not like I really give a fuck.

My stepmonster tried buying me something to wear for tonight, but I declined for obvious reasons and raided Ainsley's closet instead. Thankfully, the girl has a massive wardrobe, with items ranging from perfectly chaste all the way over to *this-would-look-perfect-with-a-pair-of-stripper-heels*. I chose a dress on the former end of the spectrum because the last thing I'd want to do is show up to a house filled with pervy old men in an overtly sexy garment.

You'd think I was completely naked, though with the way my boyfriend's gaze eats me up.

The tips of my ruby red fingernails scrape against Kingston's light brown stubble. "You keep looking at me like that, and we're never getting out of here."

"As tempting as that is, I've got a job to do." His full lips curve. "But save that thought for later."

"Uh-huh." I pat his cheek condescendingly to cover up the fact that I want to climb him like a tree. "I'll be counting the seconds until I can get you naked."

"Smartass." Kingston smacks me on the butt. *Hard.*

"Huh," I muse. "I think I can see the appeal."

He laughs. "What?"

My lips twitch. "Nothing."

He stares at me for a moment like he's trying to read my mind. "We should get going."

"Yep." I grab the little clutch purse—also borrowed—from Kingston's nightstand, shoving my lip gloss and phone inside. "Let's do this."

∼

A chill skitters down my spine as I remove my coat and hand it to the butler, shaking my head at the fact that anyone would need an actual fucking butler. Alexander Ivanov, the host of tonight's shindig, lives in a mansion in Brentwood Hills, and it's as opulent as one might expect. The weird thing is that places like this aren't shocking me as much as they used to, and I'm not entirely comfortable with that fact.

Kingston runs his finger down the crease between my brows. I didn't even realize I was frowning until he did that.

He places a hand at the small of my back and leans into my ear. "Relax."

"I'm fine," I assure him. "I was just taking in all the swanky stuff."

His hazel eyes briefly look around as he presses a hand to his chest to activate the wire. "I'm so used to it, it doesn't even faze me."

"And that's exactly what I'm afraid is happening to me," I mumble under my breath.

"Don't worry, Jazz. No matter how long you're in this world, you'll never be like *that*." He nods his head to the Real Housewives of Beverly Hills wannabes.

Holy crap! As I get a better look, I think one of them might be the real deal.

Kingston guides me through the house toward the back end, where most people are gathered.

"Have you been here before? It seems like you know where you're going."

"No." He shakes his head. "But I've been to enough of these things to know how it works. There's a pattern. Women are usually gathered off to the side in small clusters socializing while the men are somewhere else bullshitting or talking business."

"Well, that seems awfully sexist."

His shoulders lift. "It is what it is."

As I glance around, I see what Kingston's talking about. For the most part, the room is awfully segregated, save a few exceptions. One of those exceptions is Ainsley, who we've just spotted standing next to her father and a dark-haired man. My bestie gesticulates wildly as she talks, while Reed stands at her side, looking amused by her obvious enthusiasm.

Preston notices us first and waves us over, rudely interrupting his daughter. "Kingston! Jasmine. Come join us."

Ainsley's eyes fall to the polished floor, not at all surprised by her father's dismissal, which both saddens me and pisses me off. Reed's expression is leaning more toward homicidal now, which leads me to believe he feels the same. She gives me a small smile when I stand next to her and link our pinkie fingers together.

"Alexander, I'd like you to meet Jasmine Callahan." Preston inclines his head in my direction.

"Jasmine, I've heard so much about you." I'm not at all okay with the fact that these two were discussing me. Neither is Kingston if the tic of his jaw is any indication. "You weren't kidding, Preston. From what I recall, she does resemble her mother quite a bit."

I stifle the urge to cringe when Alexander takes my hand and places a kiss on top. "You knew my mom?"

Kingston places his palm on my lower spine, which lends me the strength I need to remain calm.

"Yes," Alexander confirms. "Though, regretfully, not nearly as well as some." He side-eyes Preston as he says that last part.

Preston flashes a smarmy smile. "Your father and I have been doing business with Alexander for many years."

"What kind of business?" Kingston asks.

Preston's goldish-green eyes slice to his son. "A little of this, a little of that. You know how it goes." His gaze returns to me. "Coincidentally, Alex and I met the same evening Charles introduced me to your lovely mother."

"Really?" I tilt my head to the side in question. "I didn't realize she and my father had the kind of relationship where he would introduce her to friends."

Of course, I know Preston knew my mom, but *he* doesn't know I know.

The look Preston is giving me couldn't be mistaken for anything but predatory. Even Ainsley picks up on it. Her curious eyes are volleying back and forth, but I can't worry about that right now. If Preston wants to talk about my mom, I'm taking advantage of it.

"Oh, I knew Mahalia *very* well. I'm surprised your

father hasn't mentioned it. Although he always was rather... stingy when it came to her. Constantly looking for ways to keep your mother to himself. I haven't seen him act that way with a woman before or since."

I have to literally bite my tongue to avoid lashing out at the way he speaks about my mom with such familiarity. "What's that supposed to m—"

Kingston's grip on my hand tightens. "Speaking of Charles... is he here tonight?"

My boyfriend's diversion tactic is jarring, but I know why he's doing it. Preston Davenport is getting bolder by the second. Having this conversation is proof of that. For a man who supposedly prides himself on keeping his composure and maintaining discretion, he's doing a shit job of it.

"No, he's not," Preston answers coolly. "Why do you ask?"

"Just curious, I suppose." Kingston shrugs.

"So..." Ainsley pipes in, obviously trying to diffuse the awkwardness. "Mr. Ivanov, you mentioned introducing me to a friend of yours from the LASPA?"

"Yes, of course." Ivanov smiles. "I last saw him by the parlor. Shall we see if he's still there?"

Kingston and Reed share a look before Alexander leads Ainsley and Reed off in search of his friend. I wait for them to step out of earshot before I start grilling Preston.

"When you say you knew my mom 'very well,' what exactly did you mean by that?"

His lips curve into a smug smile. "Perhaps that's a story for another time. For now... let's just say my son and I have more in common than you might think."

With that cryptic bullshit, he walks away without another word.

"You and your son are nothing alike, asshole," I mutter, turning to Kingston. "God, I literally want to strangle that man."

He glares at his father's retreating back. "Get in line. Although knowing my dad, there's probably *quite a few* other people ahead of us."

"No doubt." I snort. "What now?"

Kingston looks around the open space. "I see a few familiar faces, but they won't speak candidly if you're with me."

"So, I'll hang out here."

Kingston scoffs. "Yeah... no. I'm not leaving you alone for a second. Let's go find my sister and Reed. He knows to keep an eye on you."

"I don't need a babysitter."

"Just humor me, Jazz. I know you're smart and capable, but you're also tiny. You're not strong enough to fight off someone twice your size, no matter how scrappy you get." He points at me as I glare. "Don't give me that look. You know I'm right."

My eyes roll. "What's the worst that could happen to me in front of all these witnesses?"

He blows out a breath. "I'm not taking any chances." When I open my mouth to protest, he puts a finger to my lips. "Stop fucking fighting me. If you won't do it for me, do it for your sister. You can't protect Belle if something happens to you, right?"

My eyes narrow. "That was a low blow."

The jackass doesn't look apologetic in the least. "Then stop forcing me to hit below the belt."

"Fine. Let's go."

Kingston takes my hand and leads me through the crowd until we spot his sister. She and Reed just turned away from the man they were speaking to, so it looks like our timing is perfect.

"Hey," I say to Ainsley. "Was that the dean?"

"Yep," she confirms. "Apparently he's good friends with Madame Rochelle from my studio. She's mentioned me to him. He's going to come watch me practice sometime next week."

My brows rise. "That's a good thing, right?"

Ainsley nods. "It's a *very* good thing."

"That's awesome, Ains. So the odds of you staying in LA just got higher?"

She smiles. "Much higher."

Reed's smile is packed with pride and adoration. If I didn't know he was such a kinky fucker, I'd swear the boy is a giant marshmallow when it comes to Ainsley Davenport. Regardless, it's apparent the guy is head over heels, which makes me incredibly happy for my friend.

Kingston nudges Reed with his arm. "I saw a few people I wanted to say hi to, but I don't want to bore Jazz. You cool if she hangs with you for a bit?"

"Of course." Reed gives a stern nod.

"Duh," Ainsley adds, swinging her arm around my shoulders. "What do you say we go find the booze?"

Kingston and Reed have a silent exchange before Kingston yanks me into him and plants a kiss on my mouth.

"I'll be back soon."

I wave him off. "Do what you need to do."

I watch as Kingston weaves through the crowd. He has his eye on someone in particular, but Ainsley tugs on my arm to get my attention before I can see who he's after.

"Jazz? Did you hear me about the booze?"

"That sounds like a great idea." I could use something to take the edge off from my encounter with her father.

"So... what's up with the weird vibes I was getting earlier?"

I frown. "What do you mean?"

"I mean..." She stretches the last word out. "Why was my dad acting like a total creeper? *And he knew your mom?!* How crazy is that? What did he say after I went to talk to the dean?"

"Uh…" I look to Reed for some help.

"Babe." Reed puts a hand on Ainsley's lower back, guiding her to the bar. "Let's get those drinks. I'm thirsty as hell."

Ainsley giggles and presses up on her toes to whisper something in his ear. Reed's hand flexes around her hip, leading me to believe that whatever she said was filthy. Whatever he says back to her is likely even filthier because she's turning beet red.

Diversion successful. God bless teenage hormones.

After she disengages from the dirty talk, Ainsley's hazel eyes, identical to her brother's, roam the room. "Is it just me, or are there an awful lot of girls our age here?"

I noticed that, too, but I wouldn't exactly know what's considered atypical with these types of gatherings.

"And that's odd?"

Ainsley nods. "Totally odd. Usually, the only women present are freshly Botoxed wives or girl-friends. At least in the parties my dad has hosted at our house. They must be dancers, too, here to meet the dean."

Reed is scanning the room right along with me and based on the wary look in his eyes, I'm guessing the same thoughts are running through his brain. Could these girls possibly be trafficking victims? My recent online research has taught me that sex trades can take on many different forms. On the surface, victims could look like your average happy, healthy person.

But sometimes, beautiful women are used as high-class escorts in wealthier circles. Or they work as masseuses—not to be confused with massage therapists—through seemingly legitimate day spas or likewise establishments. You just never know because things aren't always as they seem. They even have task forces during the Super Bowl, whose sole job is to raise awareness or provide an opportunity for victims to escape during the massive influx of travelers.

Sadly, it's not always easy for a victim to leave, even if they had the chance. The traffickers keep them compliant with threats, blackmail, drugs, material things, or pretty much anything they can use as leverage. One recent study said that girls in foster care are particularly vulnerable. Is that how my mom got sucked in? Is this what she was subjected to?

Ainsley's right—a lot of these women are in their late teens, *maybe* early twenties. Kingston once told me that you can usually spot an interested buyer by watching how closely they observe others. Pay attention to their body language as they track a young woman or, even more disturbing, little girls. As I attempt to do that, I think I spot one.

The man isn't even that old—maybe thirty at best —but he's giving off strange vibes. The redhead he's talking to flattens her palm over his chest, before lifting up on her toes to whisper something in his ear. When he pulls back, he nods and watches her walk away. Another woman—this one blonde and closer to his age than mine—comes up to him with fire in her eyes.

I'm guessing this may be his wife or girlfriend who just happened to witness his interaction with the other woman. The man's face flushes as she presumably rips him a new asshole before stomping off. With slight hesitation, looking down the hall the younger woman walked down just moments ago, he chases after the blonde. I look down the hallway and spot the redhead disappear behind some French doors. My gut's telling me something's not right. I need to make an excuse to step away so I can follow her.

"I need to pee real quick."

"Okay," Ainsley says.

"Hold on a sec," Reed adds.

The man from the ballet school approaches us. "Miss Davenport, may I have another word? It'll be brief; I promise."

Reed looks back and forth between Ainsley and me.

"I'll be fine," I assure him, hitching a thumb over my shoulder. "I think the powder room is right there. I'll only be gone a minute or two."

Reed reluctantly allows Ainsley to pull him aside

while talking to the man. I see him running his thumbs over his phone screen, probably texting Kingston, but I don't waste any time hanging around. I head down the hallway and find the doorway the mysterious woman walked through. It leads to a small brick patio right off of a beautiful courtyard. I get a quick flash of her coppery hair as she disappears into what appears to be a large hedge maze.

I have a feeling I'm going to regret this, but that doesn't stop me from going in after her.

chapter eight

JAZZ

Well, one thing's for sure, this is definitely a maze. I've lost count of how many times I've rounded a corner, and there's no end in sight. I'm trailing behind the woman just enough to avoid being seen, but not too far where I could lose her. The outdoor lighting barely reaches this area, so the darkness helps conceal me, but I still need to move cautiously. Thankfully, whoever designed this thing thought to pave the path, so it's easier to navigate in these damn heels I'm wearing.

My phone is vibrating like crazy in my purse, but I'm not going to risk pulling it out and scaring this chick off. I may have no clue where we're heading, but she certainly does, and I intend to find out what's at the end of this labyrinth. Just when I think this will go on forever, the hedges open up to a patio, like the one at the other end. Behind this one, though, is a small cottage. It seems rather odd to have your guests go through all that to get here, but what do I know? I suppose it would afford them privacy.

The woman walks through the front door without knocking, so I'm guessing she's the person staying in the house. I turn around to begin the long trek back when a familiar voice catches my attention.

What the hell?

I whip my head around and see the redhead had left the door slightly ajar. I slowly creep closer, my eyes darting back and forth to ensure the area is clear. I plaster my back against the stucco siding just to the right of the door and listen carefully. The unmistakable sounds of sex are echoing throughout, and if I had to guess, I'd say there's more than a few bodies inside. It sounds exactly like what I heard outside of the boathouse by the lake.

What is it with these rich people and their orgies?

My ears perk up when I hear the voice that drew me here.

"What took you so long?" the woman asks.

I quickly peek through the crack, and sure enough, Madeline is standing right inside the door, talking to the auburn-haired girl. She's wearing a short, bright red dress that hugs all her curves with a pair of skyscraper heels. I can't hear the other woman's reply over the grunts and groans behind her because she's talking too quietly, but I do hear what my stepmother says next.

"If you want more, you know what you need to do to earn it." Oh shit, she's walking this way. "Were you raised in a fucking barn, Nadia? Close the damn door when you come in."

I press a hand to my chest as Madeline slams the door shut, willing my racing heart to calm down. Fuck, that was too close. I stay crouched down and duck walk to the other side of the house. There's a sliding glass door back here that allows me to see inside. I know it's risky as fuck, but I need to know what the hell is going on in there. Group sex, obviously, but why is Madeline just standing there fully clothed? Staying as close to the exterior wall as possible, I approach the glass to get a better look.

I stifle a gasp when I catch my first glimpse. There aren't many people inside, but it's obvious *why* they're there. I expected to see comfy furnishings, maybe a small kitchen like in Kingston's house, but none of that is here. No, this place has one purpose and one purpose only, and I doubt there's any sleeping or lounging around going on. *Ever.* The lighting is subdued, but still bright enough where I have a clear view of everything.

There are three different contraptions spread out through the open space. The first one is a weird kind of bench off to the right. It almost looks like a neck massage chair, but instead of a set lower seat, the middle section is raised higher with bondage straps attached to each end. A gorgeous naked woman is strapped to the bench, ass high in the air, while a much older—also nude—man ruts into her from behind. I'm pretty sure his dick is up her ass, but I can't quite tell because his rather large, jiggly belly is getting in the way. I wouldn't exactly say the woman is unwilling, but I also wouldn't say she's an active participant. She's just lying there, taking it, occasionally opening her mouth to scream. Whether it's in pleasure or pain, I don't know.

The second setup is a sex swing hanging from exposed rafters on the left side of the room. It's occupied by a young woman with two men about the same age as her sandwiching her in. Her top half is inverted, probably to better accommodate the dick in her mouth. One guy is pounding her from the front, while the one fucking her face is tweaking the nipples on her giant breasts. Just like the first girl, she doesn't seem like she's resisting, and she's definitely awake, but she doesn't seem to be enjoying it either.

In the center of the room, there's a massive four-poster bed. A man with a slightly graying beard is on his back, pumping a hand over his erection. The redhead I followed here approaches him, and they exchange a few words. In the next moment, she lowers the straps of her dress and shimmies out of it, leaving her naked as the day she was born. She then crawls onto the mattress beside him and lowers her head over his cock. He fists her long hair to watch as she Hoovers his dick for a few moments, before slapping her ass, prompting her to climb onto his lap where she rides him, reverse cowgirl style. Without a condom, mind you, which totally ups the ick factor. My eyes widen in panic when her eyes flicker to me, but I don't think she actually *sees* me. She's kind of just staring out into space, going through the motions.

God. What the fuck did I just stumble on?

The entire time, Madeline is standing against the wall, observing each coupling, with a look of sick satisfaction on her face. The front door suddenly opens, and none other than Preston Davenport walks in, surveying the room as he stands in the open doorway.

Fuck, fuck, fuck.

This is exactly the kind of evidence Kingston needs. I fumble with my purse to dig out my cell, but Preston steps into the house as I open the text window. I damn near drop my phone in shock because my boyfriend follows behind him, saying something to his father. Preston beckons him over to Madeline, and the three of them start discussing who the hell knows what while watching an orgy. Whatever it is, their body language tells me it's actually a pleasant conversation, which confuses me even more.

After a few minutes, a fourth naked woman appears from the hallway and approaches Kingston. She trails her talon-like fingernails down his chest, smiling at him coyly. My fists clench as I watch this girl flirt with him, and I could swear he's flirting right back, seemingly unconcerned that she's not wearing a stitch of clothing beyond a pair of stilettos. In fact, if I'm not mistaken, he looks like he *appreciates* that fact. I can't help but notice how many similar features she and I share, from her small stature to her long dark hair, to her bronzed skin. The only drastic difference is the augmented breasts she's jutting toward my boyfriend. Preston says something to his son, and both men laugh while leering at said breasts.

Naked Chick leans into Kingston's ear, pressing her huge boobs against his torso. As she pulls back, he nods, which seems to excite her. Now, this girl is either a great actress or *much* happier to be here than the other three working girls in the room. My eyes practically bug out of their sockets when she drops to her knees right there and eagerly starts undoing Kingston's belt buckle.

Finally—*finally*—Kingston places a hand on her wrist as she pops the button on his slacks. She looks confused for a moment as he says something before she stands, once again smiling. Kingston's hand snakes out and grips the back of her neck, pulling her into him. He can't possibly be.... Tears well in my eyes when he slams his mouth against hers, and they proceed to engage in some tonsil hockey. Bile rises in my throat, but I can't look away if my life depended on it. When Kingston breaks the kiss, Naked Chick takes his hand and leads him down the hallway. The entire time this shitshow is going down, a smug smile is plastered across both Preston's and Madeline's faces.

What in the ever-loving fuck is happening right now?

It takes everything inside of me not to charge after them, telling that bitch to get her hands off my boyfriend. Then again, said boyfriend just *kissed her*, and he didn't exactly seem to mind following her down the hallway, presumably to a bedroom. I squeeze my eyes shut to ward off the looming tears. I want to trust Kingston. I honestly do. But what I just saw was pretty hard to excuse, no matter how you spin it. Has he been playing me this whole time? Was that story about his mom just a bunch of lies? Has *everything* been a lie? I need to get the fuck out of here.

I pull off my shoes and start booking at full speed back toward the maze. I'm running blindly with tears streaming down my face, landing myself in one dead end after another. I can't seem to think straight long enough to focus on where I'm going. My lungs burn from the exertion, the soft pads of my feet are sore from running barefoot on pavement, and my heart aches from what I just witnessed. As I round another corner, I slam into someone, soliciting an "Oof!" from both of us. My back scrapes against branches as I fall into a bush before catching my balance.

"Jazz, are you okay?" a deep voice asks.

I blink my eyes into focus and find Reed and Ainsley, both looking at me with concern. I feel like a giant dumpster fire right now, so I can't exactly blame them. It must've been Reed that I bumped into because it felt like slamming into a brick wall and not the tiny little pixie that is Ainsley.

"Jazz." Ainsley tugs on my arm. "Are you okay? Why are you crying?"

I furiously swipe at the tears on my face. "Yeah... uh, I'm fine. I just got scared because I've been trying to find my way out of this damn maze, and I can't. I guess I kind of freaked out a bit." Neither one of them looks like they believe me, but I do my best to control my emotions. "What are you guys doing here?"

"We were looking for you," Reed answers, holding out his phone. "Kingston gave me the login for his tracker app when you never returned from the bathroom."

I look at the screen, and there are two little green dots right next to each other. Shit, I almost forgot about the tracker he installed on my phone.

"Why didn't *he* come looking for me?"

If Kingston's playing me, who's to say Reed isn't in on it?

Reed briefly looks at Ainsley before replying. "Because he's tied up with something."

Yeah, tied up being wrapped around a whore.

I scoff. "Right."

Fuck. Do not cry, Jazz. Do. Not. Cry.

"He, uh..." Reed grabs the back of his neck. "Said he'll be a while, so he gave me the keys to his Rover so I can drive you home."

Ainsley bites her bottom lip. "Jazz? You ready to go home?"

Well, isn't that a loaded question? I'd do anything to go back home, but the thing is, Sperm Donor's mansion isn't the place.

"Sure. I'm tired, anyway." I sniffle, looking around. "Do either of you know how to get the hell out of here?"

"Yeah. I'm actually freakishly good with mazes. Piece of cake." Ainsley taps an index finger to her temple. "Built-in GPS."

I throw my hand out. "Lead the way."

Ainsley wasn't exaggerating. She leads us out of the maze without any hesitation or errors. I'm quiet the entire drive back, using exhaustion as an excuse the few times she questioned me. The more I think about what I witnessed at that house of horrors, the more I tell myself to take it at face value. Nobody

105

forced Kingston to kiss that girl. To ogle her naked body with such a lust-filled gaze. To take her hand and disappear into a back room, doing God knows what. Oh, who am I kidding? I know *exactly* what they were doing.

Just as we're pulling in the driveway to my house, a text comes in from my boyfriend, forcing me to choke back a sob. I guess I shouldn't call him my boyfriend anymore, considering he's a liar and *a cheater*. I can forgive a lot of things, but the latter isn't one of them.

Kingston: You make it home yet?

I battle my inner smartass, wanting so badly to respond with something sarcastic, but I manage to control myself.

Me: Yep. Just pulled in the driveway. I'm tired, so I'm going to bed. Talk to you later.

Kingston: You sure? I'm about to head out. I can swing by on the way, and you can stay at my place.

Yeah, right. That's not happening.

Me: I'm sure. Really tired. Goodnight.

Instead of another incoming message, my phone rings. I hold it up as I open the car door, showing Reed and Ainsley Kingston's name flashing on the screen.

"I've gotta take this. I'll see you guys later. Thanks for the ride."

"Night, Jazz," they say in unison.

I take a seat on the front stoop as I hit the button to accept the call. "Yeah?"

"You sure you're okay? You sound weird."

"How can I *sound* like anything through a text?"

I'm pretty sure he growls. "You know what I meant, Jazz."

Actually, I'm not sure I know anything about you.

I sigh, telling myself not to cry again. "I'm fine, Kingston. Just really tired. I'll talk to you tomorrow, okay?"

"Reed said you were crying when they found you."

That fucker.

"It's no big deal. I just panicked because I got lost. I'm fine."

"Why were you in that maze, Jazz?"

Why were you in that house, Kingston?

"I thought it looked cool, so I went in to check it out."

He's silent for a moment. "How'd you end up outside when you said you were going to the bathroom?"

"Why does it matter?"

"What do you mean, 'Why does it matter?' You know I didn't want you alone for any reason."

"Why not? Because you were afraid I'd see you doing something you shouldn't have been doing?"

"What the fuck does that mean?"

"Don't yell at me."

"Don't piss me off, and I won't."

I unlock the front door and step inside. Thankfully, no one is loitering in the foyer.

"And on that note, I'm done with this conversation. Goodnight, Kingston."

My phone rings one second after I hang up on him, but I decline the call. He tries three more times before sending a text.

Kingston: Pick up the fucking phone, Jazz.

Not gonna happen, buddy.

Kingston: If you don't pick up the phone, I'm driving my ass over there, and I'll drag you out of the house if I have to.

I know that's not an idle threat, so I move fast. I trade my fancy dress for some black jeans, a matching hoodie, and some Chucks, pulling my hair in a low pony before sliding a beanie over my head. I look like I'm getting ready to do a little B and E, but I suppose blending in is precisely what I'm going for here. I thumb through the contacts on my phone and pull up the one I need.

The deep voice I know as well as my own answers on the first ring. "Jazz. I didn't expect to hear from you anytime soon. What's up?"

I step into my bathroom and flip on the fan in case anyone's watching the camera feed. Fuck, for all I know, Kingston is the one responsible for that camera. "I need a favor. Can you come get me?"

"At your new place?"

I nod. "Yeah. Well, no... but close to it. I'll text you the address to a gas station. Can you pick me up there?"

"Babe, it'll take me at least an hour to get up there."

"That's fine," I assure him. "It'll take me a bit to walk there anyway."

"Why don't you want me to pick you up at your house? Embarrassed to be seen with me?"

"Not at all. It's more like I need to get the hell away from this house as fast as possible."

He sighs heavily. "Okay, baby. Text me the address, and I'll haul ass to get you."

"Thank you." I blow out a breath. "Shawn? There's one more thing."

"What's that?"

"I'm leaving my phone at home, so after I text you, you won't be able to reach me. And don't text me back."

He chews on that for a moment. "What aren't you telling me?"

"I'll explain when I see you. You know I'm good for it."

"Trouble with the rich folk, huh?"

"Something like that. Look, I gotta go. I'll see you soon. Bye, Shawn."

"See you soon, Jazz."

I forward the address to the Chevron, then delete our text thread and the call log before setting my phone on the charger. Going back into my closet, I stuff my ID and some cash in my pocket and grab a jacket off the hanger. At the last second, I grab my backpack off the floor and throw a change of clothes into it. Better to be prepared than not. Good thing I've taken to running outside lately because I've familiarized myself with the area quite a bit. Now, I just need to make sure I stay out of sight during the three-mile walk in case Kingston drives by. I may have a thousand questions running through my head right now, but one thing I'm sure of is that he's coming for me.

chapter nine

KINGSTON

What the fuck is going on with Jazz right now? I don't buy the tired excuse for one second. Reed said she was definitely upset when they dropped her off, and he doubts it had anything to do with getting lost. Why was she in that maze? Did Jazz see my dad and me as we passed through? More importantly, did she overhear our conversation? Is that why she's ignoring me?

Fuck.

All these unanswered questions are driving me crazy. Thank God Reed found her when he did. Who knows what could've happened if my dad and I ran into Jazz? Or, if she made it through to the end of the maze and stumbled on that house? My father was on a mission to test my loyalty. If Jazz saw what was actually going on in that house... there would've been no coming back from that, on several levels.

At least now, my plan can move forward. I may have had to do some things that made me uncomfortable tonight, but I gained quite a bit of ground in the process. As far as my dad is concerned, fucking that woman proved to him that my feelings for Jazz aren't as deep as he thought. That while I'm possessive of her, it's because I don't want to share my toys, not because I'm hopelessly in love with her.

I scrub a hand down my face, shaking my head. I still can't believe they're running a prostitution ring. He didn't divulge many details, and I wasn't going to risk suspicion by pushing it, but he did say what happened in that house only scratched the surface of what he has going on. That sex sells, and he's become incredibly wealthy because of that. He hinted at more business opportunities that he and I could tackle *together*. When I asked about Charles' involvement, he simply said Charles wasn't involved in *everything*, and he planned on keeping it that way. When I inquired about where the women came from, he assumed I didn't like what I saw and said, "There's plenty to choose from if you'd like a more *diverse* selection." That's when he called that Latina chick over, telling her to give me the *golden treatment*.

There was no way in hell I would find out what that meant in the middle of a sex den, especially in front of my father and Madeline, so I asked if there was somewhere more private we could go. Thankfully, he confirmed there was and told the girl to show me to a bedroom. According to my dad, that room is for clients who require the utmost discretion to indulge certain *inclinations*, and they pay handsomely for privacy. I'm guessing those preferences are pretty questionable considering what was going on out in the open like it was perfectly normal. Knowing my dad, though, he probably just didn't want his fuck buddy, Madeline, to see my dick because then, she'd dump his ass so she could attempt to ride me.

I shudder at the thought. I have nothing against a hot MILF, but that woman is the true definition of a femme fatale. No pussy is worth your inevitable demise. Okay, maybe *one* pussy could take me down, and I'd likely be smiling the whole way, but that's less about the organ and more about the person attached to it. Christ, the guys were right. I *am* pussy-whipped. Not that I'd ever admit it, especially to the owner of said pussy. I'm having a hard enough time dealing with all these goddamn emotions she makes me feel.

Like right now, I feel crazed as I park my Rover in front of her house. I don't know why, but my gut tells me that something is very, *very* wrong, and the longer I wait, the worse it's going to get. Thank God Reed thought to drop my car off before he and Ains drove back to his place in hers. My Agera or my bike aren't exactly quiet, and anyone inside would've heard me coming down the road.

It's late, so I use the key Peyton gave me long ago to let myself inside through the garage's side door. I creep through the mudroom and into the kitchen, careful to listen for any signs of people. I've taken this route so many times when I used to sneak into Peyton's bedroom at night, the darkness doesn't impede me one bit. This time though, I bypass Peyton's room entirely and stop in front of Jazz's door. I press my ear against the wood and hear nothing but silence. I test the handle, breathing a sigh of relief when I find it's unlocked.

The second I open the door, my panic increases tenfold. The bedside lamp is on, so I can see Jazz's phone resting on the charger. Both the closet and bathroom doors are wide open, so it's pretty apparent Jazz isn't here. I check the game room across the hall and the basement and back yard for good measure, but I know it's pointless. Jazz isn't anywhere on the property, and she intentionally left her phone behind so I couldn't find her.

What the fuck is going on?

She's obviously running, but why? Jazz is a smart girl, and her survival instincts are spot on. What could've possibly made her feel so desperate to do something so reckless? With no phone and no ride, she couldn't have gone far. I stash her phone in my pocket, head back to my car, and dial Bentley as soon as I start the engine.

"Yo, bro, what's up? You home from the party?"

"Is she with you?"

Bent's silent for a moment, probably trying to figure out why I'm yelling at him. "Is *who* with me?"

"C'mon, man, don't fuck with me. Is Jazz with you? Did she call you?"

"Dude. Back the fuck up. I thought Jazz went with *you* to the party. Why would she be with *me?*"

I grit my teeth. "She *did*. But Reed and my sister drove her home because I was held up with my dad. By the time I got to Jazz's, she was gone, and I have no idea where she went."

"So? Track her phone. Problem solved."

I slam my hand on the steering wheel. "I *can't* fucking track her phone because she intentionally left it in her bedroom. What does that tell you, Fitzgerald?"

"That she's ghosting you." He clears his throat. "What'd you do, dickhead?"

"I didn't *do* anything!" I shout. "Well, not anything she could possibly know about, anyway."

"What does that even mean?"

"Fuck!" I step on the gas as soon as I pull out of our gated community. "Are you home? We're going hunting for feisty princesses. I'll explain everything when I get there."

"Word. Give me just a few, and I'll meet you out

front." He belts out a laugh, although, for the life of me, I can't figure out what he'd find so amusing. "Oh, and Davenport?"

"What?"

"You might want to rethink that little nickname you have for her. Because by the way she rules your ass, Jazz is a motherfucking queen."

I grunt. "Just hurry up and get ready."

I hang up the phone and continue the short drive to Bentley's house, thinking about his parting comment the entire way. He's not wrong—Jazz *is* a motherfucking queen. But he left out one very important distinction.

She's *my* motherfucking queen.

~

"What are you going to do now?" Bentley unfastens his seat belt as I pull in front of his house.

We've been driving all over the place for the last three hours. Bent and I stopped at every nearby park and twenty-four-hour business in the area, which was limited to gas stations, a diner, and a pharmacy, but there was no sign of Jazz anywhere. Reed was stationed in front of Jazz's house just in case she came home, and Ains hung out in my pool house in case Jazz showed up there. About fifteen minutes ago, Ainsley called to tell me that Jazz had reached out to her. Jazz blocked the number she was calling from, but she said she was safe for the night and that she'd talk to Ainsley tomorrow. My sister immediately relayed the message to me, so we'd call off the search.

The fact that I have no idea where she could be pisses me off. It makes me realize I don't know much about Jazz's life before she moved here. She's never mentioned any friends from her old neighborhood, but that doesn't mean she doesn't *have* any. Ainsley said Jazz and that dickhead ex of hers had a pretty friendly vibe—which that in itself really shakes up the hornet's nest inside of me—but my sister doesn't think Jazz was with him when she called.

Whatever Jazz said to her gave Ainsley the impression that she's crashing in a hotel for the night, which marginally settles me. I don't think Jazz would go through the trouble of contacting my sister, knowing she'd be worried about her if she wasn't genuinely safe. I don't understand why Jazz didn't call *me*, though, and why she ran in the first place. It's driving me nuts. Unfortunately, I don't think I'll get those answers until I corner Jazz, which I have every intention of doing later on this morning.

I rub at the knot forming in the back of my neck. "The one thing I'm sure of is that Jazz won't miss spending the day with her sister. We pick her up at eleven every Sunday morning, so if Jazz doesn't come home before then, I'm going to camp out in front of Belle's house until she shows up there. One way or the other, I'll get to her."

"I hate saying this, but you know I'm gonna give it to you straight."

I make a *spit it out* motion with my hand.

Bentley shrugs. "I think you fucked up... at the party, I mean."

"How did *I* fuck up? I was doing exactly what we went there to do. And I made more progress in a couple of hours than I have in the last two *years*. My dad's finally letting me in. He put a lot of trust in me by bringing me to that house."

"I know that," he assures me. "And that's a *really* good thing. But the hooker part? Seriously, man?"

"I didn't have a goddamn choice." I blow out a breath. "If I didn't accept his *generous gift*, as he called it, my dad would've known I was lying to him. It was his way of testing my loyalty to him, and I *passed that test* with flying colors. It had to be done, man."

"Yeah, but what if Jazz finds out?"

"There's *nothing* to find out," I argue. "And even if there was, my dad or Madeline wouldn't say shit because they'd have to explain their role in that whole situation."

"I still think you need to come clean. Didn't you two agree that you wouldn't keep secrets from each other anymore?"

"She wouldn't understand this." I shake my head. "If I told Jazz, the only thing that would accomplish is hurting her, and she's had more than enough pain over the last few months. I'm not going to add to it."

"I think you're making a mistake, man."

"It's my call to make. Stay out of it, Bent."

"I care about her, too, you know. I have a right to be concerned."

I scratch the light stubble forming over my jaw. "I know you do, but it's still my call. *Drop it.*"

His brown eyes narrow. "I don't get it. Wouldn't you rather have Jazz hear about it from your point of view? It's not like you—"

I hold a hand up, cutting him off. "I said, *drop it.* Unless you or Reed tell her—" I glare right back at him, "*which neither of you will do*—she won't know. It's better this way."

Bent shakes his head. "I think you're making a big mistake."

"Yeah? Well, then I guess it's my mistake to make, isn't it? Since she's *my* girlfriend."

He frowns. "You're a dick. You know that?"

I scoff. "Trust me, buddy. I'm *well* aware."

chapter ten

JAZZ

"You sure about this, babe?"

I sigh and turn to Shawn. "I just told you about all the shit I'm dealing with. Why would you even question my need to protect myself?"

He sucks on his full bottom lip for a moment. "Who would've ever thought your life would be *more* dangerous moving out of the projects? If I didn't know you so well, I'd swear you were making this shit up."

I scoff. "My life has become a telenovela. Why would *anyone* make that shit up?"

Shawn's lips twitch, probably remembering all the time we've spent bingeing Latinx soap operas on Netflix. We used to make fun of all the preposterous storylines, and now I'm living one. How's that for irony?

He reaches over and fingers a lock of my hair. "I happen to have some fond memories involving those ridiculous shows."

I suck in air when his eyes darken. More often than not, Shawn and I would only make it through half an episode before we'd wind up screwing on his bed. Chemistry was never a problem for us, and it's clearly still not an issue for him, but I'm not on the same page. Hell, I'm not even in the same book.

Pushing his hand away, I say, "Shawn, don't."

"C'mon, Jasmine, forget about this crazy-ass plan of yours. Why don't we turn around and go back to my place? You know I can make you feel good."

I undo my seat belt and pull the door handle. "Please don't make me regret asking you for help. You're the only person I have."

Great, now he looks pissed. "You said it yourself. He cheated on you tonight. He's probably been lying to you all along. That pretty boy doesn't deserve you."

I pinch the bridge of my nose. "That doesn't make it hurt any less, and two wrongs don't make a right, Shawn."

"And you think meeting up with Tiny will make it right?"

"Nooooo. I think meeting up with Tiny will give me some reassurances that I desperately need right now. You're the one who always preached about never relying on someone else to protect me. That if anyone ever comes at me, do what I need to do to save myself. *This is me doing that.*"

Shawn pulls his hat off and turns the brim backward before putting it back on. "I don't fucking like this, Jazz."

"Duly noted. But I'm still going in there."

He curses. "If you insist on doing this, I'm not letting you walk away until I know for sure you can handle the damn thing. We'll go to a range or something in the morning."

"Can't." I shake my head. "Sundays are the only days I get to see Belle."

"Well, then we'll go Monday."

"I have school on Monday."

"You're going back there? Seriously?"

I rub my temples. "I have to. You know I can't walk away from this."

"If something happens to you..."

"*I can't not try.* Besides, something can happen to any one of us when we least expect it. My mom is a perfect example of that. She waited at that bus stop almost every damn day without incident *for years.* I bet she didn't think she'd get caught in the middle of a drive-by on her way to work that morning and never make it home. I doubt anyone thinks that when they're going through their regular a.m. routine."

"I wouldn't say *no*body," he argues.

I roll my eyes. "You know what I meant."

Shawn grabs my arm to halt my progress when I try getting out of the car. "Hold up a second, a'ight? If we do this, you need to promise me that you'll be careful."

"I promise. You know I overthink almost everything. I'll be safe."

Shawn yanks the keys from the ignition with a nod, and we both make our way over to the worn-down apartment building. Shawn raps on the door in a one-two-one pattern. After listening to several locks disengaging, it swings open a moment later. The man filling the doorway is the exact opposite of small, which makes his nickname hilarious. Seriously. Dude's six-and-a-half-feet tall and easily three-hundred pounds. To most, he's a scary mofo, but to me, he's just Shawn's brother from another mother.

Tiny steps aside and flashes a toothy smile. "Damn, girl, you're getting better with age."

I smirk. "Thanks, Tiny."

Shawn punches his arm. "Back the fuck off."

His best friend takes a step back and holds his palms out. "Chill. Didn't realize you two were a thing again."

"We're not." I shake my head.

Shawn scowls at that, which makes Tiny laugh.

"So, to what do I owe the honor?" Tiny gestures for me to have a seat on the brown leather couch.

My ex-boyfriend takes a seat on the cushion

beside me. "Jazz needs a piece. Something small and easy to handle, preferably."

"You don't say..." Tiny's brows raise in surprise. "Someone giving you trouble, shorty?"

I nod. "You could say that."

Tiny cracks his knuckles. "All right, then. Step into my office."

He gestures for me to follow him into a bedroom. At first glance, it seems like a standard guest room/office combo. There's a daybed against one wall, a small bookshelf, and a desk on the opposite wall. I'm confused as he pulls out the trundle under the bed until he reveals an army green storage container in the hollowed-out section of the mattress. Tiny fiddles with the lock before lifting the top off, revealing an assortment of handguns, neatly organized from largest to smallest. He picks up a little black one, checks the magazine, and hands it to me.

"These are all ghosts, so you don't need to worry about anyone tracing it. This one has minimal recoil and great accuracy. The only real downfall is there are only six rounds, but it's perfect for someone your size. I don't usually sell ammo—don't want to risk anyone turning a loaded weapon on me, ya know? But since I know you're cool, I'll hook you up. The State of California has really strict buying laws, so come see me when you need more."

"I'd appreciate that." I test the weight of the gun in my hand. "How much?"

Tiny rubs his chin. "Normally, I'd say six hundred, but you qualify for the family discount. Can you do four?"

I dig into my pocket and pull out the cash I brought with me. After this, I'll only have one-hundred and forty-two dollars left to my name. I really need to get a job.

I peel off four Benjamins, which he stuffs in his pocket and begins the process of closing up shop. Once the bed no longer looks like an armory, Tiny turns around and places a small box of 9mm bullets in my hand.

"Be careful, girl. It was good to see you."

"Thanks, Tiny. You, too."

$\approx$

Shawn digs a rectangular tin out of his pocket and slides it open. "My shop got this awesome new strain from Colorado. It's potent as fuck. The pre-rolls came in yesterday, so I grabbed a pack before they sold out. You wanna give it a try?"

Ah, the benefits of working at a dispensary. You get to sample all the best weed first.

"Why the hell not? It'll probably help me sleep. There's no way that's happening naturally at the rate my brain's running."

"Hey, flower's a-hundo-percent *au naturel.* Anyone who says otherwise is spreading fake news."

I incline my head. "Touché."

He lights the J as it hangs from his lips, permeating the air with a skunky smell. After taking a puff, he passes it over so I can do the same, then we repeat the process a few more times. Shawn offered his couch for the night, which I gladly accepted. By the time we left Tiny's, it was already after midnight. Shawn's place is less than a mile from my sister's, so this makes it much easier for me to get to her in the morning. I'll just have to take her somewhere we can get to by foot or bus and figure out how I'll get home after.

"You really think this Ainsley chick has no clue?"

"I wouldn't have called her if I didn't. She's a good friend and an even better person. I knew she'd be freaking out, and I didn't want her to worry about me all night." My head swims as the weed suddenly hits me. "Whoa, this *is* good shit."

Shawn laughs before taking another hit. "It really is. You know my tolerance is through the roof, but this shit hits me a lot quicker than anything else I've tried."

I get teary-eyed when his statement makes me think of Bentley. "Can I use your phone again?"

"Jazz. It's after two."

"I know."

"I'm not giving you my phone so you can call that prick."

"Not calling him."

"Then, who?"

"Shawn." I hold my hand out, palm up. "Please."

When he hands the phone over—albeit reluctantly—I open the internet browser and log into my email account. I can't remember who suggested this once, but ever since, whenever I store a new number into my phone, I always email myself a copy of the contact card and keep it in a saved folder. People rarely dial full phone numbers these days, which means they rarely have the chance to memorize them. This ensures I'll never be without someone's info if I lost my phone. Or you know, had to purposely leave it behind because someone installed a tracker on it.

I pull up Bentley's number and dial it after masking the caller ID. Shawn gives me a weird look as I step out onto the back deck, but I don't have the brainpower to figure him out tonight.

"Hello?" Bentley's voice is groggy like maybe I woke him up.

"Were you sleeping?"

I can hear him shifting. "Jazz? Where you at, baby? You okay?"

"I'm okay," I assure him.

"Where are you?" His deep voice is more alert now. And harder.

"Remember when you promised you'd never lie to me again?"

He clears his throat. "Yeah, I remember."

I lean against the metal railing, staring at a flickering streetlight. Shawn lives in a second-floor apartment, so I have a lovely view of the parking lot that belongs to the complex behind his. And a prostitute's ass cheeks while she's propositioning someone at the curb. Southern California has some breathtaking coastlines, but the so-called City of Angels definitely lives up to the term *concrete jungle*. It's busy, loud, and bright, even in the middle of the night. I never minded it before, because it was all I ever knew, but living in the west hills these last few months has shown me something different. I've grown used to the quiet—the stillness.

"Jazzy? You still there?"

I shake out of my weed fog. "Sorry. Been smoking a little."

"By yourself? *Where are you, Jazz?* You scared the shit out of us earlier."

"My location doesn't matter. I'm somewhere safe. Swear."

He sighs heavily. "Why'd you leave, baby girl? What happened?"

"I think you know, Bentley." I choke back a sob. "And I need you to be honest with me."

"Are you crying? Tell me where you are, and I'll come get you."

I shake my head before realizing he can't see me. "Tell me, Bentley. *Please.*"

He releases a pained groan. "You and Davenport really need to learn how to communicate better. It'd prevent a shit ton of problems. I don't want to get in the middle of this, Jazz. I wouldn't *have to* get in the middle of this if your stubborn asses would just *talk to each other.* C'mon, Jazzy, you know Kingston has a reason for everything he does. It may not always be the right thing, but he does genuinely believe it's the *best thing* to do, whatever the circumstances."

"So, you're telling me the best thing to do in this situation was *fuck some rando?*"

He doesn't say anything for at least thirty seconds. "You followed them to that house, didn't you?"

I belt out a sardonic laugh. "No, I actually followed someone else and got there *before* them. But yes, I saw Kingston and his father enter the sex club, or whatever it was. I had a clear view of everything from the back door, which means I also saw my supposed boyfriend *fooling around with a naked girl right before he disappeared with her down the hall.* "

Damn it. I didn't mean to tell him that. My high is obviously making me more loose-lipped than usual.

"Jazz, please call him. It isn't what it looks like. He's in a really fucked up place right now, worrying about you."

I sigh. "Am I a hypocrite, Bent? Am I crazy for feeling so betrayed, considering what happened between the three of us that night?"

"Naw, baby. There's a big difference between stepping out on your boo versus the two of you inviting someone in to play with you. *Talk to him,* and you'll see it's not what it seems. I know my boy, and I know he'd never do something like that to you. You're his world, Jazzy."

I look over my shoulder when the door slides open, and Shawn steps out. "You okay out here?"

"Who the fuck is that?" Bentley shouts angrily.

Shawn scowls, obviously hearing Bentley's words through the phone.

I hold up a finger, asking him to give me a minute.

"Bent, I need to go. I think I just need to sleep this off. I'll talk to you later, okay?"

"Jazz, wait. Don't—"

I end the call and pass it back over to Shawn. "Thanks."

His eyes bounce between mine. "You okay?"

"I really think I need some sleep." A yawn escapes, further proving my point.

He jerks his head over his shoulder. "You can take my bed. I just changed the sheets."

"I'm not going to take your bed."

Shawn puts a hand on each one of my shoulders and starts guiding me down the hallway. "You're

133

taking the damn bed. I'll sleep on the couch. Malakai should be home any minute now, and I can't guarantee he'll be alone. It'll be quieter in my room."

"Fine," I concede. "But only because your couch really sucks."

"Go to bed, Jazz. We'll talk in the morning."

chapter eleven

JAZZ

"Thanks for the ride. And for everything last night."

Shawn pulls his navy blue BMW 328i up to the curb, two houses down from Belle's. The sedan is over ten years old, but the boy keeps it obsessively clean. Boys and their cars, amiright?

"You sure you don't want me to drive you two somewhere?"

"I'm sure." I nod, leaving out the part that Belle probably wouldn't be happy to see him. She liked Shawn well enough while we were dating, but she *loves* Kingston, and I'm afraid seeing Shawn would confuse her.

"At least reconsider the ride home. There's no point in paying for one when I can do it for free." He looks at the backpack on my lap. "You can leave that with me, and I'll bring it back."

That'd probably be the smart thing to do considering the Glock I have wrapped in the shirt I wore last night. It's not loaded, but still. I don't like the idea of carrying a weapon when I'm spending the day with my sister.

"Yeah... okay. Maybe meet me back here around five?"

Shawn searches my eyes for a moment. "I can do that."

I offer him a soft smile. "Thanks again, Sha—" Movement down the street catches my eye. "Ah, fuck."

Shawn's gaze follows mine. His shoulders stiffen the moment he notices Kingston coming right at us, glaring holes through the windshield. Damn it, I should've known he'd show up here.

"Oh, fuck no." Shawn practically rips the keys out of the ignition and opens the car door.

"Shawn, don't."

He scoffs. "Sorry, Jazz. I'm not backing down on this. That preppy fuck has some nerve showing up here."

I scramble out of the car, catching up with him right as Kingston reaches us. The two men stare each other down, the animosity between them tangible. A muscle jumps in Kingston's cheek while Shawn clenches and unclenches his fists. Neither one of them says a word. They just square off, trying to murder each other with their eyes.

I insert myself directly between them. The last thing I need right now is to have them throw punches at each other, then have to deal with someone calling the cops. Both men are pretty evenly matched in size, and Shawn has legit street smarts, but after seeing Kingston fight at Peyton's birthday party, I think he could actually do some real damage to his opponent.

"Jazz, move," Kingston grits out.

"Don't talk to her like that," Shawn retorts.

A cruel smirk forms on Kingston's lips. "Or what?"

I hold my arms out on either side as they both take a step forward. "Both of you. Knock it off."

Kingston's eyes meet mine for the first time. "Is this who you've been with all night?" His eyes are bright green today, almost glowing with intensity as he awaits my answer.

I pop a brow. "So, what if it was?"

His eyes narrow. "Then we're going to have a problem."

I scoff. "Oh, we *already* have a problem, Kingston."

Kingston's gaze shifts to Shawn. He couldn't look more unimpressed if he tried. "You can take off now. I'd like to have a word with my girlfriend alone."

Shawn charges forward again but stops when my

palm presses against his puffed-out chest. "Fuck you. I'm not going anywhere. And the way I see it, she ain't your girl anymore." He releases a sardonic laugh. "But don't worry; I took care of her *real good* last night."

Shit.

He just had to go and rouse the beast, didn't he? In one second, Kingston's pulling me out of the way, and in the next, his fist is connecting with Shawn's jaw. Shawn fires back immediately, landing a solid blow in roughly the same spot.

"Stop it!" I scream. "Somebody's going to call the cops, you idiots!"

Of course, they don't listen and continue trading punches. When I see the neighbors peeking their heads through their curtains, I know I need to end this fast before both these fools get thrown in jail. I'm not stupid enough to risk my face being collateral damage, so I do the first thing I can think of. I take off my shoes, right there in the middle of the street, and hurl one at each one of their heads as hard as I can.

"Ow!" Shawn shouts, rubbing his forehead.

"What the fuck?" Kingston grumbles at the same time, staring at one of my fallen Chucks on the concrete.

I prop a hand on my hip. "You assholes deserved it."

Shawn's nostrils flare as he wipes the blood away

from his lip. "Did you seriously throw your shoe at my face?"

I roll my eyes. "*Hell, yes*, I threw my shoe at your face. Quit being such a baby. It's not like it hurt worse than a *fist*, but clearly, the element of surprise knocked some sense into you morons."

Shawn winces. "That's harsh, babe."

"Call her that again and see what happens." Kingston spits blood on the ground.

Shawn juts his chin out. "I'm not afraid of you, playa."

I throw my hands up. "Oh, shut the hell up, both of you. If you'd stop measuring d—"

"Jazz!"

All three of our heads whip in the direction of my sister's voice. She's barreling down the sidewalk toward us with a huge smile on her face.

I crouch down and open my arms to pull her into a hug as soon as she's within reach. "Hey, kiddo. I missed you."

Belle squeezes me tighter and buries her nose into my neck. "Missed you, too."

I glare at both guys over Belle's shoulder, silently telling them to get their shit together.

I finger a lock of her loose hair. "You took the braids out. How'd you get the curls to look so pretty?"

My sister nods. "Monica works at a beauty salon. She gets to take home all sorts of stuff to try. She gots me some new oil that smells like sunscreen." Belle lifts a lock of her hair, waiting for me to take a sniff. "See?"

I take a whiff of the coconut fragrance. "Mmm, you smell good enough to eat." I playfully snap my teeth near her neck, making her giggle.

Belle pulls back and frowns when she finally notices Shawn. "What's *he* doin' here?"

Shawn laughs at her accusatory tone. "Hey, there, shorty. Long time, no see."

Belle balls her fists and parks them on her hips. "I am *not* short."

He holds his palms out in surrender. "My mistake. Will you forgive me?"

Now Belle crosses her arms over her chest and harrumphs.

Of course, Kingston's loving the fact that my sister is giving my ex a less-than-warm reception. "Hey, kiddo."

A smile stretches across her face, right before she launches herself into Kingston's arms. Shawn's not the only one right now who's uncomfortable with the fact that Belle adores Kingston so much.

Kingston stands with Belle proudly propped on his hip. He tugs on one of her curls and says, "Your hair looks really pretty."

"Thank you." Belle gingerly presses her fingertips to the corner of his mouth. "You have an owie on your lip."

Kingston's tongue snakes out, wiping the little droplet of blood away. "Don't worry about me, sweetheart. It doesn't hurt *at all*."

Shawn and I both shake our heads at Kingston's obvious dig.

I tell my stupid heart to stay firm when Kingston boops her on the nose. "You feel like going to the children's museum today?"

Motherfucker.

Belle's face lights up. "Yeah!"

"Actually... Belle, I was thinking you and I could have a sisters-only day. Maybe hop on the bus like old times and go somewhere fun?"

Her brows draw together. "But I wanna go to the children's museum."

"Yeah, Jazz, she wants to go to the museum." Kingston smiles victoriously.

I mentally flip him off. "Well, then we can take the bus to the museum and still have our sisters' day."

"Or I can drive you," Shawn offers. "Promise I won't get in the way. I'll just be your chauffeur."

Belle looks at Shawn first, then me, then Kingston. I think she's finally sensing the tension in the air. Her brow furrows as she pulls on Kingston's sleeve, prompting him to let her down.

"Are you mad at me?"

I shake my head. "Of course not, honey. Why would you think that?"

"Because everyone looks really mad, like the time I spilled juice all over the couch, and Daddy yelled at me and made me go to bed without dinner."

I have to work really hard to conceal my hatred toward my sister's father. Another reason I need a job: So I can consult an attorney to see what my chances of getting partial custody are.

Kingston kneels down. "Hey, princess. No one's mad."

Belle points to Shawn. "Then why's his lip bleedin' too?"

Kingston doesn't even spare Shawn a glance. "We were just playing around."

Shawn uses the bottom of his shirt to wipe the blood off. Thankfully, the shirt's black, so hopefully it won't stain. He winks when he catches me staring at his abs, which are a *helluva* lot more defined than they used to be. I may not want to be with him, but I'm sure as shit not blind. Unfortunately, Kingston catches me looking too, which earns me a glare.

I give him one right back. "Don't even start with me."

Belle grabs my hand. "Jazz?"

I sigh. "Honey, I promise no one is mad at you. And we'll do something super fun, but I need to have some grown-up talk with the boys first. Why don't you go back inside, and I'll come get you in just a few?"

"Then, you, me, and Kingston will go to the children's museum?"

I give her a reassuring smile. "We'll get that all figured out, okay? Just go back inside, and I'll be there soon."

Belle twitches her nose. "Fine."

Nobody says a word until she's back inside the house. As soon as she closes the door, all bets are off.

"You need to leave," Kingston tells Shawn.

Shawn scoffs. "Fuck, no."

I hang my head in resignation. Both guys watch me as I duck into Shawn's Beamer and grab my backpack.

"Jazz—" Shawn starts.

I hold up my hand. "I know what I'm doing, Shawn. Thank you for last night. I'll call you later, okay?"

He looks between Kingston and me incredulously. "Are you kidding me right now? You're taking *his* side after what he did?"

I pinch the bridge of my nose. "I'm taking *my sister's* side. And what's best for her right now is to avoid causing a scene and confusing her further."

"I don't like this." Shawn adjusts the brim of his ball cap.

"It'll be fine, Shawn. I'll call you later. I promise."

He releases a heavy breath before hooking me around the shoulders and pulling me into a side hug. Kingston looks murderous as Shawn kisses the top

145

of my head, but fuck him. He has *no right* to say shit right now.

"If I don't hear from you tonight, I'm coming up there."

Shawn points two fingers to his eyes, then back at Kingston. "I'm watching you, fucker."

Kingston's square jaw tics. "Right back at you."

Kingston and I stand in silence while Shawn gets behind the wheel and drives away. When he's down the street, I start walking toward Kingston's Rover.

"I'm not talking about this out here. Is the car open?"

I hear the locks disengage when we get closer. "It is now."

I open the driver's door and toss my bag over the seat into the cargo area. When I see the question in Kingston's eyes, I say, "I don't trust you not to drive off if you get behind the wheel."

The asshole smirks as he rounds the car to climb in on the passenger's side. "Whatever you say, Jazz. But I'm holding on to these so you can't run off." He dangles my shoes by the laces, laughing when I unsuccessfully try grabbing them.

I point a stern finger at him. "You don't need to be a dick about it."

"Quit behaving like a spoiled brat, and maybe I won't."

"Excuse me?!" I rear back. "You have some fucking nerve."

"You wanna tell me what the disappearing act was about? And *why the fuck* you'd go to that asshole?"

My eyes narrow. "Don't pretend like you didn't already talk to Bentley."

"Humor me." Kingston throws out his hand. "Tell me what you *think* you saw, and I'll tell you what you *really* saw. Then, we can move on to how fucking stupid you were for following someone to that house in the first place."

"Wow." I shake my head. "Just... wow."

"Nothing to say?" He raises his eyebrows. "Fine. I'll go. I made a huge breakthrough with my dad last night. *Huge*."

I golf clap. "By fucking some chick in the middle of a sex club? Congratulations."

"I didn't fuck *anyone*," he grits out.

I roll my eyes. "Fine. Got your dick sucked. Whatever."

"I didn't do *anything* with anyone, Jazz."

My jaw drops. "I was there, Kingston! I was at the back door, looking in. *I saw you stick your tongue down some naked chick's throat!* Right before she dragged you down a hallway."

He closes his eyes for a moment. "That's the last thing I wanted you to see, but it had to be done. And *nothing else happened*."

"Right." I fold my arms over my chest. "Why

147

should I believe you? Because you've been so honest up until this point?"

He growls. "I'm fucking dead serious, Jazz."

"Fine. Then why don't you tell me what *really* happened? And why you *had to* kiss some naked rando?"

"Because my dad was testing my loyalty. He was questioning me about you... about my feelings for you. When I assured him he imagined things, he asked me how far I was willing to go to prove myself." Kingston rubs the side of his jaw. "I told him I'd do whatever it took to ease his concerns."

"And his answer to that was bringing you to an orgy?"

"It wasn't an orgy. I mean, technically, I guess the fucking occurred all in the same room, but those women weren't there for the fun of it."

"What's that supposed to mean?"

"They were *working*. My dad and Madeline run a prostitution ring. The real reason behind Ivanov's party was to invite guests to their newest fetish room. Apparently, they have regular clientele who need excuses to get away from their significant others. Or, some of them just get off on the knowledge that their spouses are nearby while someone else is sucking their dicks, I don't know. So... Alex, or one of their other *hosts*, as he called them, throws a party.

"Enough people are invited where it wouldn't be

noticeable if a few disappeared for a while. And it's not uncommon for men to branch off at these parties to discuss business, which is likely the excuse they use. My dad said it was only one of *many* things he had his hands on. I got the impression they were going behind your dad's back on this one; hence, why he wasn't invited."

I scrub a hand down my face. Sadly, everything Kingston's said to this point is believable, considering the players and what I saw. It still doesn't excuse his actions.

"Kingston, that still doesn't explain the girl you were with."

"Yeah, it does, Jazz. I already told you my dad was testing my loyalty to him. His way of doing that was to get me to screw someone else to prove my thing with you is purely physical. Honestly, I think he was also looking for something to hold over me. I don't know if you noticed, but there were cameras in every corner. My dad said they were there if any of his *guests* wanted a memento, but I think he uses the footage for blackmail. I wouldn't be surprised if he planned on sending a video of me with that woman to you to further whatever his agenda is.

"When my dad called her over to us, and she dropped to her knees right there, I knew I couldn't say no, but I also wasn't going to actually let her touch me. That's when I asked if we could go somewhere more private. I think my dad was going to argue until he saw Madeline practically drooling over my open fly. I don't know what his deal is with her, but I do know my dad doesn't like competition."

I clench my jaw. "Kissing *is* touching, Kingston. And you still followed a naked woman into what I assume was a bedroom."

He sighs. "You're right; I did follow her to the bedroom. *Where there weren't any cameras.* My dad assured me that room wasn't being filmed, but since his word means shit, I checked with my detection device to confirm."

I scoff. "And what about the prostitute?"

"The second we got in that room and I knew it was clear, I threw a blanket to her and told her to cover herself up. That *nothing* was going to happen."

"And she was perfectly okay with that? What about when your dad asked what happened?"

"At first, I was just planning to pay her off, but then she asked me if I was gay, and I went with it. Told her that I was afraid to come out of the closet; that my dad would never understand and disown me. I played on her sympathies. Asked her to pretend we fucked, and she agreed. We stayed in there for a while and made appropriate *noises* so it'd be believable. Then I took off."

"How can you be so sure it worked? That she went along with it?"

"Because she told me her little brother was gay and he was in the same boat with their parents.

Wound up committing suicide at fourteen. She said she'd do it for him."

"Kingston, why should I believe anything you say?"

"Because I'm telling the truth."

I shake my head. "I saw how you looked at her. *How you kissed her.* You sure as hell looked like you were into it."

"Because *I had to* look like I was into it!"

I'm glad the windows are closed to muffle the volume because our voices are becoming increasingly louder.

Tears prick at my eyes. "I'm not going to be the stupid girl who'd rather feign ignorance than accept that her boyfriend is a cheater."

"I'm not a fucking cheater!" His eyes are manic. "I've *never* been a cheater. Jesus-fucking-Christ, Jazz. You think I *liked* kissing that woman? I was trying not to fucking vomit! The thought of kissing someone else, being with someone who's not you, makes me physically ill! *It was all part of the act!*"

"How do I know *this* conversation isn't an act?" I flick my finger between us. "That *everything* you've said to me isn't an act?"

"Because if you'd get out of your own goddamn head for a second, you'd see the truth staring you in the face. You just need to *look*, Jazz."

"And what's that?"

"That I fucking love you, all right? I didn't want to.

God knows I fought it, but I couldn't stop it. I. Fucking. Love. You." Kingston rakes a hand through his thick hair. "If you don't want to take my word for it, my mic was on the whole time I was in that house. Listen to the recording."

I blink several times. "I don't know what to say, Kingston."

My head falls back against the seat as I close my eyes, processing. I open them again when I feel Kingston's thumb brushing against my cheek.

"Jazz." His voice is raspy. When our eyes meet, I see that his are also filled with tears. "Don't shut me out."

I put my hand over his. "I don't want to, but it fucking hurts. I can't just bleach the memory of you with that girl out of my brain."

"I know, baby. And I'm so fucking sorry." He scoots closer and rests his forehead against mine. "I need you, Jazz. We're so close, but I can't do this without you."

I pull back and check my reflection in the mirror. "We need to get Belle. She's been waiting in there for too long."

"Are we good?" Kingston brushes some hair away from my face. "Because I can't ever have you take off like that again. I was scared to death."

I turn my face into him. "If you're ever in a situation like that again... you need to find another way, Kingston. I won't be okay with you touching someone else—not even kissing—even if it's all part of the front. *I can't.*"

"I swear on my fucking nuts. It won't happen again."

I jerk my head toward the house. "Well, then, let's get Belle to that museum. We can talk more later."

He nods. "Okay."

chapter twelve

KINGSTON

The last twenty-four hours have seemed like days. When I had no idea where Jazz was, I imagined the worst. Then, when Bent told me she called and that he heard some dude's voice in the background, I wasn't exactly relieved, considering what she witnessed earlier in the evening. I spent the rest of the night wondering if she was going to seek refuge in some other guy's arms because she thought I fucked someone else.

When I saw her sitting in the car with her asshole ex this morning, I was even more concerned and instantly irate. Jazz wouldn't be the first person to fall back in bed with an ex because the familiar provides comfort. I still don't know what happened, and quite frankly, I don't think I *want* to after she was struck silent when I dropped the L-bomb. I didn't mean to blurt it out like that—hell, I didn't even realize it until the words left my mouth—but once it was out there, it was too late to take it back.

The fact that she had *nothing* to say in return... well, fuck. I don't know what to do with that. I'm not surprised she didn't immediately return the sentiment, but I also can't say I'm not butthurt by that. I've never said those words to any woman besides my mom or sister. And with Jazz, they carry an entirely different meaning. Fuck, I'm so tied up in knots over this girl, it's not even funny.

"Are you sure you don't want to just go pack a bag and stay at my place?" I shift my car into park in front of Callahan's mansion.

"I'm sure, Kingston. Just like I was the first five times you asked." Jazz unbuckles her seat belt and turns toward me. "Thank you for making another Sunday special for my sister."

My eyebrows lift. "Special for Belle... but *not* for you?"

She pulls her bottom lip between her teeth. "I've just got a lot going through my head right now. I had a nice enough time, though, so thanks."

"A *nice enough* time," I repeat. "Just what every guy wants to hear when he takes his girlfriend out for the day."

Jazz sighs. "Goodnight, Kingston. Don't worry about me in the morning. I'll have Frank give me a ride to school."

I watch, dumbfounded, as she hikes her backpack over her shoulder and exits the vehicle. Jazz doesn't look back once as she approaches the front door or steps inside the house. I'm not sure how long I stare at that door, waiting for her to come back before I launch into action. I use my key to go through the side door and make my way over to the staircase. I don't run into anyone on the way, but unfortunately, my luck runs out when I reach the upper level.

Peyton freezes just outside her bedroom as she sees me. She pulls on the doorknob, shutting the door behind her. "Kingston. W-what are you doing here?"

I take in her disheveled hair, kiss-swollen lips, and sticky skin. Based on her appearance and the distinct smell of sex wafting from her, it's obvious Peyton isn't alone in her bedroom. Usually, she'd rub that in my face, because she's holding out hope that one day I'll care, but Peyton's being oddly cagey right now, which tells me she doesn't want me to know who's in there.

"We'll get to that. I'd like to know what you're trying to hide first."

She balks. "Why would I try to hide something from you?"

I jerk my chin over her shoulder. "Who's in your bedroom, Peyton?"

Peyton glares. "None of your business, Kingston.

Unless *you* want to be in my bedroom, you lost the right to ask."

"What if I said I *did* want another chance? Would you let me in?"

Her eyes widen. "Uh... I mean, I'd have to think about it."

I scoff. "You'd have to *think* about it, huh? So, if I told you to turn around, walk back into your room, and bend over the bed so I can pound you into the mattress, you'd have to *think about it?*"

Peyton's nipples harden through the short, silk robe she's wearing, telling me she likes that idea very much. I, however, am trying not to lose my dinner all over the floor.

"Well... I mean... if you really wanted to..."

"All you need to do is tell your current company to leave, Peyton." I finger the collar of her robe. "Then, I could remind you what a solid fucking really is."

Her cheeks pinken. "Uh... if you can just give me a few minutes."

I lean against the opposite wall and cross my arms. "I'll be waiting right here."

Peyton slips inside her room, and within seconds, I hear a deep voice shouting. Not too long after, a seriously pissed off Lucas Gale steps into the hall, flashing a venomous glare in my direction.

"Fuck you, dude. Not cool at all."

When the door opens again, imagine my surprise

when the piece of shit I beat up at that Malibu party comes out. I laugh when Barclay Baker scurries by without a word. After about a minute, a third *and fourth* guy—this time Christian Taylor and David Wright—come out. They, too, can't get away from me fast enough.

"Jesus Christ," I mutter to myself. "Peyton's pussy is like a goddamn clown car."

Peyton finally returns after another minute, looking a bit more put together, with a giant smile on her face. "So... uh, maybe I should shower first or something. Do you want to join me?"

I shake my head. "Peyton, you really are dumber than you look. I had *zero* intention of touching you beforehand, but I definitely wouldn't be interested now even if I had. Maybe if you get on your knees and grovel, it's not too late to call your harem back."

Her entire face reddens so much, it's nearly purple. "You're an asshole!"

I give her a wry look. "So everyone likes to tell me. If you're going to insult me, at least put some effort into it."

"Why are you here, Kingston? Did you just come here to cockblock me?"

I smirk. "Nah. That was just a bonus. Although, while I have your attention, I'm going to do you a solid and give you some advice."

She parks both hands on her hips. "*What?*"

"You don't know what you've gotten yourself

into with these... alliances you've formed. You may think you have it made because you have some powerful people behind you, but let me assure you, Peyton, you're just a measly puppet on a much grander stage."

"I have no idea what you're talking about." She averts her eyes like she always does when she's lying.

"Sure, you don't. But while you're in denial, think about this: If you—or anyone on the wrong side of this war you're waging, for that matter—fucks with what's mine, the meanest, most dangerous mother-fuckers you've encountered thus far will be like kittens compared to what I'll do to you. If you're smart, you'll tuck tail now and move on with your life. Because if you don't... you might not live to see another birthday."

Peyton makes another loud screeching sound as her eyes fill with tears, but I'm not sure she's actually forming words.

Jazz's head peeks out of her bedroom. "Kingston?" Her eyes bounce between Peyton and me. "What's going on?"

I incline my head in Jazz's direction, but I'm still looking at my pathetic ex. "Now, for the *real* reason I came here. If you'll excuse me."

"I hate you!" Peyton screams, before slamming her door shut.

Jazz steps aside when I approach, to let me into her bedroom. "What the hell was that about?"

I shrug, shutting the door behind me, making sure I turn the lock. "That was me being unable to resist fucking with her."

She shakes her head. "As amusing as that is, why are you still here, Kingston? I was just about to take a shower before heading to bed."

"Perfect." I back her into the bathroom, shucking my shirt along the way.

"What do you think you're doing?"

I don't miss the way Jazz's eyes darken as she looks over my naked torso.

"I'm solving our problem."

Jazz rolls her pretty brown eyes. "Not everything can be magically solved with sex."

"Maybe not," I agree, raising her arms so I can remove her shirt. "But with us... it seems like the most effective way to cut through the bullshit and communicate."

I step out of my shoes and pants next, while Jazz does the same, clearly agreeing with my statement. I reach behind her and turn on the water, right before I lose my boxer briefs. Jazz licks her lips, eyeing my erection as it springs free. I shove her panties over her hips while she unclasps her bra and tosses it to the ground. I back her into the shower, directly under the spray, until she's pressed against the tile.

Water drips off her inky lashes as I crowd her against the wall. "You don't get to run from this,

Jazz." She gasps when I cup her pussy. "You don't get to run from *us*."

I watch her face as my fingers slip inside, while my thumb works her clit. There's so much honesty in her expression—*pure need*—and I'm sure she can see the same reflected in mine.

"I wasn't running," she argues. "I just needed time to think."

"What's there to think about?" I pull her bottom lip with my teeth. "I. Fucking. Love. You." I punctuate each word, thrusting my fingers in and out. "What's so complicated about that?"

"It's not." Jazz gasps as I drop to my knees and start tonguing her pussy. "I...just..."

"You..." Lick. "Just..." Lick. "*What?*"

"I... just..." Her hands slam against the wall. "Fuck! Right there!"

I smile against her heated flesh, licking and sucking her into a frenzy. "You like that, baby?"

"God, yes," Jazz groans.

I get her to the brink right before I stand. Without any prompting, Jazz jumps up and wraps her legs around my hips. At the same time, I thrust into her in one smooth motion. I pinch her clit between my fingers, and she's instantly spasming all around me. Jazz digs her nails into my shoulders, chanting my name over and over. When she relaxes, I pick up the pace and continue toying with that bundle of nerves until she's once again choking my dick with her tight cunt.

"Fuck." I rest my forehead on Jazz's shoulder, watching the spot where our bodies are joined.

"Kingston." Jazz cups her hands over my jaw, lifting my gaze to hers.

I slowly work my cock inside of her, in no hurry to get to the finish line. "Yeah?"

She traces a finger over my eyebrow. Fuck, I don't know why, but I love it when she does that. "I'm sorry I didn't say it back."

My lips curl upward. "Say *what* back?"

Her eyes lift to the ceiling. "Oh, God, you're going to make me work for it, aren't you?"

I thrust harder. "It seems like I'm the one doing all the work right now."

I can't help myself when Jazz's chest juts forward, putting her pretty brown nipples on display. I seal my lips around one, sucking hard enough that I know I'll leave a mark behind.

She holds me to her chest like she never wants me to stop. "God, that feels good."

I release her with a pop and lift my head. "Let's get back on topic. Now, what were you saying?"

Jazz's chocolate eyes twinkle. "You're a pain in the ass."

I slide my hand between Jazz's round cheeks, dipping lower to gather her arousal before pressing an index finger against her puckered hole. "I'd *love* to show you what a pain in the ass really feels like. Although, I promise the pain part won't last long."

Jazz squirms in my arms as I work the digit in, the water making our bodies extra slippery. "Fuck. If it feels even close to that good, I'll let you do it in a heartbeat."

I move the finger I have in her ass in tandem with my dick in her pussy. "Have I ever made anything not feel good when I'm inside of you?"

"Nope," Jazz pants. "You're definitely great at the sexing."

I laugh. "Good to know. Now, *you were saying?*" My finger slides out of her ass, my palms cupping the firm globes as I stop moving entirely. "Jazz. Look at me."

She cups my jaw again, leaning forward to kiss each one of my eyelids, then my cheeks. Our lips touch briefly before she pulls back and meets my gaze. "I love you, too, Kingston."

I couldn't fight the smile stretching across my face if I tried. "Yeah?"

Jazz nods. "Yeah."

"Good." I squeeze her ass cheeks. "Because if you didn't, that would've been really fucking awkward."

She laughs, which makes her pussy vibrate around me.

I groan. "No more talking. Let's finish up here so we can go back to my place and do it again."

"That sounds like an excellent plan." Jazz winks.

chapter thirteen

JAZZ

"Hello?"

"Hi, is this Jasmine Rivera?"

"It is," I confirm. "But please, call me Jazz."

"Hi, Jazz. My name is Misha. I'm the manager at Calabasas Coffee. Are you still interested in the barista job we have open?"

"I am," I say excitedly. "Very much so."

"Great. When can you come in for an interview?"

"I get out of school at two-thirty each day, so any time after then would be fine."

"Perfect. How about three o'clock tomorrow afternoon?"

"Awesome. Thank you for the opportunity."

"I look forward to meeting you, Jazz."

I end the call and set my phone on the breakfast bar.

"Who was that?" Kingston slides a plate of scrambled eggs in front of me.

"The manager at Calabasas Coffee. I have an interview tomorrow at three."

He frowns. "Why do you have a job interview? I didn't even know you were applying for jobs."

"Uh... because I need money." I give him a *duh* look. "I've been looking for a while, but this is the first place that's called. I think my limited availability with school isn't helping."

Kingston takes a large gulp of juice. "Jazz, if you need money, I have plenty."

"I'm perfectly aware, Kingston, but you're also not responsible for me." I take a bite of my eggs, moaning as the flavors explode on my tongue. I don't know what he does to make eggs taste so good, but the boy can cook.

He scoffs. "The fuck I'm not."

I point my fork at him. "Don't go getting all alpha male on me again. You should know me well enough to know that I don't accept charity."

"It's not charity, Jazz. I want to take care of you, and I have the means. It's as simple as that."

"And *I* want to be the one to take care of myself and my sister. It's as simple as *that*."

"Stubborn ass woman," he mumbles.

"Quit bitching and finish eating before we're late for school."

"You're really testing my nerves right now." Kingston glares at me as he chews.

"What are you gonna do? Spank me?" I wiggle my brows. "Because I might be into that."

His fork clanks against the plate as he drops it. "That's it. Now, you're really asking for it."

I hop out of my chair and push it down as I run away. I make it no more than ten feet before Kingston's strong arms are banding around me, lifting me into the air. He tosses me onto the bed, face down, ass up. I shiver when he flips my uniform skirt up to my waist, rubbing his hands over my newly exposed skin. I'm wearing a thong today, so there's *a lot* of exposed skin back there.

"Fuck, you have a beautiful ass." Kingston's large hands flex, gripping my butt cheeks.

I wiggle my butt. "I thought you were going to spank me? Or was that all a bunch of—"

Thwack!

I squeal from the surprise when the crack of Kingston's hand meets my flesh. I moan when he rubs the same spot right before he does it again to the other cheek.

"Shit," I pant.

"Too much?" This time, when he soothes my warming skin, he dips a finger between my thighs, stroking my clit over my panties.

"Nuh-uh." I shake my head emphatically. "It's hot."

Kingston groans. "We're definitely going to be late now."

"I'm okay with that."

~

"Where were you two this morning?" Ainsley grills Kingston and me as soon as we sit down at the lunch table.

My cheeks heat. "We, uh... I accidentally turned the alarm off."

"You're a shit liar, baby girl." Bentley laughs before shoving a bunch of fries in his mouth.

I kick him in the shin, which only makes him laugh harder. "Shut up."

"Anyway..." I direct my attention back to Ainsley. "I finally got called in for a job interview. It's at that coffee shop we went to last week."

"Nice." Ainsley steals one of Bentley's fries and takes a bite.

"Why do you need a job?" Bentley asks.

"That's what I said!" Kingston feels the need to add.

I slam my hand over my boyfriend's mouth. "Because I need the money, and no, I'm not going to just let this jackass bankroll me." Kingston licks my palm. "Ewww!"

He laughs when I wipe the slobber on his pants.

"What's wrong? You normally love it when I drag my tongue d—"

I pinch his lips together. "Don't even."

"Nice one, dawg." Bentley reaches over my head to high-five Kingston.

I rub my temples and groan. "Why do I even bother?"

Ainsley flicks her finger between Bent and her twin. "With those two, I have no idea."

Kingston narrows his eyes in Reed's direction. "Don't act like he's Mr. Innocent."

"Oh, trust me, I *know* he's not." Ainsley giggles when Kingston makes a face.

Reed smirks and plants a kiss on the side of her head, which makes Ainsley sigh wistfully as she leans into him.

I point at them. "You two are adorbs."

"Maybe one of these days, I won't be a fifth wheel," Bentley complains.

"Aw, baby, you can play with my balls any time you want." Kingston coos. "Just name the time and place."

Bentley flips him off. "Fuck you, dude."

I scoot out of the way when Kingston pulls Bentley into a headlock. The boys are so busy wrestling, they don't notice Headmaster Davis approach our table until he speaks.

"Enough, you two." He waits for the guys to

break apart before he turns toward me. "Miss Callahan, I'd like to see you in my office, please."

"Right now?"

"Right now." Kingston stands when I do, but Headmaster Davis holds his hand up. "*Alone*, Mr. Davenport. This doesn't concern you."

I'll be fine, I mouth to Kingston as I follow the headmaster out of the dining room.

"What's this about?"

His beady eyes narrow over his shoulder. "You'll find out when we get to my office."

We walk into the administration office and through the door leading to Headmaster Davis' personal office.

He pulls out a chair before rounding the desk to take his own. "Have a seat, Miss Callahan."

I do as he says and wait expectantly. I've learned over the years to never speak unless spoken to when dealing with authorities. Too many people incriminate themselves with nervous chatter. Not that I have anything to be concerned about, but considering I have no idea why I'm here, I'd rather be safe than sorry.

"Do you have any idea why I called you in here today?"

I shake my head. "None."

Headmaster Davis steeples his bony fingers. "Your attendance has been quite concerning lately. You do realize class participation accounts for thirty percent of your grade, do you not? I'm under the impression that graduating is of the utmost importance to you. Is that accurate?"

I frown. "I've missed a few classes since the beginning of the year. I don't understand how that's concerning considering we're into December."

His lips curve into a cruel smirk. "Actually, according to my records, you've missed several *weeks* of class already."

My jaw drops. "Are you referring to the time I was *hospitalized* and subsequently healing from significant injuries? The same time period in which I *kept up with all of my assignments?*"

"That, among others," he confirms. "Like, this morning. Your first and second-period teachers marked you absent. Care to explain?"

I fold my arms over my chest. "I slept in."

He raises his eyebrows. "And did Mr. Davenport *sleep in* as well?"

"*Excuse me?!*" I glare. "What exactly are you insinuating, Mr. Davis?"

"You will address me as *Headmaster Davis*, young lady, and I'm not insinuating anything. I was simply asking a question."

"Well, you'll have to ask Mr. Davenport about his whereabouts because I can only speak for myself."

He considers that for a moment. "Very well. Now, normal protocol dictates that I call a student's parents whenever they're marked unexcused from a class. However... there are other ways you can make up for it."

"Such as?"

"Such as... earning extra credit. Some students opt to help out in the office after school. Filing things for me and such."

"What's my other option?"

"There *is* no other option."

I stand up. "Well, I guess you're going to have to go ahead and call my so-called father. Anything else? I'd like to finish eating before the period is over."

His eyes narrow. "That will be all, Miss Callahan."

I give him a flippant wave as I exit the office. Kingston is waiting for me as I step into the hall, fully working the broody boy angle.

"What was that about?"

"He wanted to give me shit about my attendance. Threatened to call Charles. I told him to have at it."

He scowls. "Because you missed a couple of classes this morning?"

I roll my eyes. "No, apparently, the headmaster has an issue with me missing *weeks* of classes. You know, when I was in recovery."

"Fucker," he mutters.

"Agreed."

Kingston extends his hand. "You wanna finish eating?"

"What's the alternative?"

He pulls me into him and whispers against the

shell of my ear, "You can let *me* eat *you*. I may have made a copy of Bentley's master key. I'm sure there's plenty of empty classrooms right now, and it'll definitely help get your mind off your conversation with Headmaster Douche."

"Option two. Let's go with that."

I'm laughing as he drags me down the hall into the first darkened room we find. It happens to be a science classroom, so instead of individual desks, rectangular tables are spread throughout the room.

"Perfect." Kingston's white teeth flash in the shadows as he pats the hard surface. "Hop up."

I use a stool to boost myself up until my ass is parked on the table. "Now, what?"

Kingston flattens his hand in the middle of my chest and presses down. "Now, lie back and relax."

He plants himself on the same stool I used and yanks my legs until they're propped over his shoulder.

"We don't want to be late for Lit, so this is going to be fast."

I barely have time to process Kingston's statement before he's pulling my panties aside and swiping his tongue right down my center. My back bows as he eats me out, hard and fast until I'm pressing my lips together, trying to stifle my screams. When he's done, he uses the little sink off to the side to clean up, helps me off the table, and leads me to the door, just as the bell is ringing.

"Perfect timing. I'm pretty sure that's the fastest I've ever made you come." He plants a kiss on the tip of my nose and pulls back with a smile. "Although, if you ever want to set a new record, you just let me know."

I press my lips against his. "I love you."

Kingston smiles. "Say it again."

"I." Kiss. "Love." Kiss. "You."

Kingston fists my hair as he ravages my mouth until we're both panting, wanting more. "Damn it, we need to get out there. You go first. My goddamn dick won't go down with you in the room."

I laugh. "See you in there."

Thankfully, our next class is only two doors down, so I make it with plenty of time. However, Kingston is a good ten minutes late, and based on the lazy smile he's sporting as he walks through the door, I'm guessing he had to take matters into his own hands to make his boner go away. I squirm, rubbing my thighs together as our eyes meet, and I see his lust-fueled gaze. God, what is it about Kingston Davenport that turns me into a puddle of thirsty girl goo? It's like all common sense flies out the window when he gives me that look. I have to pointedly ignore him through the rest of the class so I can actually focus on what our teacher is saying.

chapter fourteen

KINGSTON

"Rafe is thrilled with the audio you got."

"Yeah?"

"Yeah," John confirms. "Have you talked to your dad since?"

"No, he never came home that night, as far as I know, and he skipped town the next day. When I called his office, his secretary told me he'd be out the entire week."

"Did she say where he went this time?"

"Miami, supposedly revisiting some high-dollar clients, but who knows if that's true."

"If he gives you anything else, or invites you somewhere, call me right away. In the meantime, I'll keep an eye on the Callahans."

"Will do. Thanks, John."

"Your PI?" Jazz slides into the seat of my car and buckles up.

"Yeah. How'd the interview go?"

"Really well." She smiles. "He offered me the job on the spot. He was even cool when I told him about Sundays with Belle and didn't have a problem with me having those days off, provided I don't mind working after school. He wants me to start this Saturday."

"That's great." I shift into gear and pull out of the coffeehouse's parking lot.

"Why does your tone sound like it's anything *but* great?"

I quickly glance her way. "Because I still don't like the idea."

"Kingston, don't be like that."

"I can't help it. Maybe I'm a selfish ass, but your working means I have less time with you, and it also means I can't keep an eye on you. I'm pretty sure your boss would have an issue with me hanging out there every time you have a shift."

"You absolutely *cannot* do that." Jesus, I can feel her glare burning into the side of my face.

"Relax, all right? I'm not an idiot."

"It'll be fine. I know things are crazy right now, but what's the worst that can happen in a public place? It's not like they're going to leave me to run the shop by myself."

I shake my head. "I still don't like it."

"Well, too bad."

"Yeah, yeah, I know. You're going to do whatever you want anyway, so I might as well accept it."

"I'm glad you're finally catching up."

I give her a dirty look out of the corner of my eye. "No need to be a smartass, Jazz. You won this round." I reach out to grab the tip of her tongue when she sticks it out at me. "Rest that tongue for later."

I don't need to look at her to know her eyes are rolling. "You wish."

I shrug. "Not going to deny that."

"Hey, you feel like swinging by Ainsley's studio since it's right up the road?"

"We can do that."

I pull into the shopping plaza where my sister's dance studio is located and find a parking spot. When Jazz and I make our way inside, it's apparent classes are in session. The lobby is filled with parents peering through the large observation windows, oohing and aahing over little kids dressed in pink leotards and tutus.

"Her first class doesn't start until five, so she's probably back in the private studio warming up." Jazz points down a hallway.

"I didn't realize you had her schedule memorized."

"It's not hard when you pay attention."

Hell, even I have no clue which class Ains takes

when. I just know she spends half of her life in this studio. Sure enough, when we get to the back end of the building, there's a single door with a small window, and my sister is inside dancing her heart out in front of a wall of mirrors. Unsurprisingly, Reed is inside, sitting against the back wall, watching her. When Ainsley sees us peeking through the window, she motions for us to come inside as well.

"Damn, the soundproofing is legit," I observe as we open the door, and music I hadn't heard before now pours through the overhead speakers.

Reed and I fist bump as Jazz and I slide down the wall next to him.

Ainsley pauses the music, wiping droplets of sweat away from her forehead with a small towel. "Hey, guys. What are you doing here?"

"I just finished my interview down the street and wanted to pop in on the way home."

"How'd it go?" my sister asks.

Jazz smiles. "I start this Saturday."

Reed gives me a look, and I mouth, *later.*

"Nice!" Ainsley opens her arms. "An air hug will have to suffice unless you want to get all sweaty and gross."

Jazz wrinkles her cute little nose. "The air hug's fine."

Ainsley's eyes find mine. "You haven't stepped foot in this place for years. Who knew it'd take another girl to get you to start taking an interest in my life?"

I give her the finger. "Screw you. Just because I don't watch you dance a million hours per week doesn't mean I'm not interested in your life. I've never missed a single recital, have I?"

Ainsley's studio isn't large enough to hold recitals, so they rent out the auditorium at this private university nearby.

Jazz's head turns toward me. "You haven't? *Really?*"

"Really," my sister confirms. "He's been to every single one since we were six."

I shrug like it's no big deal. "Who else is going to show? It's not like my dad or any of his wives care."

Jazz punches me in the arm. "Ass."

I rub the spot she hit. "What? I'm not saying anything that isn't true."

"Well, you could be a little less callous about it," Jazz chastises.

"It's fine, Jazz. I'm used to it." Ainsley takes a big chug of water before setting the bottle down on a stool. "Kingston's not trying to be a dick. It just comes naturally to him."

Reed and Jazz both laugh at that.

"Yeah, yeah." I wave my hand. "Are you going to impress us with your skills, or what?"

My sister beams. "You bet your ass I am. You

wanna see the lyrical routine I'm working on for the next recital?"

"Duh," Jazz sasses.

Ainsley laughs and cues up the music before walking to the center of the room. The moment she gets into position, I swear to Christ, the air in the room shifts. When Dua Lipa's "Homesick" starts playing, my tiny sister, who weighs maybe a buck-oh-five soaking wet, becomes larger than life. She floats across the small space in a series of kicks and leaps, long, graceful lines and complicated spirals that she makes look absolutely effortless. There's not a single doubt in my mind that this is what she was born to do.

I glance over and see Jazz and Reed watching Ains with the same rapt attention. She has that effect on you when she's on a stage, or this case, in a studio. Ainsley doesn't simply dance—she mesmerizes. Jazz looks like she's about to cry, and my best friend couldn't possibly look more in love. Fuck. I really didn't stand a chance of keeping them apart, did I?

Reed's one of the most stand-up guys I know. He's my brother in almost every sense of the word, but Ainsley's my other half. You don't get much closer than when you share a womb with someone. If Reed ever hurt my sister, I'd have to drop him from my life, and that's something I never want to do. I guess at this point, I just have to hope that neither one of them fucks it up.

At the end of the routine, Ainsley is lying on the floor, pure anguish written all over her face. I know she absorbs every emotion built into her choreography, and it takes her a minute to shake out of it. The three of us give her time to piece herself together again, and the moment it happens, she springs up, with a massive smile on her face, bubbly as ever.

"Well, what'd you think?"

Jazz wipes at the corner of her eye. "It's beautiful, Ains."

"Why, thank you." Ainsley curtsies. "Now, get the hell out of here. You're all distracting me."

Reed's chest shakes with laughter as he stands up and approaches my sister. They exchange quiet words, and whatever he says to her makes the flush on her cheeks deepen.

Jazz tugs on my sleeve. "C'mon, let's give them a minute to say goodbye."

I hold my hand up. "Later."

"Later," Ainsley and Reed reply in unison.

Jazz pauses by one of the observation windows on our way out. It looks like a new class started because now the room is filled with children who are maybe ten at most, dancing to hip hop.

"When I start getting regular paychecks, I'd love to get Belle signed up for a class like this. There used to be an after-school program like it, and she's a natural. Sadly, the teacher who volunteered her time moved, and she hasn't had anything like it since." Jazz bites her bottom lip. "I'd have to figure out transportation, too, though, because I doubt I could rely on Jerome to take her."

"What about his girlfriend? She seems pretty stable."

"She is," Jazz agrees. "And Belle *loves* her, which I'm so thankful for. But from what I understand, Monica usually doesn't get home from work until after dinner time on weekdays, and she works every weekend. Plus, you know, I honestly think it's only a matter of time before she dumps Jerome's ass. I just hope I can get some type of custody arrangement in place before that happens."

I open the car door for Jazz. "We'll make it happen. I can call some people."

She waits until I'm in the driver's seat before replying. "As much as I appreciate the offer, I need to do this on my own, Kingston."

"No. You don't."

Jazz levels me with a glare. "Yes. *I do.*"

I shift into gear and pull away from our parking spot. "Look. I understand why you want your independence. And I respect the fuck out of it, Jazz. But money makes everything easier. And when it comes to things like this, connections don't hurt either. I have plenty of both. My mom would love knowing the money she left us went to something good like this. If it makes it easier to accept, don't do it for my mom or me. Do it for *your* mom and your sister."

She stares out the window. "I'll think about it."

I reach over and squeeze her denim-clad thigh. "That's better than nothing, I guess."

"What did John have to say earlier?"

I give her a wry look. "Nice change in topic."

Jazz raises her eyebrows expectantly.

"He basically said the FBI guy was happy with the audio I got from the party. My dad's gone for the week, so John's going to keep an eye on your dad, Madeline, and Peyton and see if they give him anything useful."

"So, we're back in a holding pattern?"

"Yep."

"*Awesome.*"

This girl speaks sarcasm as fluently as I do.

"You feel like grabbing something to eat?"

"I could eat." Jazz digs through her purse and pulls out her phone. "Maybe we should call Bentley and see what he's up to? Boy's been moody AF lately."

"You can say that again."

"What do you think his deal is?"

"Dunno." I shrug. "Maybe he's just getting sick of pretending like he's okay all the time."

"Poor Bent." She pouts. "We need to find him a girlfriend."

I scoff. "Uh... *no, we* don't. I've never played

matchmaker a day in my life, and I have no intention of starting now. If Bentley wants a girlfriend, he's perfectly capable of finding one on his own."

"So, what you're saying, is I should recruit Ainsley for this particular mission."

I laugh. "That's *exactly* what I'm saying."

chapter fifteen

JAZZ

"Two things you never want to forget, always make sure the bean hopper is topped off, and wipe off the steam wand immediately after each use."

Misha, my new manager, runs a quick blast of steam and uses a rag to demonstrate the latter. "Any questions?"

I shake my head. "I think I got it. Now, if I can memorize the drinks, I'll be set."

He laughs. "It's easier than you think. Most people stick to the basics. Although, this is Cali, so don't be surprised if someone asks for a half-caff, sugar-free, grass-fed goat milk latte."

"Well, of course. Isn't that how you're supposed to drink it?"

Misha makes a face. "That's sure as hell not how *I* drink it. I'd much rather run five miles every morning so I can have my full-fat, extra-sugary lattes, thank you very much."

"I hear ya."

The bell dings above the doorway, indicating a new customer has arrived.

"You wanna try this one?" Misha nods his head to the man walking up to the counter. "I'll take his order, and I'll be right here if you need help with the drink."

I freeze when I follow Misha's gaze and see the man standing in front of the register.

"Jazz?" Misha prods. "You got this?"

At the sound of my name, the asshole jock turns toward me with a smarmy smile.

I nod. "Yep. No problem."

Misha takes his order and hands me a cup marked for a salted-caramel mocha. I hit the button to brew some shots, pump chocolate and caramel syrup into the cup, and pour milk into the carafe for steaming. I dump the espresso and milk into the cup and give it a good stir to combine. Once I'm sure the lid is secure, I call out the customer's name.

"Salted-caramel mocha for Lucas."

Peyton's fuckboy covers my hand with his own as I'm setting the cup on the pick-up bar. I focus on remaining calm, even though the hairs on the back of my neck are standing on end. This guy seriously gives me the creeps. Ever since Kingston humiliated Lucas by making him clean the dining hall floor in his underwear, Lucas never wastes an opportunity to undress me with his eyes, which I'd think he was doing to egg my boyfriend on, but strangely, he only does it when Kingston *isn't* around to witness it.

"When did you start working here?"

Mindful that my manager is eyeing us curiously, I pull my shoulders back and infuse some cheer into my tone.

"Today's my first day."

"Interesting." Lucas takes a sip of his coffee, licking foam off his lips. "Peyton didn't tell me."

"I doubt Peyton knows." I shrug. "I don't exactly talk to her much."

He pulls out his wallet, deposits a hundred dollar bill in the tip jar, and holds his cup up. "*Perfect* latte, Jasmine. I'll be back soon."

After Windsor's star QB leaves the store, Misha plucks the Benjamin out of the jar and stashes it under the register tray.

"You know that guy?"

"We go to school together. And he sorta dates my stepsister. Does he come in here a lot?"

Misha nods. "Every morning, sometimes twice on weekends. Is that going to be a problem? I was getting weird vibes off you two."

I gulp. "Nope. Not at all."

"I'm glad to hear it. Especially if he keeps tipping like that." Misha inclines his head to the woman who just walked in. "You ready for your first mid-morning rush?"

I nod. "Absolutely."

∿

"You did great today, Jazz. Have a good night."

"Thanks, Misha. I'll see you on Monday after school."

When I make it outside, Kingston is waiting right out front, idling in his Rover. I hear the doors unlock as I approach and climb in on the passenger side.

"Thanks for picking me up. You really didn't have to, though. I told you Frank said he's more than happy to take me."

"And I told you, it's no big deal." His gold-flecked eyes dare me to argue. "How was your first day?"

"Really good. It's pretty crazy during the rushes, but the job itself is easy enough, and my shift went by fast."

"You smell like coffee."

"I should hope so considering where I've been for the last six hours." I sniff my hair. "What's the matter? Do I repulse you?"

Kingston's eyes leisurely travel the length of my body. "Jazz, you could roll around in a giant pile of dog shit, and you'd still get me hot."

"Ewww." I scrunch my nose. "You couldn't have

picked something else for me to hypothetically roll around in? *Any*thing else?"

He laughs. "Nope. I'm sticking with dog shit."

"Such a romantic," I quip.

"Baby, you couldn't handle me if I pulled out the romance." Kingston winks.

"Oh, God," I groan. "So cheesy."

"Speaking of cheesy... how do you feel about dropping in on a Windsor party tonight?"

"Seriously? I thought we agreed to pause on the parties for a while after what happened at the last two."

"We did. But this one is at Lucas Gale's house."

I scoff. "All the more reason *not* to go. That guy gives me bad vibes. He came into the coffee shop today and was acting like a total creeper. Apparently, he's a regular."

Kingston frowns. "Well, that's even more of a reason to go. If we show up on his turf, it sends a message to everyone, especially him and Peyton, that we're in charge. And if I happen to have words with Lucas about finding a new place to get his caffeine fix while we're there, so be it."

"I don't know, Kingston."

He reaches over the console and grabs my hand. "It'll be fine, Jazz. Trust me. I wouldn't suggest it if I wasn't sure."

I groan. "Fine. But I need to shower and change first."

"We have plenty of time."

When we arrive at the Gale residence, the party is already in full-on rager mode. A group of guys are yelling at the TV while playing video games, red cups litter the floor, the music is loud, and scantily clad drunken girls dance on tables. I'd say it's your typical rich kid party, but Lucas' party has one noticeable difference: The gangbang they have going on right when you walk in the front door. There's a line of ten girls, naked from the waist down, bending over, while a group of guys sticks their dicks into each one of them, pumping a few times before moving on to the next girl.

"Whoa." Bentley whistles. "I'm all for playing some pussy roulette every once in a while, but this is crazy. Even *I* know to take that shit to a semi-private location."

I throw my hand out toward them. "What's the point of th—"

"And freeze!" The music cuts off abruptly right before the DJ yells his command.

"Damn it!" a guy with his dick hanging out yells.

The dude standing next to him pats him on the back. "Sorry, bro. Better go jerk it in the corner."

"And go!" the DJ says right before the music starts up, and the thrusting begins again.

Ainsley's jaw drops. "Oh my God, are they playing some sexed-up version of musical chairs?"

Bentley nods. "Looks like it."

Just then, one of the girls currently getting pounded notices our group. "Bentley! You should join the next game."

Bentley rubs the back of his neck, and if I'm not mistaken, he actually looks embarrassed. "Uh, no thanks. I'm good." He starts making a beeline toward the bar. "I need a drink."

The rest of us eagerly follow him, trying to put as much distance as possible between us and the orgy.

Reed turns his head to my boyfriend. "A hundred bucks says this shit's uploaded to Pornhub within the hour."

Kingston scoffs. "Why the fuck would I take a losing bet? I'd say no more than half an hour."

"That's seriously some of the stupidest shit I've ever witnessed," I say. "None of those dudes are wearing condoms."

"I'd imagine it'd get a little annoying switching them out every thirty seconds," Bentley offers.

"Should we take bets on who gets which STD?" I ask.

"Or knocked up?" Ainsley adds.

"I think I just saw Gale heading out back. Let's make sure he sees us." Kingston jerks his head to the side.

The pool is closed up for the season, but there's a

firepit in the middle of a brick patio, which is where most people seem to be congregating. Sure enough, Lucas, Peyton, and their entire preppy posse are all sitting around the fire with Solo cups in their hands.

Lucas stands the moment he sees us, causing Peyton to land on her ass since she was sitting on his lap. "What the fuck are you doing here?"

"Why else would we be here?" Kingston replies smoothly. "We came to party."

"Yeah?" Lucas questions. "Who invited you?"

"Kings have a standing invite to any Windsor party." Bentley gives Lucas a cocky grin. "And since Davenport, Prescott, and I are the kings, we're automatically welcome, along with anyone we choose to invite."

"Well, it's a stupid fucking rule." Lucas' statement was directed at Kingston, but he smiles when his eyes wander over to me. "Well, if it isn't my favorite new barista?"

Kingston's fingers flex around my hip. "Don't talk to her."

Lucas takes a sip from his cup. "It's my house. I'll talk to whoever I want. Your royal decree can't prevent me from doing that, can it?"

Peyton brushes herself off and takes a seat in the chair Lucas vacated. "What are you talking about, baby?"

Lucas holds his arms out. "Oh, you didn't hear? Sweet, sweet Jasmine here is now a working girl."

"I'm pretty sure she was *already* was one of those," Whitney Alcott, AKA Bentley's bitter ex, mutters.

I flip her off in reply.

Lucas points at Whitney. "Sadly, that theory has yet to be proven. But, she *is* the newest employee at Calabasas Coffee." He turns to me and flashes a smarmy grin. "You know, our favorite coffeehouse in the valley? The one we all go to *practically every day?*"

Fuuuuck. Why didn't I think about having to serve the assholes I go to school with when I started applying for jobs? I don't hide my displeasure fast enough, because Lucas' smile grows when he sees that he's getting to me.

"We're going to love having Little Miss Crenshaw slinging drinks for us. Although I'm sure since she's so new, it'll probably take her a while to get the orders right. Might have to send the first few back." He looks around. "Won't we?"

I park a hand on my hip as the lemmings murmur their agreement. "I'm from Watts, dickhead."

Lucas shrugs. "Same thing."

Uh, no, it's *not*, but this idiot wouldn't know the difference.

Kingston flashes a murderous glare. "Find a new place to get your coffee. If any of you show up at Jazz's work and cause trouble for her, you'll answer to me."

"And me," Bentley adds.

"And me," Reed echoes.

I stand a little taller when the sheep no longer look amused.

"Does Daddy know you got a *job?*" Peyton says that last word the same way I imagine she'd say *off-the-rack wedding dress.*

"No, but I'm sure you'll take care of that for me the first chance you get." I wave my hand dismissively. "Not that he can do anything about it since I'm eighteen."

Peyton's eyes narrow into slits. "Daddy is well connected. If he doesn't want you to work, nobody within a fifty-mile radius will hire you."

I roll my eyes. "Yeah, we'll see about that."

"Hey, Peyton," Kingston calls out, diverting her attention. "I'm surprised you're not enjoying the festivities up front. You know, seeing as gangbangs are your thing now."

Peyton's eyes widen. "I have no idea what you're talking about."

"Really?" Kingston laughs. "So, that wasn't Gale, Baker, Wright, and Taylor that I recently caught you fucking at the same time?"

"*What?!*" Imogen and Whitney shout simultaneously.

Peyton looks at her two friends nervously. I'm guessing they didn't know she was screwing their new boyfriends.

"It's not as bad as it sounds," Peyton argues.

Whitney turns to her boyfriend. "Christian? Is it true?"

Christian Taylor looks away. "Uh... sort of?"

"Sort of?" Whitney screams. "What does that mean?"

"She only blew me. We... ah... got interrupted before it could go any further." Christian inclines his head to the guys sitting on his left. "But yeah, she fucked the others. It was actually pretty impressive how she took all three dicks at once. I've got a video if anyone's interested."

Peyton gasps. "*What?!*"

"How could you do this to us, Peyton?" Imogen whines, leveling her so-called friend with a glare. "We're supposed to be besties for life! C'mon, Whit, let's get out of here."

"Gladly." Whitney looks me over with distaste. "Apparently, being a whore runs in the family."

"Watch it, Whit," Bentley growls.

"*Or what*, Bentley? You gonna dump me? Oh, wait, you already did that!" She laughs, looking around the group. "I'm *so* over high school dick. Older guys only from now on."

"Totally," Imogen agrees.

Peyton stands up and screams as the other two girls hightail it out of Dodge. "Why are you trying to ruin my life, Kingston?"

"Uh... I'm pretty sure you're doing a damn fine

job of that yourself, Peyton. Don't blame my brother because you're trying to bang your way through the entire senior class."

Peyton glares at Ainsley. "Shut up, bitch. Nobody asked you."

Oh, hell, no.

I charge Peyton, but Bentley pulls me back. "Claws in, baby girl."

I struggle in his hold. "Lemme at her, Bent. I think she's due for another nose job. I'm just gonna help her out."

At this point, we've gathered quite the audience. Peyton looks like she's going to be sick when she notices how many people have witnessed her humiliation.

I'm instantly calm when Kingston grabs my hand. "C'mon, Jazz. We're done here. They're not worth it."

"You're right." I nod.

The five of us leave the party, not sparing a backward glance to the drama we left behind. Now, the question is, why do I feel like we just invited a lot more trouble into our lives?

chapter sixteen

JAZZ

"I will never understand how that big voice came out of little Jenny Humphrey."

"Who's Jenny Humphrey?"

"Uh... from *Gossip Girl*?" Ainsley nods to the display on the dash when she sees how clueless I still am. "The singer from The Pretty Reckless. She plays Dan's little sister Jenny on *Gossip Girl*."

"Is that like, a show?"

Ainsley gasps. "Please tell me you're kidding."

I shrug. "Sorry. Never heard of it."

"X-O-X-O ring a bell?"

"Nope." I pop the P at the end.

"Holy crap. As soon as I get back from Portland, we are bingeing the shit out of it. It totally changed the television landscape of teenage dramas. It's a classic." She sighs. "I can't believe I'm not going to see you for a whole week."

Ainsley shifts her car into park and reaches over to hug me. She insisted on driving me to work this afternoon since she and Reed are flying to his sister's tonight for Christmas.

I give her one last squeeze before pulling back. "I know. It's crazy to me that it's already winter break, and our trip to Disney is almost here."

"Belle still has no clue where you're taking her, huh?"

"None." I shake my head.

"You promise you'll take lots of pictures and send them to me?"

"Promise." I open the car door and grab my purse off the floor. "Thanks again for the ride."

"Of course. Have a good shift."

"Text me to let me know you landed safely."

Ainsley nods. "Okay. Bye, Jazz."

I shut the door and wave to her as she pulls away from the curb. When I step inside my work, I immediately go to the backroom to stash my purse and grab my black barista apron. This is only my second week, but I absolutely love working here. My boss and co-workers are amiable, and making coffee is surprisingly fun. We're allowed to experiment with the different syrups and sauces, trying to invent new specials whenever we have some downtime. I smile when I see today's special of the day on the chalkboard.

Candied Peppermint Tuxedo Mocha

That would be the drink I came up with the other day: Two pumps of white and dark chocolate sauce and one pump of peppermint syrup, topped with whipped cream and crushed peppermint candies. It's not only delicious, but the combined flavors make a perfect holiday drink. Considering we're only a couple of days away from Christmas, it's fitting.

"Hey, Jazz."

I smile. "Hey, Java. Has it been busy?"

Yes, that's her real name. I thought she was joking when she first introduced herself. Only in Los Angeles, I swear. There's also a Racer, Maple, and Denim that work here. Oh, and Alley.

Java shakes her head. "Not too bad. I think people are still out there shopping."

"Is it just the two of us?"

"Yeah." She nods. "According to Misha, the last two weeks of December are typically the slowest of the year because so many people around here leave town. Racer was supposed to be on shift for another hour, but he left a little early. We're never supposed to be here alone, so if anyone asks, he wasn't feeling well."

"What's the real reason?"

Java rolls her eyes. "He had to bathe his ferret and

clean the cage before his girlfriend came over. Race lives in like a four-hundred-square-foot studio, so space is tight, and as you can probably imagine, bad smells spread pretty easily. Apparently, she refuses to give him head if the rodent stinks, so Lil Wayne—the ferret, not the rapper—is getting a bath. Can't say I blame her. The last time he and I hooked up, I almost passed out from holding my breath too long because I was trying not to smell the thing. Those little guys are cute as hell, but they start to reek pretty fast."

"Wow... that's more information than I ever needed." I laugh.

"Sorry." She blushes. "Sometimes, I forget to censor."

My lips twitch. "It's all good. Your honesty is refreshing."

The bell above the door dings as a small group of twenty-somethings walks in.

"Duty calls," she singsongs.

～

"What else needs to be done?"

Java sets the mop in the bucket and looks around. "I think we're good after we empty the garbage."

"I can handle that."

"Thanks, girl. There's new bags are under the bathroom cabinet, and the dumpsters are in the back lot by the fence. Ours is the green one. It should be open from the mid-day run, but make sure you lock it when you're done."

"Got it."

After I finish putting a new liner in the last trash bin, I gather the bags and head out the back door. Damn, it's kind of creepy back here. I heave the garbage into the dumpster and make sure the padlock is secure. As I start to walk away, I swear I hear a shoe scuffing against the ground, kicking up gravel. My head snaps to the side, looking around, but it's too dark back here to really see anything. I hurry my ass back inside and take a few breaths to calm myself.

Java frowns when she walks into the back room and sees me. "You okay? You look spooked."

"Yeah." I turn on the tap to wash my hands. "I just thought I heard something out there and got freaked out for a second."

"Oh, that's probably the squirrels."

"Squirrels?"

"Yeah." She nods. "There are tons of them that live in the trees behind the property line. Horny little bastards, too. I was taking out the garbage once, and I heard the strangest noise coming from up high. It was super loud and kind of sounded like an animal dying. As I got closer, I found two squirrels goin' at it like rabid monkeys." Java shivers. "I had to get *really* stoned that night to blur the memory. Sadly, it's happened at least two dozen times since, so now it's permanently etched into my brain."

My lips twitch. This girl and her lack of filter are definitely amusing.

"Wow. That's... interesting."

Java looks around the strip mall parking lot as we exit the store. "Your ride's not here yet?"

I shake my head. "No, I didn't tell him we finished up a little early."

"Oh." Her gaze falls to her boyfriend's Audi. "Let me just tell Ian real quick, and I'll wait with you."

"Thank you, but I'm fine." I incline my head toward the other end of the lot, where there's an open sub shop. "I'm just going to grab a sandwich while I wait."

"You want a ride over there?"

I shake my head. "I'm good."

"Okay, girl. Have a good night."

I wave. "You too."

I start walking faster when I notice a black Escalade pulling out of a parking spot. Now, that in itself wouldn't be odd, considering we're in a shopping center, but the only place that's still open is the sub shop, which is quite a few doors down. When the SUV starts heading directly toward me, I break into a run. I only make it about fifty feet before the driver slams on the brakes, and the cargo door flies open. A big guy wearing all black, including a ski mask, jumps out of the car and lunges for me.

Oh shit.

I struggle in his hold, but the guy is too damn strong for me. He clamps a hand over my mouth and nose, practically suffocating me as he wrestles me into the back of the Cadillac. I want to cry out at the unfairness of it when my purse falls to the asphalt, knowing the gun I bought for this very purpose is in there. My phone is in there, too, which means Kingston won't be able to track me.

Well, isn't this some fucked up déjà vu?

The second the doors are closed, he yells, "Go!"

Wait a second... I know that voice.

The masked driver steps on the gas and peels out of the parking lot. I know how screwed I am if I let these guys take me to a different location, so I kick and bite and fight as much as I can.

"Hurry the fuck up and get there," the guy who's holding me commands.

"I'm trying!" the driver yells.

I know that voice, too. What in the actual fuck?

What seems like only a few minutes later, the Escalade takes a sharp right, knocking the beefy guy and me off balance. The rear seats are flattened, so I'm thrown toward the side door, while he stumbles toward the back one. I don't give a shit that the car is in motion, I reach for the door handle, but the child locks must be engaged because it doesn't open.

"Fuck!"

The car takes another sharp turn down a bumpy road before coming to a grinding halt.

The big guy tackles me, smooshing my body against the carpeted floor. "Leave us!"

Driver guy hesitates. "What are you going to do, man?"

"What do you think I'm going to do?" Meathead squeezes the back of my neck. "I'm going to teach this bitch a lesson. Go back to your dorm, Taylor. And leave the keys."

I knew it! The guy behind the wheel is Christian Taylor! Ainsley once told me he lives in a dorm room at Windsor. Is that where we are? If the driver is Christian, that means the one on top of me must be—

"Lucas, man, you said you were just going to scare her. That's the only reason I agreed to help you."

Lucas peels off his ski mask and tosses it to the side. I guess there's no point in trying to conceal his identity now. "I said, *get the fuck out.*"

"All right, all right. Just... I don't know. Just be careful, man."

As soon as the door closes, Lucas' meaty paws are flipping me over, so I'm on my back, and he's sitting on my torso. Fuck, he weighs a ton. He quickly slams his hand back over my mouth and pinches my nostrils, just to prove he can steal my breath if he wants.

"You really fucked up by showing up at my house, bitch," he growls. His face is mere inches away from mine, so I can smell the alcohol on his breath. "I was going to listen to Peyton and leave you alone, but you just had to push me. That boyfriend of yours just couldn't leave well enough alone. Well, he might be untouchable, but guess what. *You're* not."

My scream is muffled against his palm as he shoves his free hand down my leggings, roughly grabbing my crotch. Tears trickle down my cheeks when he moves my panties aside and stabs me with two thick fingers.

"Fuuuuuck. Your pussy is even tighter than I imagined. A little dry, though. We'll need to work on that before you take my dick. I've been dying to get a piece of you since that night at the lake. I can't get the thought of your naked, helpless body out of my mind." Lucas gives me an evil smile as he continues pumping his fingers in and out. "Oops, did I just admit that? I guess there's no point in denying it now, considering you've probably figured it out already. In case there's any doubt, Christian was the one with me that night, too, but he was too much of a pussy to take what he wanted. Lucky for you, I don't have that problem."

The windows are tinted so dark, only the faintest bit of light comes through the moonroof, but it's enough to see how maniacal his expression is right now. The dude's lost it, for sure, which does not bode well for me.

"Now, I want you to listen real carefully on what's about to happen. Blink twice if you understand."

I glare at him.

Lucas shrugs. "Eh, good enough. Now, in just a moment, I'm going to remove my hand from your mouth. When I do, I'm going to take my dick out, and you're going to blow me until I'm ready to stick it in your cunt."

Jesus Christ, this fucker is delusional.

"Then..."

I'm relieved when he removes his disgusting fingers from my body, but it's short-lived when he sucks them into his mouth and moans.

"Damn. I don't normally waste my time eating a bitch's pussy, but I might make an exception for you. Maybe you *do* have some kind of voodoo snatch. Maybe fucking you will convince me to consider your debt paid after we're done here. Provided you cooperate, that is." He digs his fingernails into my jaw. "But don't get any crazy ideas. If you bite me while my dick is in your mouth, I will knock your fucking teeth out. If you try screaming for help, I will choke you until you lose consciousness. And don't think I have anything against fucking an unconscious girl. It certainly wouldn't be the first time." He squeezes my nipple painfully over my shirt. "Are we clear?"

There's no way in hell I'm just going to lie here quietly while he rapes me, but I think this psycho's lost the plot just enough to believe me when I nod.

"Good girl." He smiles as he removes his hand from my mouth.

I greedily gulp in as much air as possible with well over two hundred pounds of weight on top of me. I don't move a muscle as Lucas unbuttons and unzips his jeans, pushing them over his hips. Of course, he's going commando—better to rape someone, after all—so his dick springs free right away. I have to literally bite my tongue, telling my inner smartass that now is not the time to point out that the pencil dick struggle is real. Maybe I've just been blessed with the few I've seen before now, but not only is Lucas' dick short, but it lacks girth. No wonder Peyton needs someone else to satisfy her. I highly doubt this guy can get the job done.

Totally oblivious to my inner monologue, Lucas strokes himself, groaning as he twists his hand over the head.

"Lift up your shirt. Show me those pretty little titties I've missed so much."

"You're on my arms," I point out.

"My bad." He releases his dick and repositions his knees so they're pressing my arms into the floor even more.

Lucas lifts his ass up just enough to pull my t-shirt until it's above my boobs, then he shoves my bra up as well. My nipples pebble from the cold air, drawing Lucas' attention to them. I have to remind myself that I'm only going to get one shot to escape, and I need to make sure it's the right time to make a move. I feel like I'm going to puke as he eyes my naked breasts, grinning like a madman as he fondles me.

"Don't be coy, Jazz. I know you want it. And if you do an excellent job sucking my cock, I might trust you enough to let you use your hands. From what I've seen, your performance shouldn't be a problem." I fight my gag reflex when he rubs the head of his penis over my peaked tips, smearing his precum all over my skin.

I don't know how I'm remaining so calm as he shifts his pelvis, bringing his dick closer to my face, but I'm thankful. The last thing I need right now is a panic attack.

"God, you have no idea how many times I've jerked off to that video of you in the shower with Davenport." He gives himself another long stroke. "Oh, speaking of... can't forget to record this so that fucker can see how much you're going to love having me inside of you."

What?!

My eyes widen when Lucas pulls his phone out

of his jeans pocket and holds it up. "Say cheese, Jasmine."

I blink rapidly as I'm blinded by the flash.

He turns the screen toward me, showing me the picture he took of my naked chest with his dick hovering above it. He makes sure I see him switch it to video mode before turning the screen back toward him.

"Open wide, you little slut."

I pinch my lips together as he comes closer, turning my head away when his nasty dick touches my mouth. I can't stop the gag this time when I taste the salty wetness he left behind on my lips.

"Nuh-uh." Lucas grabs my jaw and squeezes, forcing my head back to the center. I swear to God, it feels like he nearly cracked the bone. "Open your fucking mouth before I *make you* open it, bitch."

Just when I think I might have to suffer through this so I can at least get the use of my arms back, his phone starts ringing.

"Fuck off!" he yells, silencing the ringer.

A moment later, it rings again, and he denies the call a second time. When it rings a third time, Lucas blanches when he looks down at the screen.

"Shit." Lucas sits back, causing me to grunt when his weight drops on my stomach, but I'll take that any day over his dick in my mouth. He slides his finger over the screen and holds the phone up to his ear. "Hello?" I can't hear what the caller says, but Lucas gets more and more agitated as the conversation goes on. "No, sir. I was just having a little fun. Yes, sir. Yes, I understand. Of course." His jaw drops. *"Right now?!* Um... sure."

Both of our gazes swing to the approaching headlights glaring through the window. Who the hell is he talking to?

Lucas gulps, suddenly looking very scared. "Yes, sir. I see them." He quickly tucks himself back into his pants and zips up. "Yes, I understand. I'll step out of the car and leave Jasmine unharmed."

Seriously, who the fuck is on the other line?

Lucas hangs up the call and mutters, "Fucking Taylor. He just had to play the goddamn saint. I'm going to kick that fucker's ass." His eyes narrow in my direction. "You got lucky tonight, but don't think this is over. Your cunt is mine, bitch."

I scoot out of the way as he hops over the console into the driver's seat and exits the vehicle, leaving me behind. I put my clothing back into place as fast as possible as I watch Lucas approach the dark sedan. He exchanges a few words with the driver before he gets into the back seat, and they drive away. What in the hell is happening right now?

Right as I'm climbing out of the Escalade, the familiar hum of an engine greets me. I crouch down until I can be sure it's not someone else I need to run from. As soon as I see Kingston's Agera, I break into a sprint. He slams on the brakes, opening the door the moment the car comes to a complete stop. Kingston catches me mid-air as I jump into his arms and wrap my legs around his waist, but the momentum from my run forces us to the ground. I start sobbing uncontrollably into his neck as he smooths his hand down my back.

"How'd you know where to find me?" I hiccup.

"I got a text." Kingston squeezes me and places a kiss on the side of my head. "I don't know who sent it, but they said to get here fast and that you were in danger. I found your purse in the parking lot a minute beforehand, so I knew it wasn't a joke." He carefully palms my face and lifts my head up. "What happened, baby?"

I wipe the tears away from my eyes. "I'll tell you, but please just get me out of here. I need to get out of here."

Kingston nods. "Of course."

As we leave the Windsor gates behind, I think about the first time I saw them and how screwed up my life has become since then. Kingston squeezes my hand, reminding me that something positive has come out of this new life as well. Someone once told me that you have to experience some bad to truly appreciate the good things in life. What I'd like to know is how many godawful things I need to experience before finally getting some peace? I'm so stinking exhausted fighting demons at every turn, I don't know how much longer I can hold on.

chapter seventeen

KINGSTON

Jazz hasn't said a word the entire ride home, which is killing me. I need to know what happened, but I know pushing her to tell me before she's ready won't do either of us any good. As soon as we step into my house, she practically runs to the shower, turning the tap to scalding. She's not even fully undressed before she's under the spray, scrubbing furiously at her face and chest.

I quickly remove my clothes and join her. "Hey. Slow down. Let me help."

I reach in front of Jazz to turn the temperature down a bit. I like hot showers just as much as the next guy, but when her naturally tanned skin is bright red within seconds, you know the water's too damn hot.

"I just need to get it off," she sobs.

"Get *what* off?" I help her out of her pants, which is easier said than done because they're soaked and molding to her legs.

"*Him*." She starts shaking as she grabs the bottle of body wash and squirts it on the bath sponge. "His scent... his touch... his... his..."

I grab the pouf out of her hand and try my damnedest not to react. I want to bombard her with questions about what happened, about why she has a *loaded gun* in her purse, but I don't want to make it worse. "Baby, we don't need to do this right now. Let's just get you cleaned up. We can talk after you've slept a little."

She shakes her head. "No. I need to get this out now. I just want it all out there. I *need* to get it all out there."

I take a deep breath. "Okay, if that's what you really want. Just... take your time and give me as much, *or as little* information as you want."

Her red-rimmed eyes lift to mine. "It was Lucas."

I clench my jaw, slowly running the sponge over her body. "*What* was Lucas?"

Jazz dips her hair under the water. "He was the one. At the lake. At the Malibu party. Tonight. *He's the one*. I can't believe I didn't piece it together before, but he actually admitted it, so there's no question. And Christian was his accomplice. Lucas was *boasting* about nearly raping me, Kingston. Telling me how much I was going to love it. He

222

started recording us on his phone, saying that he was going to send it to you. I mean, what kind of sick fuck does things like that?"

I damn near crack the shampoo bottle down the middle as I pour some into my hand. I take a moment to bring it to a lather before transferring it to Jazz's hair. Her body relaxes as I massage her scalp; meanwhile, I'm grinding my teeth together so hard, I'm surprised they haven't turned to dust.

"How did you end up at Windsor?"

She turns around and rinses the shampoo from her hair before replying. "We finished up early at work. It was only fifteen minutes. I knew you were probably already on the road, so I decided to just hang at the sub shop at the other end of the plaza and grab a sandwich. I was going to text you as soon as I got there, but about halfway across the lot, they pulled up in that Escalade—Lucas and Christian— and Lucas pulled me into the car. I tried fighting him off, but he used his weight advantage to immobilize me like the last two times. Tonight, he was crushing me *and* cutting off my air supply.

"When we stopped... at the school, I guess... he... shoved my shirt up." Now that her skin isn't so red, I can see the fingerprint-shaped bruises forming on her jaw. "He...put his fingers *inside* of me. He pulled his pants down and..." She gags. "Oh, God."

I'm going to fucking kill him.

"He took his pants down and *what*, Jazz?" I intentionally keep my voice soft to counteract the violent storm brewing inside of me.

"Rubbed his dick over my chest. My lips. He was about to force it into my mouth right before those guys showed up to take him away."

I squeeze my eyes shut, trying to ward off the images running through my brain. I can't make the rage stop. I need... I need something to tamp it down.

"Motherfucker!" Jazz screams as I turn around and slam my fist into the wall, splintering the tiles, coating them with my blood. Shit, that hurts.

"I'm gonna be sick." I turn back toward her right as she's cupping a hand over her mouth.

Yeah, me too.

Jazz falls to her knees on the shower floor and starts heaving, but nothing comes out. Scratch that. Here it comes... and... there it goes, right down the drain.

"Shh." I crouch down and rub my hand along her back. I hiss when the water hits my flayed knuckles, mixing blood with vomit as it swirls down the drain.

The beast inside of me is roaring, demanding vengeance, but leaving Jazz right now isn't an option. The second I get my hands on that motherfucker though, he's dead. I mean it. Literally fucking dead. I will make sure it's nice and slow, too, so he can feel every bit of terror and pain he inflicted on her.

Finally, when her body is no longer convulsing, Jazz stands back up and sobs while I rewash her body and rinse the remaining vomit down the drain. I shut the water off, grab a towel, and begin the process of drying her off.

"Damn it." My hand is really fucked. I'm pretty sure I broke some knuckles, and blood is getting all over the terrycloth.

"Kingston, let me help. You're hurt." Jazz reaches for my hand, but I pull back.

"No. You have enough to worry about. Just give me a sec."

I head to the linen closet and grab a hand towel, wrapping it around my knuckles. Once it's secure, I wrap a larger towel around my waist and help Jazz out of the shower. I start leading her back to the bedroom, but she pauses by the sink.

"Hold up. If I don't get this taste out of my mouth, I'm going to wind up puking again."

I nod and wait quietly while Jazz brushes her teeth and rinses her mouth out. I smile, despite the shitty circumstances, when she places her tooth-brush back in the holder. She stubbornly refuses to stay every night like I want her to, but she's brought several personal items over to make her more comfortable when she is here. I can't say I hate seeing her stuff mixed with mine.

Jazz immediately wraps herself around me, not leaving an inch of space between us, once we're secured under the covers. We're holding on to each other like a lifeline, neither one of us willing to let go.

I kiss the top of her head. "Do you think you can answer a few more questions?"

She nods slightly. "I can try."

"You said someone came to get Lucas. Who?"

"Dunno. When he was about to... his phone started blowing up. He talked to the person on the other line for a bit, called him sir, so I know it was a man, but that's all I got out of it. Then, a car suddenly showed up, parking right behind the one we were in. Lucas stepped out of the Escalade, sat inside the other car, and they drove away. I don't know who the mystery man was, but they scared the shit out of Lucas. That part was obvious."

I frown, processing everything. It takes me a minute, but all of a sudden, the puzzle pieces start clicking together. If Lucas is Jazz's original attacker, that must be who my dad was referring to in that video with Peyton. My dad said that if Peyton's lapdog goes after Jazz again, he will make him pay. Is my father the mystery man? But how would he know where Jazz was or what was happening at the time?

Fuck.

Why do all the goddamn answers lead to more questions whenever my dad is involved?

Jazz shifts her body, and my dick reacts from the

friction. I try to pull away, but she clings to me, tangling our legs together and rubbing against me more purposefully.

"Jazz."

I feel her delicate fingers pulling at the towel around my waist. "Kingston, please. I need this."

I groan as she loosens the towel and begins stroking my length. "Baby, you should try to get some rest."

"I will." Jazz places her lips against my collarbone at the same time her thumb sweeps over the precum leaking from my tip. "After I ride you."

She gets up on her knees and removes the towel she had wrapped around her. Her lithe, beautiful body sits before me, ripe for the taking. From her bronzed skin to the delicately sculpted muscles of her abdomen to her perfect, perky tits begging for my attention. My fingers trace the two horizontal marks on Jazz's torso, leaving goosebumps in their wake. The scars are much lighter now, no longer raised up and angry looking. Pretty soon, it'll almost be as if they were never there.

"They're healing so well."

"Kingston, I don't want to talk right now. I just want to feel you inside of me. Please don't make me beg."

I'm trying not to take advantage of Jazz's vulnerable state, but it's damn near impossible when she looks like she wants to eat me alive. I know the feeling because I've never wanted anything or anyone more than her. Jazz leans forward, her long, damp hair tickling my arms as our lips meet. I suck her full lower lip into my mouth, clamping my teeth down as she moans. She sucks my tongue into her mouth, and my dick jerks, imagining her giving it the same treatment.

Jazz straddles me as we kiss, rubbing her wetness along my shaft, up and down, down and back up until I don't think I can hold out anymore. If we're going to do this, I need to make sure she's well taken care of first, and that's not going to happen if I shoot my load before I can even get inside of her.

I tap her hip with my uninjured hand. "Come sit on my face." When she hesitates, I add, "What's wrong? Do you want to stop?"

"No." She shakes her head, emphatically. "It's just... I just remembered something he said to me. He wanted to go down on me... said he doesn't normally, but he'd make an exception for me."

I count to ten in my head, trying to remain calm. I don't know what the right thing to do here is. I *do* know she loves having *my* face between her thighs, but the last thing either of us wants is for her to be thinking about her would-be rapist right now.

"Baby. Don't feel obligated to do this. To do *anything*. I just want to make you feel good. If you need time, I get it."

She gives me a soft smile. "I know I don't *have* to

do anything, Kingston. Not with you. But I *do* want this. If I let that bastard ruin something that I enjoy so much, he'd win, and I'm not going to let that happen."

Jazz scoots up my body and combs a hand through my hair as she hovers above me, positioning a knee on each side of my head. She releases a curse when I lift my head off the pillow and swipe my tongue through her folds.

"Good?"

Jazz nods. "*So* good."

"Then drop down, baby. Let me eat that pretty pussy. Let me make it feel even better."

"God," she pants as I swirl the tip of my tongue over her clit.

After a few tentative licks, to make sure she's still on board with this, I devour her slick flesh, licking and sucking, loving every little whimper and expletive that's ripped from her mouth. I moan right along with her as her sweet cream explodes on my tongue. Jazz claws the headboard each time she orgasms, screaming my name over and over.

After I make her come for the fourth time, Jazz flops to the side, panting. "No more... soooo good... but too sensitive."

I use the towel that was around my hand to wipe my face. Thankfully, the bleeding has stopped, but my aching knuckles are swollen as fuck.

I roll over and place a kiss on her hipbone. "Does that mean you're done with me for the night?"

She pulls on my shoulders, prompting me to move up her body. "Hell, no. Just no more love button action."

"Love button?" I laugh.

Jazz gives me a warm smile that makes my breath stutter. "Get inside of me, Kingston."

I pull her nipple into my mouth, swirling my tongue around the tip as I withdraw. "Whatever you say, my queen."

"Queen? What happened to princess?" Jazz gasps when I give her other nipple equal attention.

I push up on my arms to look her directly in the eye. "*My* queen. No one else's."

"No one else's." Jazz cups both sides of my jaw as she repeats my words. "*Ever.*"

I stare down at her for several beats, neither one of us compelled to fill the silence. We're perfectly content, merely enjoying the closeness of each other's body. This feeling inside of me, the one that's making my chest expand, should've been my first clue on how much I worship this girl. No matter how fucked up my life can get, when I'm like this, with Jazz, I'm genuinely happy. I *live* for these little stolen moments.

"I love you," she whispers.

I grin. "Of course you do. I'm such a nice guy, what's not to love?"

Jazz shakes with laughter, tears springing from her eyes.

"You are *not* a nice guy. Most of the time, anyway." She pulls me closer and nibbles my earlobe. "But you are *mine*. Now, kiss me."

I groan into her mouth as I slide into her wet heat. Jazz's hips chase mine as I pull out almost to the tip, before sinking back in. Our pace is unhurried, lazy almost, but neither she nor I mind one bit. I'm not usually a fan of missionary because it's such an intimate position—and quite frankly, not nearly as much fun as others. But right now, I wouldn't want her any other way. Being able to feel Jazz's body flush against mine, our sweat-slicked skin rubbing against each other with each motion. Watching her expressive eyes tell me how much pleasure I'm giving her. How much she wants me. How much she *needs* me.

I'm not a *making love* kind of guy, but if I had to give this a label, that's what it would be, no doubt. My dick and tongue give everything I have and take anything she's willing to offer in return. My hands caress every inch of skin I can reach, while hers do the same to mine. I've never been more attuned to someone than I am at this moment. There could be a riot right outside my door, and I probably wouldn't notice. After Jazz comes apart one last time, I pick up the pace just enough to reach my own release. My head is tucked into her neck as I come, and out of nowhere, I have an epiphany.

Jazz Rivera is *the one*. The *only*.

I want this woman to have my babies. I want her face to be the one I see every morning when I wake up, and every evening before I fall asleep. I want to laugh with her, hold her when she cries, fuck her until she sees stars. I want us to grow old together and watch our children have their own children. Some people would probably say I'm naïve, that eighteen is far too young to know when you've met the person you're going to spend the rest of your life with, but I'd tell those people to fuck off. There's not a doubt in my mind, she's *it* for me.

"Holy fuck," I mutter.

"I know," she pants. "That was *amazing*. I'm spent."

I pull out and use one of the towels to help Jazz clean up. When we're done, she turns her body toward mine and places a kiss right over my heart.

"You're it for me, too, Kingston."

Huh?

I'm confused for a moment until I realize I must've said that part out loud. I squeeze Jazz tighter, petting her hair as she snuggles into me. When her breathing starts to even out, I close my eyes too, giving myself a few moments to soak it in before I have to do what needs to be done.

chapter eighteen

JAZZ

"God, I'm so excited for tomorrow."

"Me too. I can't wait to see the look on Belle's face."

I smile. "She's going to be ecstatic. I know I said it before, but thank you so much for planning this. My mom and I always tried to separate Belle's birthday from the holiday, and I was worried her dad wouldn't do the same. Since this is her first birthday without our mom, I wanted it to be extra special. You really nailed it, Kingston. I seriously can't think of anything more perfect."

Kingston pulls me into a hug. "I imagine it'd be tough being a Christmas baby, especially when you're younger, and that's a holiday you celebrate. It's easy to get lost in the mix."

"Right." I nod. "That's why we always had a

tradition of celebrating the holiday on Christmas Eve, and on Christmas Day, it was all about Belle."

"I think it's a great tradition." He kisses the top of my head. "I'm happy to help keep it going."

"How's your hand?" I carefully lift his hand to inspect his knuckles. "It looks a little better."

"It doesn't hurt nearly as much as it did. The ice helped with the swelling. Don't let me forget to call someone to repair the tiles after we get back from Disney."

"I won't." I shake my head, still a little shocked he punched the wall last night. "Have you heard anything from John yet?"

"The Escalade is no longer at Windsor, but that's all we know so far."

Apparently, after I fell asleep, Kingston called his PI to give him the scoop on everything that happened to me last night.

I take a seat on the nearby stool. "And John doesn't think going to the police will help?"

"He thinks it's better to leave them out of this, for now, considering the cover-up from your original attack."

"Right. Who could forget about that?" I mutter.

Kingston stares at me thoughtfully. "Is that why you had a gun in your purse?"

Shit.

Wait... *had* a gun in my purse?

I glare. "Why were you snooping through my purse?"

"I wasn't *snooping* through your purse," he insists. "When I found it in that parking lot... I opened it to check the ID. To make sure it wasn't someone else's that looked like yours. Where the fuck did you get an unmarked gun anyway?" I see the moment it hits him. "Shawn. He gave it to you."

"No, he didn't *give me* a gun. I *bought it* from a friend of his."

"Oh, that's *so* much better." Kingston gives me a wry look. "Why would you even want one?"

"Why do you *think*, Kingston? I want to feel safe."

"And you think a gun will do that?"

"It's better than nothing." I shrug.

"Not if you don't know how to shoot one," he argues. "So... *do you know how to shoot one?*"

"Not *exactly.*"

He points an accusing finger at me. "And *that's* exactly why it's staying locked up in my safe."

"What?" I shout. "You can't do that!"

Kingston's eyes flare with anger. "Watch me."

"It's not your call, Kingston!"

He exhales harshly. "Look. I'm all for the right to bear arms. If you really want a gun because it makes you feel safer, then I'm okay with that. But we're going to do it the *right* way. You're going to learn how to safely handle a gun, and you're going to have one that's registered.

"I refuse to allow you to put yourself at risk by carrying around a loaded weapon that you have no idea what to do with. Especially an *unmarked* weapon. Christ, if a cop caught you with that thing, you'd be screwed. Do you have any idea how strict California gun laws are? Do you really think having a criminal record looks good when you're trying to obtain custody? C'mon, Jazz. You're smarter than this. I can't believe that fucker let you go through with it."

"For your information, he *didn't* like the idea either, but unlike you, he *allowed me to make my own decision* because he knows I'm a big girl."

"Jazz. You know I'm right. And you know I'm coming from a good place. I'm not saying you can't have one. I'm just asking you to be smart about it. I don't want to lose you. I *can't* fucking lose you."

I groan, resting my head on the breakfast bar. "Fine. We'll do it your way."

"Thank you." He places a kiss on the back of my head. When his phone buzzes in his pocket, he pulls it out and says, "That's John."

I sit up.

"Yeah?" Kingston frowns at whatever the private investigator is saying. "When?" Now, he's scrubbing a hand down his face. "Nothing on Gale yet?" His hazel eyes flicker to mine as he listens to John, becoming increasingly more agitated. I have a feeling whatever John came up with so far isn't good. "Sounds good. Keep me posted."

"What'd he say?" I pepper him with questions as soon as he hangs up the phone. "Did he find Lucas?"

Kingston shakes his head. "Not yet. But Christian Taylor was found dead in his dorm room this morning. They're calling it a self-inflicted gunshot wound."

I gasp. "What?!"

"Yep. Police are saying it's pretty cut and dry. Christian left a note."

"Does John know what the note said?"

He gulps audibly. "Two words: I'm sorry."

"I'm sorry?" I repeat. "Sorry about what?"

"For participating in your assault? Cheating on his calculus test? Letting Peyton suck his cock? Who knows?"

"Holy shit." When I glance up, Kingston has a bizarre look on his face. "What's that look for? What are you thinking?"

His lips thin. "I think Christian's suicide may have been a setup."

"By who?"

"Any one of the major players? But my top suspect is my father."

I frown. "What makes you think that?"

Kingston grabs a bottle of water out of the fridge and takes a sip before handing it to me. "The video of my dad with Peyton. He said if Peyton's lapdog—

which all signs point to Lucas being that lapdog—went after you again, he'd pay. Even though Christian didn't directly assault you last night, he was an active participant in Lucas' plan. Knowing my dad, he'd consider that action a personal slight and seek revenge on all parties involved."

"So... if that's true... you think Lucas is next?"

Kingston nods. "Exactly."

"But... isn't your dad in Mexico for Christmas?"

"He is. And he flew commercial, so I know he's actually there because John verified it. But he could've easily sent one of his goons on his behalf." Kingston nods his head toward the window. "He was in the middle of the Caribbean when my mom died, remember?"

"I remember." I sigh, looking out the window toward the pool area where his mom was found dead.

"So, what now?"

"John's going to keep looking for Lucas, and we'll go from there once we know more. He said he passed everything on to his FBI contact in case my dad is responsible."

"Basically, we wait. *Again*." I grab the tie off my wrist and pull my hair back into a pony. "Do we continue to *act normal* like John suggested?"

"That's exactly what we're going to do. It's Christmas Eve. We're not going to let them ruin that, or our trip. I say we go back to your place to get your bag like we planned, then come back here to have our mini celebration."

"Is Bentley still planning to drop by even though Reed and Ainsley are up in Oregon?"

"He said he'd be here. We've been doing this thing since middle school. Ainsley and Carissa started the tradition and made a big deal out of it every year. Dinner, gift exchange, Christmas movies, cookies... the works. The guys and I were just indulging them at first, but we started to enjoy it somewhere along the way. After Rissa died... Ainsley insisted on keeping up with it. She needed that normalcy, and I think Bent did, too."

"It's nice you guys have your own special way to celebrate."

He brackets my hips with his palms and leans down to kiss me. "*We* have our own special way to celebrate. You're part of that now."

I link my fingers behind his neck and pull him into me for another kiss. "You wanna join me in the shower before we head out?"

Kingston flashes a toothy smile. "I *definitely* want to join you in the shower."

～

"You're sure this is everything?" Kingston holds up my overnight bag. "We're going to be gone for two-and-a-half days."

"Um... yeah. That's it. Why?"

He shakes his head with a smile. "I'm just used to women packing a lot more shit. Ainsley always has *at least* one suitcase for her shoes alone. And she's the lowest maintenance girl I know, behind you."

"Yeah, but Ainsley's *really* into fashion. Which is good for me, I suppose, since I have no clue what to do when I need to dress up."

Kingston grabs the back of my head and pulls me into a kiss. "I think you're selling yourself short. But if you ask me, you don't need to dress up."

"Says the boy who's always ready to attack me seconds after seeing me in a fancy dress."

"What can I say? I like the easy access." He shrugs unapologetically.

"I'm so sure." I laugh. "Well, I guess we should g—"

A blood-curdling scream pierces the air, interrupting my train of thought.

"What the hell?" Kingston rips open my bedroom door and peeks down the hall where the noise came from.

When I look over his shoulder, I see Peyton sitting against the wall across *her* open bedroom door. She's crying hysterically with her knees pulled to her chest, rocking back and forth, mumbling to herself. "What happened?"

Kingston takes a few steps in her direction. "Peyton. What's going on?"

Her watery eyes narrow on him when she snaps out of it. "Did *you* do this? Is this that payback you were talking about?"

Ms. Williams appears at the top of the stairs, pausing for a moment to catch her breath. "Miss Peyton. Are you okay?"

Peyton throws her hands out. "No, I'm not okay! Why would I be okay? What kind of sick joke is this? Kingston! *Are you responsible for this?!*"

Ms. Williams steps forward when Peyton gestures to her bedroom and peeks inside. She goes white as a sheet and stumbles backward. "Oh, my. I think... someone call the police. *Now.*"

Kingston closes the gap between my bedroom and Peyton's and follows Ms. Williams' line of sight. Once his eyes latch on to something, he, too, looks like he's about to be sick. "Oh, fuck. *Is that his....* Damn, that had to hurt." He steps back and turns his head to the side as he cringes.

"*What* had to hurt? What is that awful smell?"

Kingston tries holding me back when I approach Peyton's room, but I squirm past him and catch a glimpse. I cover my mouth, choking back bile at the horror show in front of me. In the middle of Peyton's no-longer-pastel-pink canopy bed is Lucas Gale, naked as the day he was born, arms stretched wide, cuffed to each post. He's lying in a puddle of blood, eyes frozen open in abject terror. I'm guessing that has something to do with the fact that his genitals are no longer attached to his body.

Lucas' bloody flaccid penis sticks out of his mouth like a Grizzly biting the head off a salmon, held in place by a strange leather gag that's crusted over with dried vomit. I'm assuming those are his severed testicles placed on each of his upward turned palms, the surrounding sheets, and wall splattered with blood. If I had to guess, I'd say whoever did this slit Lucas' throat *after* they mutilated his body. It looks like some kind of ritualistic sacrifice, but I know that's not the case. This whole gruesome scene is perfectly staged for dramatic effect. It's a message, plain and simple—a very bold, incredibly macabre warning to the owner of this bedroom.

"I-I'm going to go call the police," Ms. Williams stutters. "I-I'll be right back."

"No," Charles' voice booms. "Nobody is going anywhere."

I turn to the right and see my father observing the situation in the same cold, calculating way he assesses everything. *When did he get here?* He calmly removes his cell from his suit jacket's breast pocket and presses a button to call someone.

A moment after he places the phone against his ear, he says, "We have a problem. I need a cleanup at my house ASAP."

Peyton's and Ms. Williams' heads swivel in my

father's direction. *Cleanup?* Like a *dead body* cleanup? What in the actual fuck? When my eyes travel over to Kingston, he doesn't look surprised in the least.

"Yes, the mansion, and at least two, possibly more." Charles pauses for a moment. "Good. See you soon." He closes Peyton's door as he ends the call and levels each one of us with an icy glare. "None of you will breathe a word about this."

"Mr. Callahan... I know it's not my place to—"

"You're right, Darlene. It's *not* your place." His jaw tics. "Are there any other staff members on the premises?"

"No, sir. You gave them the day off to spend the holiday with their families. Remember?"

Charles nods. "Call them immediately and tell them to take the entire week off with pay. It's my holiday gift to them. Do *not* say a word about what you saw here, and do not speak to anyone else, *especially* the police. Go straight to my office and wait for further instruction when you're done."

"Y-yes, sir." Ms. Williams hangs her head and scurries down the stairs like her ass is on fire.

He turns his angry gaze on Peyton. "What the hell happened?"

"I don't know!" Peyton cries. "I just got home and found him like that!"

"You *just* got home?" Charles raises his bushy eyebrows, glancing at the face of his Rolex. "It's almost two in the afternoon. Where were you?"

She dabs her eyes and sniffles. "The girls and I had a slumber party at Whit's house."

I snort. She sure as shit wasn't with Whitney or Imogen the same night they found out she was screwing their boyfriends. And I have a sneaking suspicion she knows *exactly* who did that to Lucas.

Peyton's baby blues quickly flick to me, but then back to Charles. "Daddy, what are we going to do?"

"*You* are not going to do *anything*. Let the men handle this. I don't trust you not to fuck this up."

Her eyes widen. "But, Daddy."

"Not a word, Peyton!" he shouts. "If I hear a peep out of you about this, trust me when I say you will *not* like the consequences. Now, go to the guest bedroom and do not come out until I say so."

"But..." she tries again.

He points his finger toward the guest room. "*Go, Peyton!*"

She bursts into tears again and runs to do as he says.

Once Peyton is behind closed doors, Charles turns his attention to Kingston. "I trust I can depend on you to handle this with discretion?"

Kingston nods. "Yes, sir. Of course." He turns to me. "Get your bag, Jazz."

"What?" I ask incredulously. "We can't just—"

"Shut your goddamn mouth and get your shit!" he yells. Kingston's eyes widen, imploring me to read between the lines.

I grit my teeth. *"Fine."*

I give him the meanest glare I can manage before stomping into my room to get my things. When I return to the hallway with my bag over my shoulder, Kingston and my father have their heads together, exchanging quiet words. They stop talking when they notice me and pull apart.

My father straightens his tie. "Jasmine. I understand you're going away with your sister for a few days. Have a good trip."

"Really?" I scoff, throwing my hand toward Peyton's closed door. "We're just going to pretend there's *not* a dismembered corpse in there?"

"Jazz," Kingston growls. "Do I need to teach you another lesson in respect?"

I nail him with a look that says, *you keep it up, buddy, and fuckboy in there isn't going to be the only one that got castrated.*

The asshole smirks in return.

"Whatever," I mumble. "My apologies for being such a disrespectful asshole. You can punish me later."

My father claps Kingston on the back. "I see you've finally been able to teach Jasmine how a woman should behave in this world. Good for you, my boy. Although it seems like her language still needs some work." He raises his brows at me in a challenge, like he's daring me to talk back.

Kingston belts out a disgustingly haughty laugh.

"I'm not a miracle worker, Charles. You've got to give me some time for that."

You'd think my boyfriend was doing standup based on how loudly my father is laughing.

I think Kingston can sense I'm about to lose my shit because he grabs me by the elbow and steers me toward the stairway. "Let's go. You have a lot to atone for before we leave in the morning."

Charles flat out guffaws at that.

The second we're in the car, I lay into him. "You're lucky I can read you so damn well, or you would've gotten a swift kick to the balls for speaking to me like that!" I punch him in the arm. "Asshole!"

"Jesus," he mutters, rubbing the spot I just hit. "Calm the fuck down. You know exactly why I did that."

"You could've given me some kind of heads up."

Kingston pulls out of the driveway. "Really? When would I have done that? Before or after we made arrangements to cover up a murder?"

I cross my arms over my chest. "I'm still pissed at you."

"Well, then I'll just have to fuck that right out of you when we get back to my place."

"Whatever."

Kingston reaches over and squeezes my thigh. "Are you done pouting so we can actually talk about what happened back there? I've gotta say, you handled that whole thing freakishly well. I was waiting for you to start panicking at any moment."

I shove his hand off, still irritated with him. "Is it bad that I don't feel upset about it? Like, *at all?* I mean, seeing him like that was *disgusting*." I shudder. "But I was processing it with this odd sort of detachment. Like... I was watching a movie or something."

He glances at me out of the corner of his eye. "I can see that. As soon as I got over the sympathy pains, I kind of felt the same way."

"What was Charles saying to you when I went to get my stuff?"

"He's taking Madeline and Peyton to their house in Vail until the new year, to give this some time to blow over. Then, he suggested I do the same with you, which is when I told him about our trip to Disney. He added some, *don't disappoint me, son* garbage, then he wanted to know how I planned to keep your mouth shut if you were difficult."

"Oh, I'd *love* to hear how you responded to that."

Kingston shrugs. "I kept it vague, but I basically implied that I would punish you into submission if necessary."

I scoff. "I'd like to see you try."

He smirks. "Hard pass. I prefer my balls intact, thank you very much."

"Here's my question. How did someone even get Lucas in Peyton's room without being caught? He's a big guy. And if Charles and Ms. Williams were in the house when that happened, how could they have not heard it? Lucas had to have been screaming bloody murder. *Literally*."

"Your guess is as good as mine, but *my* first choice would be some type of fast-acting benzo or paralytic. The O-ring gag would've helped with the noise, especially if they shoved something else in Lucas' mouth before feeding him his own dick."

"Wow... it's kind of scary how quickly you answered that question. And that you knew what type of gag they used." I rub my temples, trying to figure out if I'm genuinely disturbed or turned on by Kingston's deviant side. I think it's a little of both. "I hate to say this, but I'm relieved he's dead. I'm *glad* vengeance was served, Kingston. I feel sort of cheated that I didn't get to witness his suffering. What the hell kind of person does that make me? I'm no better than the bad guys."

"Fuck that," he growls as he pulls his car into the garage and kills the engine. "I don't *ever* want to hear you say something like that again. You're *nothing* like any of those people."

"How can you say that?" I challenge. "I wanted him dead. I'm *happy* he's dead."

Kingston grips my chin and turns me toward him. "Your feelings are one-hundred percent justified, Jazz. Lucas Gale severely beat, stabbed, and violated you. He attacked you *multiple times*. If someone didn't show up to haul him off last night, he would have likely succeeded in *raping you*. There's no way you were his only victim.

"I have no doubt that if Lucas were still alive, there would've been *more* women who suffered at his hands. Someone who behaves like that without conscience, and with such determination, is a goddamn psychopath. Lucas reminded me of our dads, which is why I've never liked him. Knowing he was the man behind the mask only proves that my instincts about him were spot on.

"You have one of the biggest hearts of anyone I've ever met, Jazz. You should *never* question who you are, especially because of this situation. People like Lucas Gale or our fathers don't deserve your sympathy."

"Maybe you're right." I sigh. "Maybe I'm just conditioned to believe violence is a bad thing, no matter what."

"There's no *maybe* about it." Kingston shakes his head. "Hey, if nothing else, consider this one less problem we have to worry about. Merry Christmas to us."

My lips curl up in the corners. "Merry-fucking-Christmas to us."

chapter nineteen

KINGSTON

"Merry Christmas Eve, baby girl." Bentley swoops Jazz into a hug as he steps inside the pool house.

My eyes narrow when his hands slide a little too close to her perfectly heart-shaped ass. "Watch the hands, asshole."

Bent laughs. "I have no idea what you're talking about."

"Sure, you don't." I swear to God, he does this shit to fuck with me on purpose.

"Bentley, stop antagonizing him," Jazz chides.

Apparently, I'm not the only one who's picked up on the fact that Fitzgerald's a shithead.

"That's okay, baby," I call out. "The more Bentley pushes my buttons, the more I get to go caveman on your ass later."

Jazz whacks Bentley's chest with the back of her hand. "Now, you *really* have to stop. Kingston doesn't need more incentive to revert back to his Neanderthal self."

"All right, all right." My dumbass friend holds his hands up. "I'll be good."

"We'll see how long that lasts," I grumble.

Bentley falls back on the couch. "When's the food gonna be here? I'm starving."

Jazz grabs the tray of cookies we grabbed from her work and sets it on the coffee table. We were planning to make some ourselves—I know, how domestic of us—but the whole abduction/murder thing happened, so we swung by the coffee shop.

"Munch on those. It shouldn't be too much longer."

"You're the shiz, Jazzy." Bentley grabs a stocking-shaped cookie and shoves the entire thing in his mouth at once. "These are de-lish-shess." Crumbs fall out of his mouth as he speaks.

"Gross, Bent." Jazz shakes her head as she pushes his feet off the table. "You couldn't wait to say that until *after* you finished chewing?"

"Nope," he says, still chewing, cookie crumbs still spewing out of his mouth.

I point at him. "You're vacuuming that shit up before you leave."

Bent looks between Jazz and me as he brushes his

shirt off. "Sheesh, when did you two become such an old married couple?"

Jazz laughs, but I don't find the humor in his statement, because I don't see anything wrong with that.

There's a knock on the door, so I answer it, grab the food, and give the delivery guy his tip. "Thanks, man."

His eyes light up when he sees the Benjamin in his palm. "Oh, wow. Thanks so much. Merry Christmas."

"You, too." I nod.

Jazz and Bentley join me at the counter as I set out all of the cartons.

"Ainsley would shit bricks if she knew we were eating Chinese takeout right now." Bentley snags a container and starts dumping its contents onto a plate. "Sweet! Orange chicken for the win!"

"Why?" Jazz gets this adorable little frown on her face. "What's wrong with Chinese food?"

Jesus Christ, did I really just think my girlfriend's frown was *adorable?* I check to see if my balls are still there. Jazz gives me a weird look but doesn't ask why I'm grabbing my junk through my jeans.

"Nothing's wrong with Chinese," I assure her. "It's awesome, and if we had our way, we'd order it every year."

"So, what's the problem?"

Bentley laughs. "Because Ainsley insists that we

eat ham and all the fixings on Christmas Eve—which the place she orders from is the fucking bomb—but it's no Chinese."

"Have you guys ever tried cooking the meal?"

Bentley and I both laugh.

I swing my arm around Jazz's shoulders and pull her into my side. "Uh... no."

"Why not?"

Bentley points to me. "Because your boy is the only one of us who wouldn't burn a pot of water, and there's no way in hell he's going to take hours to prepare a meal that's wolfed down in a matter of minutes."

"I know how to cook," Jazz offers. "I'm pretty good at it, too. I helped my mom with Thanksgiving and Christmas dinner every year."

"Davenport, you better put a ring on it before that shit gets out. If the dudes find out someone who looks as good as she does can cook, you're fucked."

I flip him off. "Very funny."

Although... the ring idea isn't so bad.

Shit. I *am* fucked.

Jazz reaches over me to grab a pair of chopsticks. "Okay, if you two idiots are done, let's dig in."

I use my finger to grab her belt loop and plant a kiss on her lips. "I love you."

She smiles. "I love you, too."

I can feel Bentley's stare burning into the side of

my face as I watch Jazz carry her plate over to the living room and take a seat.

"What?" I keep my voice low enough so it can't be heard over the TV.

"Nothing," he replies, matching my volume. "Just didn't realize you two were freely dropping L-bombs now."

I raise a brow. "Didn't realize I needed your permission."

Bentley flips me off. "Fuck off, dude. You don't need to be a dick. I was just making an observation."

We stare at each other for a few beats. Since that night between the three of us, Bent hasn't stepped over the line once. Not unless he's purposely pushing my buttons, anyway. I know he's moved on from any notion of making Jazz his girl, and I honestly think he knows he misinterpreted his feelings for her. So, why does this whole *I love you* thing matter so much to him?

"Why do you care, anyway?"

"Because you're my dawg and Jazzy's my girl." Bent rolls his eyes when I glare. "I didn't mean it like that, and you know it. I'm happy for you, man. *Both* of you."

Bentley holds out his fist, so I give it a bump with my left hand. And just like that, the tension is gone.

"You gonna tell me how the other hand got all banged up? What'd I miss in the last twenty-four hours?"

"Dude, you missed *a lot*. I'll fill you in after we eat."

"Aw, hell, I have a feeling this is gonna be some story."

I laugh. "Yeah, something like that."

"You guys coming?" Jazz calls over her shoulder. "I've got *Die Hard* all cued up and ready to go."

Bentley's jaw drops. "Wait a second... we're watching *Die Hard?*"

Jazz's brows scrunch in concern. "That's okay, isn't it? Kingston told me to pick out a Christmas movie."

Bent's lips twitch. "And you think *Die Hard* is a *Christmas* movie?"

"Uh... yeah," she says. "It's like, *the* Christmas movie."

He turns to me. "Dude, if I were you, I'd be at motherfucking Tiffany's the second they open for business."

≈

"Okay, kiddo, we're here."

"I'm going to take the blindfold off now," Jazz adds.

Jazz insisted on covering her sister's eyes right after we pulled off I-5 into Anaheim, to hold on to the surprise as long as possible. Jazz helps Belle remove the blindfold, just as we're pulling in front of the Disneyland sign.

"Look, honey!"

Belle blinks a few times after the obstruction has been removed and looks to where Jazz is pointing. Her dark chocolate eyes widen, and her face splits into a grin when she figures out where we're at.

"Disneyland?!" she screams. *"That's* my birthday present?"

Jazz laughs when Belle squeals. "Yep. We have two whole days and nights to see everything! Do you like it?"

"I *love* it!"

I glance in my rearview and see Belle practically vibrating in her booster seat as I drive around looking for a spot. Thankfully, we're here early enough that it doesn't take me too long to find one.

"What do you want to do first?" I ask.

"Princesses!" Belle shouts. "I wanna see *all* the princesses!"

I turn around in my seat. "Okay, princesses, it is. But before we do that, we have to get your special birthday badge, so everyone knows that you're an eight-year-old now. We can't have them thinking you're still a *little seven-year-old.*"

Belle's head shakes. "No way. I'm *way* bigger now."

Jazz's tear-filled eyes meet mine. *Thank you,* she mouths.

I nod, taking a deep breath in when she smiles. Fuck, she's beautiful.

The three of us make our way to the entrance, waiting for our turn at the gates. Once we're inside the park, Jazz insists on getting tons of pictures in front of the train station, gushing over how cool it is that the floral Mickey Mouse has a Santa hat. After that, we stop at City Hall to get Belle's birthday pin, and then watch her face light up as the first cast member we see calls her by name and wishes her a happy birthday.

After checking the schedule, we have an hour to kill before any princess meet and greets begin, so I drag the girls into Fantasyland to get their requisite Mickey ears.

"Kingston, no, I don't need one," Jazz insists when I tell her to pick out a hat. "You've already done so much."

I bump her shoulder with mine. "You can't go to Disneyland and not get a set of Mickey ears with your name on it. Everyone knows that, Jazz."

Belle points to a pink princess hat, complete with a tiny crown in between the ears. "Yeah, Jazz. *Everyone* knows that. *Duh.*"

Jazz laughs as she retrieves the hat from the shelf. "Okay, okay. Looks like I'm getting a set of Mickey ears."

New hats in place, we go through another round of pictures, this time in front of the Walt statue. Jazz insists on getting a selfie with me, and right before I click the button, both girls plant a big kiss on each one of my cheeks.

Jazz smiles when she sees how well the photo turned out. "That's my new screensaver."

Mine, too.

She forwards the pic to her phone, and then we're off to see the princesses. The entire day is filled with lots of squealing from Belle and countless smiles from Jazz, while I simply take it all in. Well, minus that one part when Jazz was trying to hold her lunch in on the teacups. Ainsley and I have had several nannies take us to Disney over the years, but I can't ever remember having fun like I am now. It almost feels like I'm experiencing it for the first time, through a child's eyes. We end the evening in front of Sleeping Beauty's castle, watching the fireworks. Belle falls asleep in my arms about halfway through the show, completely zonked out.

"How can she possibly sleep through this?" I ask Jazz, dumbfounded.

She laughs. "Kids, man. They'll pass out anywhere. When their little bodies are done, they're *done.*"

Jazz loops her arm through mine and rests her head on my shoulder as we watch the finale. As pyrotechnics light up the sky, it's almost too easy to forget what we have waiting for us back home. This, right here... I could stay in this moment forever.

chapter twenty

JAZZ

"You are the sweetest, most thoughtful man alive." I pepper kisses along the length of Kingston's jaw. "Thank you for such a perfect weekend."

He growls when my teeth clamp down on his earlobe. "Fuck, I need inside of you. Keeping it PG for two days straight has been killing me."

I pull back with a smile. "All the more reason for us to get *extra* dirty tonight."

Kingston's eyes glow with excitement. "*How* dirty?"

I walk backward, stripping my clothes off along the way. I'm down to nothing but a thong when we reach Kingston's bedroom, so I turn around and grip the edge of the mattress, bending over. I look over my shoulder and see his lust-drenched gaze devouring every inch of my skin.

I slowly slide my panties off and kick them away. "You gonna stand there staring all night?"

"Fuck." Kingston bites his knuckles. "I don't know where I want to start first."

I wiggle my butt. "Does this give you an idea?"

One second he's five feet away, and in the next, Kingston's large hands are pushing me into the mattress, spreading my ass cheeks. I squeal when I feel his tongue where no tongue has gone before.

"Soooooo good." My moans are muffled by the comforter, but there should be no doubt how much I'm enjoying this, based on how enthusiastically I'm pushing back into him.

Kingston points his tongue and swirls it around while he inserts a finger into my pussy, pumping it in and out. He does this until I feel like I'm going to combust, then he suddenly pulls away and flips onto his back, feet planted on the ground while his upper body is on the mattress between my spread thighs. He swipes his talented tongue through my folds, while the finger that was just inside of me moves to my backside. Kingston's finger presses against the little rosebud while he suctions his lips around my clit and pulls. Right before I fall, he eases that finger inside my ass, pumping it in and out as I ride his face through an orgasm. I tense when he adds a second finger, causing the skin to burn.

"Relax, baby," he coos. "I'm going to make you feel so fucking good."

I breathe through the pinching sensation, and sure enough, as soon as I relax my muscles back there, it no longer hurts. There's pressure, sure, and it's a foreign feeling being so full, but it's not unpleasant. Kingston continues stretching my tight hole as he licks my pussy until I'm screaming through two more orgasms. I'm a boneless heap as he withdraws his fingers and opens the drawer to his nightstand, removing a small bottle of lube, tossing it on the mattress.

"You sure about this?"

I arch my spine languidly. "*So sure*. Although, don't be concerned if I can't move all that much. I think you just turned me into Jell-O."

He smiles. "Don't worry, baby, just lie there and let me take care of you."

It takes Kingston only a matter of seconds to undress before he's kneeling on the bed, grabbing the back of my neck and pushing inside of me.

I moan. "Your aim is usually much better than that."

Kingston starts to laugh, but it's choked off by a groan. "I just need to feel your pussy wrapped around me first. You complaining?"

I shake my head, as much as his grip will allow, anyway. "Hell no."

He slides his other hand under my torso and covers my right breast. "Good. Because I don't think I could stop right now."

"Then, don't." I claw the comforter as he deepens the angle.

I'm not sure how long we go at it, but by the time Kingston pulls out, we're both a sweaty mess, and the comforter has been pushed off the bed. I shiver when his tongue trails down my spine. When he reaches my butt, he bites each of my cheeks and gets off the bed.

I look over my shoulder. "Whatcha doing?"

Kingston bends over, giving me a perfect view of his ass, making me want to return the biting gesture. When he stands, he's holding the bottle of lube from earlier.

"You shoved this off the bed when your arms were flailing about like one of those inflatable tube men."

My jaw drops. "My arms were *not* flailing like an inflatable tube man!"

His lips curve. "Sure, babe. Whatever you say."

I watch as Kingston pops the lid on the bottle and squirts a generous amount on his palm. He fists his erection, sliding his hand up and down until he's fully lubricated. I hold my breath when he kneels back on the mattress and presses the flared head against my over-sensitized nerves.

Kingston glides a hand down my back when I tense up. "Breathe, Jazz. If it gets to be too much, just say the word, and I'll stop."

"Move, Kingston."

He slips the hand that was on my back beneath me, slowly rubbing circles over my clit. "Rub your clit for me, baby. Just like this."

I moan as I take over for him, working that bundle of nerves until I can feel wetness seeping out of me. Kingston takes the hint as I push back into his cock and slowly eases into my ass, cursing under his breath the farther in he goes. I gasp when he reaches the next barrier, feeling impossibly full, but I don't tell him to stop. Kingston was right; if I just focus on breathing through it, there's pressure, but not any actual pain. His chest is pressed to my back when he finally holds still, leading me to believe he's bottomed out.

Kingston places soft kisses down the side of my neck as I adjust to his length. "You good? The hard part's over."

"Yeah, I'm good."

At first, he slowly moves in and out in short little bursts, getting me used to the foreign feeling. As Kingston's strokes get longer and faster, he slips two fingers inside my pussy, moving them in time with his dick. His fingers and cock rub against each other through the thin stretch of skin separating them, flooding my body with indescribable bliss. It's so much to process at once, I almost feel like I'm having an out-of-body experience.

Before I know it, I'm coming harder than I ever have in my life. Kingston is quick to follow, shouting obscenities as he rides the waves of his release. When he withdraws, he bands an arm around me, pulling me up to the top of the bed with him. We're a tangle of sated, sweaty limbs as our heads hit the pillows.

"God, I fucking love you." Kingston's chest heaves as he tries to regulate his breathing.

I nip his chin, which earns me a pinch on my side. "Same."

His lips form into a sleepy smile as he brushes some wet hair away from my eyes. "You feel okay?"

"*More than* okay." I run my finger along the length of his eyebrow, down to his jawline.

Kingston's hand wanders down my body, and he chuckles when he comes across the fluids trickling out of me. "We should probably take a shower. And change the sheets."

I bury my face into his neck, grinning. "Probably. But that would involve standing, and I don't think that's an option for me right now. Nap first, clean up later."

"Good plan." He nuzzles his own face into my neck as he hugs me to his chest. The growing erection prodding my stomach is sticky from the lube and our combined fluids, which I should find gross, but I don't. "Add a second round to the agenda, and you've got yourself a deal."

I wrap my leg around Kingston's hip, allowing him to slide home.

"Deal."

～

The sun has barely risen when I peel my eyes open. I wince as I stretch, my entire body sore from mine and Kingston's sexcapades last night, including my ass. *Especially* my ass. While it wasn't painful during the act, my body is definitely protesting right now. Hopefully, just like the first time I lost my virginity, that will ease with time, because I really don't want it to be a one-time thing. Who knew butt stuff could be so fun?

Kingston's breathing is deep and even, telling me he's still fast asleep. I smile when I think of the perfect way to wake him. I carefully untangle myself from his arms, sliding down to the middle of the bed. I trace the long vein running along the under-side of Kingston's cock with my tongue. We showered right before we passed out for the evening, so his salty skin still faintly smells like the body wash I love so much.

Kingston groans as I take him into my mouth. "Well, good morning to you, too."

I hum around his girth, making him curse.

Kingston gathers my hair to the side and watches through hooded eyes as my head bobs up and down.

I suck him off just how he likes it: with a lot of tongue, a little teeth, and plenty of suction until he's wrapping my hair around his fist, pulling tightly as he shoots his load into my mouth. When I'm sure I have every last drop, I release him with a pop and swallow. I sit back on my knees with a smile, wiping a stray drop from the corner of my mouth.

"I'd like to request that exact same wakeup call every morning once we're living together."

"What?!" I sputter. "Did I miss the part where you *asked* me to move in with you?"

Kingston's mouth kicks up in the corner. "Am I supposed to pretend that's necessary?"

"And when exactly is this moving in together stuff supposed to happen?"

"Ideally, the day after we bring our fathers down."

My jaw drops. "Are you conveniently forgetting about the minor fact that we're still in *high school?*"

He laughs. "Are you conveniently forgetting that we're both legal adults, and I have more than enough money to pay for it?"

"Not the point, Kingston." I give him a wry look.

"Maybe not," he concedes. "But we'll need somewhere to go after the feds seize their assets. Charles and my father have been fairly clever hiding their money, but both mansions are in their names individually, so that'll be one of the first things the feds grab."

I stare at him for a moment, dumbfounded. I don't know why the thought of this happening never crossed my mind. "So, we'll be instantly homeless?"

"I'm sure they'd give us *some* time to get out, but I'm trying to prepare before it becomes a problem." Kingston shifts our bodies so he's now hovering over me. "I have a realtor keeping an eye out for new listings. Think about it. We can get a place by the beach if you want. Belle can have her own room and decorate it how she sees fit. Ainsley, too, if she doesn't wind up shacking up with Reed or going away to school. We're together practically all the time anyway. What's the big deal?"

"*The big deal* is that moving in together is quite the commitment."

"And?" Kingston's eyebrows rise. "Are you trying to tell me you're not sticking around?"

"We're *eighteen*, Kingston."

He leans down and sucks on the skin where my neck meets my shoulder. "You and I both know we've been forced to grow up early. Age is just a number."

I gasp when his lips seal around my nipple. "I don't know... it's a lot to think about."

Kingston's tongue dips inside my belly button before peppering kisses down to the apex of my thighs. "What I heard is I need to work a lot harder to convince you."

I squeal as he gives me one long lick from bottom to top. "Oh, yeah? How do you plan on doing that?"

"I'd say this is a pretty damn good start, wouldn't you?" He circles my clit with his tongue before sucking on my heated flesh.

My back bows. "It's a *great* start."

chapter twenty-one

JAZZ

"So... what did Reed think about his Christmas present?"

Ainsley's cheeks turn bright red. "He was a big fan. *Big*, big, fan."

I laugh. "And you?"

"You could say I'm definitely sold on the idea." Ainsley smiles coyly before throwing her hands up. "Ugh! I don't understand why Blair can so easily forgive Nate, but not Serena. I don't get girls who think the hero can do no wrong."

I look at the screen and see the headband-wearing brunette bitching about something. *Again.* We're two episodes in, and I gotta say, I'm not too impressed so far. It's basically like the Upper East Side version of Windsor.

"Yeah, me neither."

"Did you get that locket for Christmas? I don't think I've seen you wear it before."

I finger the delicate silver chain around my neck. "Yeah, Kingston got it for me."

Ainsley lifts the charm from its resting spot over my clavicle. "It's pretty."

"I agree."

I leave out the part that it has a built-in GPS tracker, so I never need to worry about being separated from my phone again.

"When do your driving lessons start?"

"Right after New Year's."

"Are you nervous?"

I nod. "More excited than nervous. I've driven before—Shawn used to let me practice with his car late at night in a Walmart parking lot. I feel comfortable with the controls and stuff. Just not the whole getting-on-the-road-with-other-cars-and-avoiding-hazards part."

Ainsley laughs. "Well, that is *kind of* the most important part."

"Hence, the driving lessons," I deadpan.

She grabs the remote and pauses the show when the guys return from playing ball. Kingston sets the basketball down by the door and goes straight for the fridge, grabbing three bottles of Powerade.

"Did you guys have fun?" Ainsley asks.

Kingston chugs half the bottle in one go. "We always do."

"Ooh, *Gossip Girl!*" Bentley plops in between Ainsley and me on the couch. "Hit play, Ains."

Reed and Kingston roll their eyes while my mouth drops open in shock. "You like this show?"

"Uh, yeah! What's not to like? There's a bunch of hot chicks in it. And everybody's always banging someone they're not supposed to be banging. Who doesn't appreciate some juicy drama?" Bentley looks at me like I'm an idiot.

I raise my hand. "Me. I could live without it for the rest of my life."

"Bor-ing," Bentley singsongs. "At least in fiction. Although, one should never underestimate the power of a good hate fuck. Man, those are the best."

Kingston's emerald eyes light up with amusement. *I believe you're familiar with the concept*, they say.

Quite familiar, my eyes retort.

Ainsley leans over and sniffs the sweaty boy beside her. "Bent, you stink. Go take a shower."

Bentley sticks his nose in one of his armpits. "Eh, it's been worse."

I make a face. "You *all* reek. It smells like a boys' locker room in here."

Kingston's eyes narrow. "How would *you* know what a boys' locker room smells like?"

I stick my tongue out. "Wouldn't you like to know?"

"Considering it definitely wasn't with me... no. No, I would *not* like to know."

The other three laugh while I shake my head.

"I'm taking my bathroom." Kingston points to Reed and Bentley. "You assholes can take one in the main house."

"Fine," Bentley grumbles, grabbing the sports bag he brought with him. "You're lucky I had the foresight to bring a change of clothes. Although, I've never had any complaints about walking around in the buff." He winks.

Kingston peels off his sweaty shirt and throws it at Bentley's head. "Get out of here and go clean up, dick. The sooner you do that, the sooner we can all eat."

I absolutely do *not* check out Kingston's ripped abs or imagine tracing each ridge with my tongue.

Kingston points to the corner of his mouth as he's walking to the bedroom. "Baby, you have a little drool right here."

I flip him off. "Bite me."

He chomps his teeth. "Anytime, anyplace, sweetheart."

Ainsley hops off the couch. "I'm going to go change real quick too."

Reed chuckles as he notices the giant stain on her shirt. "What'd you do?"

Ainsley scrunches her button nose. "Jazz made

me laugh while I was taking a sip of my soda. Pepsi came out of my nose and dribbled all over my shirt."

Now, he's full-on laughing. "*Sexy.* I'm sorry I missed that."

"Oh, *shut up.*" She follows Bentley out the door but pauses at the threshold when she notices Reed isn't right behind her. "You coming?"

"Gimme a sec." Reed and Ainsley share a loaded look.

She nods, seemingly picking up on whatever he was silently throwing down. "Just come up to my room when you're done."

I look at Reed questionably once we're alone. "What's up?"

He takes a seat on the couch next to me, nervously rubbing the back of his neck. "Ainsley told me that she told you about my... uh... *preferences.*"

"Oh. Um... okay. And?"

"I wanted to say thanks for your discretion. And for encouraging her to talk to me. I feel much better about the whole thing."

I wave my hand dismissively. "It's no big deal, Reed. *Really.* You make her *so* happy, and that's all I care about. I'm just glad you believe that now."

He clears his throat. "There's one more thing."

I raise my brows. "Yeah?"

"I... uh... wanted to apologize for the whole video thing. That night in Donovan's pool house. I didn't record it because I was being a perv, or I wanted to leak it. I did it for Kingston."

I frown. "Why? So *he* could leak it?"

Reed shakes his head. "No. So he could see what we all saw from the start. That you're different. That *he's* different when he's with you. But Kingston was on a mission to push you away as fast and as hard as humanly possible because you complicated things. I wanted him to have a reason not to do that. By seeing for himself how he looked at you, how you're both so freakishly in sync with one another, even when you thought you hated each other. I didn't want him to miss out on what could've possibly been the best thing that's ever happened to him."

I smile softly and squeeze his hand. "You're a good friend, Reed."

"So are you, Jazz." He gives me a sad smile. "When Carissa died... Ainsley was a mess. She'd been burned so many times by girls pretending to be her friend, but they were really just using her to get closer to one of the guys, or me. But Carissa wasn't like that. She was everything a best friend is supposed to be, the one girl in the world who truly understood Ainsley. Who didn't want anything from her *but* friendship. They even had the ballet connection. When Ainsley lost Rissa, she was *devastated*. It killed me watching her break like that. And though she got better with time, I didn't realize how much she was still hurting until the day she met you."

I quirk my head to the side. "What do you mean?"

"She stood taller. Smiled wider. I don't know... it's just like she was more *alive* than she had been in the two years prior. *You* did that, whether you meant to or not."

I dab at the corners of my eyes. "Shit. You're making me cry."

"Everything okay in here?"

I jump, startled by Kingston's voice. I didn't even hear the shower turn off.

Reed stands up and heads toward the door. "I'm gonna go clean up. Be back soon."

I nod. "'Kay."

"Why are you crying?" Kingston pulls me up from the couch into a hug. "Do I need to kick Reed's ass?"

I half laugh, half sob into his chest. "No. Reed's awesome. We were just having a little heart-to-heart about your sister." I wipe my eyes as I look up at him. "He really loves her. You know that, right?"

Kingston brushes some hair away from my face. "Yeah, I know."

"Is she gonna be okay when everything with your dad comes to light?"

"Sadly, I don't think she'll be surprised." His Adam's apple bobs. "But yeah, it'll fuck with her. Probably a lot. She's too much of an eternal optimist for it not to."

"At least you know she's in good hands with Reed. Right?"

He nods. "I can't think of anyone better to be there for her."

I smile as I rest my head against his chest. "Me neither."

chapter twenty-two

JAZZ

"Kingston, you might want to take a look at this," Reed suggests. "Madeline just walked into your dad's corporate office."

Kingston and I join Reed at the breakfast bar and watch the feed of my wicked stepmother standing in front of Preston's desk.

"Isn't she supposed to be in Colorado?" I ask.

"Charles said they'd be there through the new year." Kingston frowns. "I guess he decided to come home early. Dude, rewind it a bit and turn up the volume."

We watch as Madeline walks into his office and shuts the door behind her.

"Well, this is a surprise," Preston says, reclining in his chair. "I wasn't expecting you back for at least a few more days."

Madeline glares. "Well, I'd hate to disappoint you, Preston, but plans change when you find out your *lover* is screwing your *daughter!*"

"Oh, shit," Kingston, Reed, and I say in unison.

Kingston's dad laughs condescendingly. "Jealous?"

"Hardly," Madeline scoffs. "Why would I be jealous of my own child?"

"Why?" Preston's brows lift. "Oh, I don't know... maybe because she's twenty years younger, her tits and ass are a helluva lot firmer, and she works my cock over better than you ever have? The young ones are always so eager to please. Maybe we should call Peyton in here so she can give you some tips."

"How *dare* you!" Madeline seethes.

"Damn, that was brutal," I remark, totally engrossed in the drama. I guess I lied to Bentley last week about it not being my thang.

Preston looks at his perfectly manicured nails. "If I were you, I'd choose your next words very carefully. This conversation is already testing my nerves. Now, I'm assuming there's a reason you're back in town early? Would you like to share with me what that is?"

She crosses her arms over her ample chest. "I came to make arrangements to send Peyton's things overseas."

"And why would you do that?"

"Because she's going to finish out high school at a

lovely French boarding school. She's flying there as we speak."

"*What?!*" Kingston and I shout in unison.

Preston steeples his fingers. "And why pray tell, would she need to leave the country so quickly?"

"She didn't have a choice unless she wanted to be cut off!" Madeline shouts. "After my husband had to clean up that little message *you* left her, she told us everything. The inheritance arrangement you two had, how she hired those two dead boys to attack Jasmine, how *you* helped cover it up. How you were *forcing yourself* on her."

He laughs. "Oh, Madeline, don't pretend Peyton doesn't share your favorite form of currency. Who do you think she learned it from? I didn't force your daughter to do *anything*. She was a consenting—*and quite enthusiastic at times*—participant."

"She can't legally consent in the State of California until she's eighteen."

"Last I checked, she *is* eighteen."

Madeline narrows her eyes. "Peyton said you've been taking advantage of her since she and Kingston broke up the first time. She was still a minor then."

"Really? And where's her proof of that? It's a bitter little girl's word against mine, and I say we didn't start fucking until *after* her last birthday. Now, as for your other accusation, I have no idea what message you're referring to, but if I *did*, I'd say Peyton should probably take it seriously and that if *someone* needed to teach her a lesson, France isn't nearly far enough away to protect her."

She straightens. "Charles is incredibly displeased you violated your agreement. *Daughters are off-limits.* How would you like it if he seduced Ainsley?"

Reed and Kingston are both squeezing their fists so tight, their knuckles are white.

Mr. Davenport's boisterous laughter is so loud, Reed has to turn down the volume. "First of all, technically, Peyton has no blood relation to him. Secondly, my daughter isn't an opportunistic whore like yours is. Charles wouldn't have a chance in hell."

Madeline's face is so red, you'd think she just ran a marathon. "And what about Jasmine?"

"What about her?"

"Peyton said you're *obsessed* with that piece of trash." Madeline rolls her eyes so far back, I swear she should've tipped over. "Just like you and Charles were obsessed with her worthless mother."

"Gold-digging bitch," I mumble. "Talk about my mom like that again, and I'll show you how *trashy* I can be."

Kingston puts his hands on my shoulders.

"The only thing I'm *obsessed* with is getting that ten billion dollars. Hell, at this point, if I have to marry Peyton and put a kid in her myself, I will. My latest divorce will be finalized soon enough."

"You most certainly will *not!*" Madeline shouts. "The executor of Pierre's estate would never believe

Peyton would marry *you* for love. You're old enough to be her grandfather."

Preston tilts his head to the side. "And? Remind me again what the age gap was between you and Peyton's father? Oh, that's right. Almost *fifty* years."

Madeline scoffs. "*Nobody* believed I married Pierre for love, least of all him. He just liked the way I sucked his limp, shriveled, old dick. Thank God for Viagra, or I might have never gotten pregnant."

I gag. "Well, there's a visual I never needed."

"Guess he didn't like it that much, since he didn't leave you a *dime*," Preston deadpans.

Madeline reaches forward and smacks Kingston's dad straight across the face. Before I can even blink, he's dragging her across the mahogany surface by her *neck*, slamming her down. Preston's other hand wraps around Madeline's throat and squeezes. Her eyes are bugging out of her head as she's clawing at his fingers, trying to pry them away.

I slam a hand over my mouth. "Oh, fuck."

Kingston starts pulling on the ends of his hair, while Reed sits there in shock. I think we might actually be witnessing a murder right now.

"Listen to me, you stupid *cunt*." Spittle flies out of Preston's mouth as he continues choking the life out of her. Madeline's eyes are fluttering shut. I think she's close to losing consciousness. "If you *ever* try something like that again, or do anything to get in my way, I will *destroy you*. Are we clear? Because if not, then I'll just end this right now."

Madeline gives the faintest of nods. She wheezes and gulps for air as Preston releases her.

"Oh, well, now look what you did," Preston chides, stroking his erection through his pants.

I quickly turn around. "I can't watch this."

A tearing sound rips through the speakers right before I hear Preston chuckle. "I knew you'd get off on that, you little slut."

"What's he doing?" I ask.

Kingston clears his throat over the wet, sucking noises. "You can probably guess. She's definitely enjoying it, though."

Madeline cries out, but her voice is weak and scratchy. A moment later, there's no question of what's occurring on that video. There's no mistaking those skin-on-skin slapping sounds or their corresponding grunts and groans. Kingston and Reed both turn away, obviously no longer able to stand watching, but none of us make a move to hit the pause button.

"You're such a greedy little whore. A real sick bitch, you know that? I could've just *killed you*, and your pussy is *dripping*." More grunting. "I bet you'd get off on watching the new girls go through seasoning. When they're screaming and crying and begging for mercy. You'd love that, wouldn't you?" Now there's feminine moaning. "Yeah, I thought so.

Maybe I'll pop in next week for an inspection and bring you along. Would you like that? Would you like to visit the warehouse, watch those girls get taken against their will over and over and over again? Watch them be beaten and starved and drugged every time they fight back?" Her moans are even louder now. *"Would you?"*

"Yes!" she rasps. "Yes! I want to see it all! I want us to fuck as we watch them get hurt!"

Preston chuckles. "Ah, Madeline, it's too bad you're a lying, cheating slut. I think we might be soulmates."

"This is fucking gold," Kingston murmurs over the grunting and moaning. "He's incriminating himself left and right. Rafe is going to have a field day with this."

"Sick motherfuckers." I wipe the tears away from my eyes, but they won't stop coming. "They're getting off to the thought of torturing helpless, inno-cent girls."

Reed reaches back and hits the stop button. "I think we've heard enough."

"Agreed." Kingston pulls out his phone and opens a text window. "Reed, what's the timestamp on that?"

"Today. 2:24 p.m."

"Got it." Kingston nods. "I just sent the info to John so he can forward it to the FBI."

"Now, what?"

Reed raises his hand. "I vote for heading over to

Bent's and getting fucked up enough to bleach our brains."

Kingston flings his arm out toward the laptop. "After that, I think it's a perfect way to ring in the new year."

Agreed.

~

"Five... four... three... two... one... Happy New Year!"

As the ball drops on Bentley's 85" TV, Kingston palms the back of my head and draws me into a kiss.

When he pulls back, he rests his forehead against mine. "Happy New Year."

I smile. "Happy New Year."

The five of us decided to keep it low-key for NYE, considering everything that's been going on. Well, four out of the five of us, I should say, considering Ainsley doesn't know the real reason behind our desire to hermit. She thought the boys were joking when they first said they wanted to chill tonight because, according to Ainsley, several Windsor kids throw huge bashes every year, but she didn't fight 'em on it. She simply shrugged and moved on to another topic. I'm guessing it's because everyone we'd want to see is already in this room. Well, besides Reed's sister or mine, that is.

"Let's hope this year is significantly less fucked up."

"Yes, that would be good." I laugh, linking my hands behind his neck. "Although it hasn't been *all* bad."

His large hands frame my face. "Move in with me. For-reals."

I search his eyes. "Kingston, we've been through this. I thought w—"

"I found a house," he interrupts. "In Malibu. It's fucking perfect, Jazz. I know you'll love it. I don't want to miss the chance to buy it."

"King—"

"Happy New Year, baby girl." Bentley hooks his arm around me and kisses the top of my head. "You too, bro."

Kingston nods. "Same."

Bentley looks between us. "Did I interrupt something?"

"I was just telling Jazz I found a house." Kingston is looking at me, but he's addressing the whole room. "You guys wanna go check it out in the morning?"

"Hell, yeah, I want to check it out." Bentley holds his fist out for a bump-slash-bro-shake.

"Me too," Ainsley and Reed say in unison.

"It's such a great place." Ainsley clinks her champagne flute against mine. "I can't wait to see it in person."

I raise my brows. "You knew Kingston was looking for a house?"

"*Of course*, I knew he was looking." Ainsley taps her temple. "Twin mind meld, remember?"

"Or, you know, I forwarded the listing to you," Kingston adds.

Ains laughs. "That, too."

I hold my palm out in a gimme motion. "Well? Let's see this supposedly perfect house."

Kingston fiddles with his phone for a sec before placing it in my hand.

My jaw drops. "Oh, wow. You didn't say it was right on the beach!"

If this house is even half as beautiful as it looks from the pictures, I can see why Kingston wants it so bad. The interior is spacious, bright, and airy, with floor-to-ceiling windows and a huge deck overlooking the ocean. The front end has a charming little courtyard with mosaic stepping stones bearing pictures of dolphins, turtles, and other sea creatures. There's even a large pergola covered in gold bougainvillea, which adds the perfect pop of color.

Nothing about this place is cold and sterile, like my father's McMansion. It's homey and beachy and not nearly as big as I was expecting. The listing says it's just over three thousand square feet, but that only makes it more perfect. It proves my boyfriend had me in mind when house hunting. He knew I'd never be comfortable in an over-the-top mansion.

Kingston smiles. "Told you. Perfect. And there

are four bedrooms. Plenty of room for us, Belle, and Ains, for however long she wants it."

"Whoa, that's pretty sweet," Bentley remarks over my shoulder. "*Nice*, Davenport."

"So?" Kingston lifts his brows. "You wanna go see it in the morning?"

"Yeah." I grin. "I really do."

chapter twenty-three

KINGSTON

"Did you hear Christian Taylor shot himself over winter break?" Ainsley asks. "I mean, can you believe that? And Lucas Gale just up and disappeared. Rumor has it, Lucas dumped Peyton and ran off with an heiress. Peyton was supposedly so distraught, she begged her parents to send her to boarding school. Personally, I think it's because Peyton's former besties wrote her off, and she knew she'd be a social pariah. Whitney and Imogen were flouncing around, acting like queen bees, making sure *everyone* knows what a backstabbing cum bucket Peyton is. It's all anyone's been talking about at school. What a crazy first day back."

Reed laughs. "Whoa there, Ains. Take a breath."

Ainsley flips him off before turning her attention to Jazz. "Do you know why Peyton suddenly went to boarding school? Like, did the 'rents say anything to you?"

Jazz shrugs. "Uh... I know that she's somewhere in France. I don't know why, though. I've been staying here, so I haven't seen Charles or Madeline since before Christmas. But I think your theory is a good one."

Fuck. I need to have a talk with Ainsley soon. I know Jazz and Reed are having a hard time hiding things from her. Plus, I need to prepare my sister for when the FBI makes their move. I've been keeping it from her because she can't lie to save her life, but I don't want her to be completely blindsided. Maybe I'll tell her once we get into the new place, and there's no chance of her running into our dad.

Jazz has been staying with me every night since the Lucas incident. She didn't even argue when I suggested—okay, maybe *demanded*—it. We went back once to retrieve her things, and haven't returned since.

"When's move-in day, dawg?" Bentley takes a giant bite from his slice of pizza.

"Just over three weeks from now."

Bentley's brows draw together. "Why sho long? I fwought you were able to get cash out of your trush fund."

"Jesus, dude. Is it that hard to wait until you've finished chewing?"

He chews a couple of more times before swallowing. "Fine. *Why so long?* Is that better?"

I shrug. "The people I bought it from needed time to pack up, so I agreed to rent it out to them for a month."

Ainsley bumps Jazz's shoulder to get her attention. "Are you excited, Jazz?"

Jazz smiles when her mocha eyes find mine. I don't know if I'll ever get used to this feeling. When she looks at me like that, like she's truly happy—*that I'm responsible for that*—I feel like the luckiest bastard on earth.

She nods. "Belle is too. She thinks it's super cool she gets her own room, even though she doesn't live with us. Hopefully, that will change one day in the near future. Kingston's going to order this beautiful princess bed and surprise her with it."

Whoever thought I'd be buying frilly little girl shit? I'm glad Jazz is finally loosening up on allowing me to spend money on her. Granted, she won't let me go overboard like I want to, but she is getting better at accepting gifts. Especially when they involve her sister. Leave it to me to fall for the one woman who has no interest in my fortune. Go figure.

I pull my stubborn girl into my side and kiss her temple.

Ainsley places an open palm against her chest.

"Aw, that's so sweet. Look at you two—all domesticated and shacking up. I can't wait to be roomies!"

I give her the stink eye. "It's not much different than it is now. Jazz is with me every day already, and you're in here at least twice as much as the main house."

"True." She points a stern finger at us. "But I'd like to set a rule for no sex on the couch. Or anywhere out in the open. I don't need to accidentally walk in on you two getting freaky."

"On second thought, maybe you should get your own place," I deadpan.

"Haha, funny guy." My sister yawns. "So, when are you going to order *my* pretty princess bed?"

I scoff. "If you want a princess bed, knock yourself out. You have plenty of money to buy your own shit."

"Yeah, but it's much more fun when someone *else* buys me shit." Ainsley stands up and extends her hand to Reed. "And on that note, I'm out. Madame Rochelle was brutal tonight. I'm beat. You coming, Reed?"

"If you're cool with that," Reed answers.

Ainsley rolls her eyes. "Duh."

Reed raises a hand as they're walking out the door. "Later, guys."

"Later," Jazz, Bentley, and I say in unison.

"I guess that's my cue to take off, too." Bentley rises from the couch and heads for the door. "I'll let you two kiddos get to the wholesome part of your evening. Have fun! Don't do anything I would do."

Jazz laughs. "Night, Bent."

"Night, baby girl." He winks before blowing me a kiss. "Sweet dreams, sugar lips."

I flip him off in reply.

When it's finally just the two of us, I wrap my arms around Jazz's back and pull her into me. "You feel like getting started on those *wholesome* activities? I've got chess, or Sudoku, or Monopoly, or—"

"Shut up and kiss me, you jackass."

I give her an exaggerated sigh. "I suppose we can do that too. If I *have* to."

"Oh, yeah. You definitely *have* to." She cracks her imaginary whip. "Get to work, buddy."

Without any warning, I crouch down and flip her over my shoulder. With a solid smack to her ass, I say, "You're going to pay for that, sweetheart."

Jazz reaches between my legs from her upside-down position and rubs my junk. "Counting on it."

This girl.

$$\approx$$

"You're never going to believe the luck we've run into." I can practically see John's shit-eating grin.

"Even better than the video of my father with Madeline?"

"We may have footage to bring Callahan in." He

clears his throat. "*And* another informant who's willing to testify in exchange for immunity. The FBI is getting close to making a move."

"Holy shit." I grab a drink from the fridge and take a seat on the couch. "*What* footage, and who's the informant?"

"Oh, nothing big. Just Charles Callahan killing one of his employees. As for the informant, that would be none other than Mrs. Callahan."

Water sprays everywhere as I choke on the sip I was taking. "Explain. Start with the employee."

"On Christmas Eve, shortly after Lucas Gale's body was found, Callahan is caught on camera injecting a needle into Darlene Williams' body. Williams was sitting in front of Callahan's desk when he came up from behind and jabbed the needle into her neck. She slumped down in the chair, unconscious almost immediately."

I scrub a hand over my jaw. "How do you know she's actually dead?"

"Because a while later, Callahan returns with two henchmen. Charles placed a finger on her wrist and said the words, 'No pulse.' Then, the mystery men rolled her up using a large piece of plastic and duct tape—which they conveniently had at the ready—and hauled her off."

"Holy fuck. What'd they do with her body?"

"No clue," John says.

"How has she been missing for two weeks, and nobody's asked about her whereabouts?"

"She lived at the Callahan house and had no next of kin. Who would bother?"

"Another employee at the mansion?"

"Callahan could've easily told them she quit or got fired."

"She worked for him for as long as I can remember, and the woman rarely took a day off. So much for loyalty, huh?"

"I guess Charles wasn't willing to take the risk when covering up a homicide."

"What's the deal with Madeline?"

"Mrs. Callahan attends the same hot yoga class three times per week. After the feds viewed the footage we sent them, they knew it was the perfect time to approach her, so they did so after her most recent class. Once Mrs. Callahan heard the FBI planned to charge her as an accomplice if she didn't cooperate, the woman couldn't spill their secrets fast enough. Madeline fell right into their hands, playing the victim card. She told them she'd do whatever she could to escape *those tyrannical monsters*."

I scoff. "Right. That woman wouldn't know innocence if it smacked her in the face."

"Agreed, and her handler is well aware. But Madeline gave them intel we've been trying to gather for years, including the location of the warehouse your father was referring to. If it all checks out, the feds will have what they need to move forward."

"What'd she tell them?"

"She validated what we knew about your father's high-class prostitution ring and the fact that Charles is blackmailing officials, though she claims not to know any details about the latter. Most importantly, though, she did confirm both patriarchs are trafficking young women, mainly from Mexico and the Caribbean. That's where the big money comes from, especially since they've joined forces with a cartel. Their operation has become such a well-oiled machine, Callahan and your father have taken a more passive role in the day-to-day."

"How does Madeline know so much? I wouldn't think they'd entrust her with sensitive information like that."

"The feds asked the same question, which is when she demanded immunity before giving them anything else."

"Why?"

John clears his throat. "Because apparently, Madeline has been actively helping them recruit young women for many years."

"Oh, shit," I mutter. "Why doesn't that surprise me? What do we do now?"

"Hang back for now. Madeline gave them an address to an old warehouse in Van Nuys. She claims she was just there last week and that a group of about a dozen young women are currently under-going seasoning. The feds are going to see if it checks out, and we'll know where to go from there."

"Is it normal for the FBI to share so much information with a *contractor?*"

"Not at all." John clears his throat. "But Rafe knows the more information we have, the more we can help, and he trusts me to decide what should and should not be shared. For him, the rewards far outweigh any possible consequences in this situation. Let's just say you're not the only one with a personal stake in this."

Huh.

"So, you'll get back to me soon?"

"I'll get back to you soon," John confirms.

chapter twenty-four

JAZZ

"You're doing great, Jasmine. When the light turns green, go ahead and take the northbound ramp up ahead."

I glance at Evan, my driving instructor, out of the corner of my eye. "But, that's an on-ramp to the freeway!"

"Exactly. I think you've proven you can handle the surface streets well enough. Let's see how well you do with merging into traffic on the interstate."

Okay, here we go.

I turn on my signal and pull into the right lane leading to the on-ramp.

"Good," Evan says. "Now, hold steady on the accelerator and make sure you check your blind spot before merging left."

I swear my pulse is racing a mile a minute, but I

manage to follow his instructions without clipping someone's side panel. Of course, the freeway is packed; this is Los Angeles, after all.

"Now what?"

I see him fiddling with his phone out of my peripheral. "Oh... uh... this is good. Just stay in this lane and watch your speed. Be on the lookout for cars in front of you suddenly hitting their brakes. We'll go down for a few miles and then pull off."

"Okay."

I check my rearview and side mirrors periodically but mainly focus on the road ahead. I get a little heavy-footed on the brakes, causing Evan to jerk forward in his seat a few times, but he's too busy playing on his phone to bitch about it. What the heck is going on with this guy? The few other times we've gone out, he's been really attentive and helpful. Today, he seems distracted.

My instructor points to the green sign up ahead. "In one mile, take that exit and keep to the right. We're going to switch, and I'll drive us back."

"What? Why? Am I not doing okay?"

"You're doing just fine, Jasmine." Evan's thumbs fly over his phone screen again before he finally tucks it away in his jacket pocket. "Traffic is getting pretty thick, so I want to take over."

"Oh. Okay."

Well, that's a bummer, but I guess I see his point. Even if the freeway is jam-packed with vehicles in

LA, people are still speeding down the asphalt like they're auditioning for a new Fast & Furious movie. I successfully make it back onto the surface streets without crashing into anything and follow Evan's instructions through an industrial area. There's hardly any traffic here—I'm guessing that's because it's Saturday and the surrounding businesses aren't open on weekends.

"Go ahead and pull against that curb."

I steer the car over toward the curb and manage to park less than a foot away from it, which is actually pretty impressive for me. For some reason, I can't judge the distance between tires and curbs. Don't even get me started on parallel parking.

"Good job, Jasmine. Go ahead and leave the keys in the ignition and step out of the vehicle."

I undo my seat belt and get out of the car. I make my way to the passenger side, where Evan is kneeling on the sidewalk, tying his shoe.

"Sorry, give me just a sec to tie this, and we'll get out of here."

"No problem."

I lift the door handle, and I'm just about to swing it open when I feel a sharp prick on my neck.

I slam my hand over the spot. "What the hell?"

Did I just get stung by a bee? I turn around, and that's when I see my driving instructor throw a syringe to the ground.

"I'm really sorry, Jasmine, but it had to be done."

"What had to be—" I stumble backward when a wave of dizziness washes over me. "Whoa."

Holy shit, did he just drug me? The last thing I see before blacking out is Evan coming at me with some rope in his hands.

～

The first thing I notice is rocking—a rhythmic, bobbing motion of sorts. Then, there's the burning ache in my arms. I try to move, but my wrists are tied together above my head.

What the fuck is going on?

I'm lying on something soft. A mattress, I think. I wiggle my fingers and find that my hands are bound with a soft rope. It almost feels like satin, but it's thick. I give an experimental tug, but it's useless. These things aren't going anywhere. Whoever tied them knows how to tie a sturdy knot. Crippling anxiety seizes me when I remember how I got into this predicament. My driving instructor obviously drugged me with something, but why? Goddammit! How do I keep ending up in these situations?

Get it together, Jazz. Okay, take deep breaths and focus. Try to figure out where you are. Damn it, it's no use. I can't see shit. My eyes are open, but it's pitch black in here. The whirring of an engine causes steady vibrations to rattle around me. When my brain connects that with the rocking motion, it finally hits me.

I'm on a boat.

"Fuck," I mumble to myself.

"Don't worry, Jasmine. There will be plenty of time for that," a deep voice purrs. "Sooner, rather than later, since we're almost ready to set sail."

I frantically search the darkness. My eyes must be adjusting because I can see a man's silhouette in the area where that arrogant voice came from.

"*You.*"

I blink a few times when the light flickers on and quickly look around. I'm surrounded by dark wood and neutral colors. Plush fabrics and expensive-looking fixtures. The front wall is made of curved windows, but they're covered in heavy jacquard drapes at the moment—blackout, I'm guessing based on their effectiveness. By the sheer the size of this room, I'd say we're in the master suite. My eyes make their way over to the posh sitting area where Preston Davenport is lounging, looking incredibly smug.

"Yes. *Me.*" I flinch when Preston stands and begins walking toward me. "Were you expecting someone else? My son, perhaps?"

God, I hope enough time has passed for Kingston to know I'm missing. I subconsciously try reaching for my locket, but the headboard I'm tied to shoots that idea down real fast.

"Where is Kingston?"

"How should I know? I'm not his keeper."

Preston takes a seat at the edge of the bed, smirking when I scoot as far away as I can. I flinch when he circles his fingers around my ankle and strokes the exposed patch of skin between my jeans and low-cut socks. I have no idea where my shoes went, but I send a silent prayer to all the gods that I'm still dressed.

I narrow my eyes. "What do you want with me, asshole? How did I get here?"

Preston tightens his grip on my leg, so much so, I know I'm going to have a ring of bruises there. "You certainly are a mouthy one, aren't you? I see my son hasn't cured you of that yet." He tsks. "Shame. Although I can't say, I won't enjoy breaking you."

The captivating eyes I love so much on my boyfriend stare back at me with lust-fueled malevolence. But instead of the warmth and love I usually feel when I'm on the receiving end of those beautiful hazels, I'm cold. Ice cold. The intent behind this sick bastard's gaze as he's leisurely roaming my body is crystal clear. He wants to hurt me and violate me, and he's going to enjoy every second of my agony. Too bad for him, I'm going to do my damnedest not to give him the satisfaction.

Preston stands up again and holds his arms out. "What do you think of your new accommodations?

You're my first guest on this particular yacht. We're about to set sail on her maiden voyage."

This jackass acts like he didn't just kidnap me or tie me to a bed against my will.

I snort. "Last I checked, you're not supposed to drug or kidnap your *guests*."

Preston leans against the built-in cabinet beside him. "Yes, that was unfortunate. But my son never seems to leave your side—boy is like a dog with a bone—so I had to take the opportunity while I could."

"By paying off my driving instructor?"

His salt-n-pepper hair brushes his forehead as he inclines his head. "You're smart, just like your mother was."

"Don't talk about my mom," I seethe. "You have no right to even *think* about her."

Preston releases a hearty laugh. "See, now that's where you're wrong. I have *every right* to think about her."

I scoff. "Oh, yeah? And why's that?"

"Because she was supposed to be mine, but my asshole business partner had to go and knock her up!"

My eyes widen in surprise, from the words and the fact that this ordinarily poised man is yelling.

Preston straightens his spine and smiles. "You didn't know that, did you? How much did your mother tell you about me? About your father?"

I know he doesn't deserve an answer, but I also

know the truth will be a *massive* blow to his ego, so I feel compelled to reply.

My lips turn up in the corners. "She said *absolutely nothing* about you. I didn't know you *existed* until after I moved in with my sperm donor."

I swear the vein on his forehead looks like it's about to blow. "Liar!"

Damn. Mr. Calm and Collected has definitely left the building. Or the boat, rather.

"Nope." I smack my lips together, popping the P.

Before I can even blink, pain ricochets through my face as he slaps me. My vision blurs as tears fill my eyes. Shit, my cheek feels like it's on fire. I yank at my restraints, instinctively wanting to cup my burning cheek, but I'm reminded once again that I'm tied to a headboard.

"Watch your mouth!" Preston starts pacing back and forth in front of the bed. "You may look almost exactly like her, but you sure as hell don't *act* like her. Mahalia was *much* more cooperative."

"What's that supposed to mean?"

"I knew there was something special about your mother from the start. Unfortunately, that bitch I was married to at the time refused to have live-in staff. I thought maybe when I knocked her up, she'd change her tune—especially when she found out we were having twins—but she had a stubborn streak a mile wide. Letting Mahalia go wasn't an option, so Charles agreed to take her into his house. Then, the prick got her pregnant within the first month and decided to keep her to himself. I should've never married Jennifer. Look what I got out of it: two ungrateful brats who are sitting on a big pile of what should've been *my* money. If only I hadn't had that foolish itch to produce an heir."

I'm suddenly glad Kingston isn't here right now to hear his father spewing vitriol.

I raise my brows. "So, my mother and father *were* in a relationship at some point?"

This man is psycho, no doubt, and I know it's only a matter of time before he's done with the talking portion of whatever he has planned. But you can bet your ass I'm going to glean as much information as possible while he's so chatty. Plus, the longer I can keep him talking, the longer Kingston has to find me.

Preston glares at me. "No, they weren't in a *relationship,* but she wasn't treated like the others. Mahalia's situation was... unprecedented. She was afforded certain... privileges, provided she cooperate. And oh, how she did *cooperate*. For a while, at least."

I ignore the comment about my mom's cooperation. I don't need to hear him say he forced himself on her to know that's what happened. If there was ever any doubt before, that's long gone.

"*What* others?"

A wicked grin stretches across his face. "If you

don't figure out how to quickly fall in line, you'll find out soon enough."

The words Preston said to Madeline in that video suddenly race through my head.

I bet you'd get off on watching the new girls go through seasoning. When they're screaming and crying and begging for mercy... girls get taken against their will over and over and over again... beaten and starved and drugged every time they fight...

I choke back bile. "Why am I here? What are you planning to do to me?"

"I plan on getting what's long overdue. I'm tired of people trying to take what's mine. First Charles, then that meathead who couldn't listen to simple instructions. Even my own son, who I thought I could depend on to be my successor, fucked up. He had to go and fall in love with you. He tried to deny it, and he put on a pretty good show, but I know him better than he thinks I do. I was perfectly fine with letting him play with you for a while, but I *will not* let him keep you. I knew it was time to make my move once it became obvious that's exactly what he intended on doing."

Jesus, this guy is unhinged.

"What *exactly* do you think is 'long overdue'?"

"Patience, beautiful Jasmine. First, I have a surprise for you."

Preston gets a maniacal look on his face before disappearing into what I assume is a bathroom. I stretch my neck to see as he returns, pulling something behind him. Oh, shit. Not some*thing*. Some*one*. Crazy Pants here is dragging my severely beaten sperm donor through the doorway, leaving a trail of smeared blood across the polished floor. Charles' face is so swollen, I hardly recognize him. At first, I think he's unconscious, but then a pained groan escapes his lips as Preston stops and drops Charles' upper body back to the floor.

"What the fuck?"

I don't realize I said that out loud until Preston responds.

"You see, Jasmine. It's time you learn the truth about how your mother *really* died. Consider it my gesture of goodwill in exchange for your future deference." Charles groans even louder this time when Preston kicks him in the ribs. "Go on, Charles. Tell Jasmine how *you're* responsible for Mahalia's death."

I'll say it again: What. The. Fuck.

chapter twenty-five

JAZZ

"What?!"

Preston rolls his eyes when Charles still doesn't produce any intelligible sounds. "Oh, fine. I guess I'll tell her since you're *indisposed*."

"What's there to tell? My mom got caught in the middle of a drive-by while she was waiting for the bus."

He nods. "Yes, that disgustingly crime-ridden area you lived in was quite convenient to make it look like an accident, wasn't it? But let me ask you this: Did the police ever mention any gang involvement? Or did you just assume?"

I don't like where he's going with this.

"Drive-bys happen all the time in LA. Why would I think any differently?"

"And *that's* exactly why it was such a perfect

cover-up!" Preston points his finger at me. "You see... when in reality, after many years living in freedom—per the agreement your father made behind my back because the sonuvabitch loved her in his own twisted way—Mahalia decided to pay Charles a visit."

"Why would she do that?"

He grins. "That's what makes this whole thing so great. Her maternal instincts apparently won out over her self-preservation. And *that* ultimately led to her demise."

I shake my head. "I don't get it."

"Mahalia got the idea in her head that she could extort money from Charles." He laughs. "Quite frankly, I think she'd been away for so long, she forgot who she was dealing with. Anyway... you see, her oldest daughter—*that'd be you*—was getting ready to start her senior year of high school. Poor Mahalia only wanted what was best for her child, who was highly intelligent, but had no hopes of going to college without a full scholarship."

No.

"Ah... I can see by your face that you know I'm speaking the truth. Shall I continue?"

I nod, too choked up to form words.

"As I was saying... she was broke, which should come as no surprise. She was living paycheck-to-paycheck in the fifteen years before her little impromptu visit, which means no college savings for you. Well, in those fifteen years, Mahalia evidently grew some balls, because she would've *never* dared to try something like this back when I knew her.

"She told your father"—he nudges Charles with his foot—"that if he didn't agree to fund your college education, she would go to the police and tell them everything she knew about our... less than legal activities. Daddy Dearest agreed to her demands, provided she sign off on a paternity affidavit. He called it his insurance policy in case she decided to go to the authorities anyway."

Okay, this is the part that never made sense to me, and I have a feeling I'm about to get my answer.

"Why would he want to claim me? I would've never known who he was. Who *any* of you were."

"Because Mahalia signed her death warrant the moment she showed up at his door. Charles told her if she ever came back, or attempted to contact either one of us, it'd cost her her life. Neither he nor I had any indication as to how much information she had shared with you. So... in order to keep an eye on *you*, Charles had to gain custody of you following your mother's fatal *accident*. And imagine my pleasant surprise when you show up, a nearly identical version of the woman who slipped through my clutches. It's like the fates were granting me a second chance to make things right."

"You're a sick fuck," I snap.

"You say that like it's a bad thing." His lips curve

into a cruel smirk. "Don't worry, Jasmine. After we get out to sea and I dump your backstabbing father into the Pacific, you and I will have some fun. For some reason, I get the feeling you *like* a little depravity in the bedroom. Lucky for you, I have *plenty* to go around."

The yacht suddenly starts moving, and Preston's eyes light up. "Oh, good. It looks like the festivities will be starting soon. If you'll excuse me, I'm just going to go check on the captain and make sure he takes us far enough away from any prying eyes." Preston nods to my father. "Make sure he doesn't leave. Oh, who am I kidding? He's not going anywhere in that condition."

"Wake up!" I whisper-shout the second Preston's laughter fades from outside the room. "If you have any paternal instincts deep down in that fucked up brain of yours, you'd wake up and untie me!"

I pull at my restraints with a frustrated growl. I keep trying and trying to yank my arms free until I'm panting from the exertion.

"Charles!" I try again, tears falling down my face. "Please *get up!* Don't let Preston get away with this! If you don't want to do it for me, do it for yourself. He's going to *kill you!*"

Sperm Donor groans again. *Finally*, some acknowledgment! Charles rolls to his side, wheezing. He slowly peels one eye open—easier said than done when it's so swollen—and locks in on me.

"Jasmine." My father coughs as if speaking took some serious effort.

"Who did this to you? Preston?"

He gives a minute shake of his head. "Hired... muscle."

Of course. Preston doesn't like to get his own hands dirty.

"Can you move?" I keep my eye on the door, waiting for Preston to reappear at any moment. "Can you untie me?"

"Can... try... don't... know... if... succeed." He has another coughing fit.

"Shh! Keep it down."

Charles army-crawls toward me with an agonizingly slow pace. Each time he moves, he makes this horrific sound that makes me think of an animal being tortured. He's wheezing loudly, beads of sweat dripping down his face. I sit up as much as I can when he's almost made his way over to the bed, scooting as far over as I can to make it easier for him to reach me. Right when he extends his arm, trying to use the bed for stability, the door opens.

"I wouldn't do that if I were you." Preston's back, with a gun pointed directly at my father.

I curse internally when Charles slumps face down in defeat. I was *so close*. I don't know how far I could've gone since I have no clue how far offshore we are at this point, but I would've tried. I'd rather drown while attempting to flee than lie here and allow Preston to abuse me.

Preston tsks. "Oh, Jasmine. What am I going to do with you? It seems like you need a lesson in who you're dealing with." Before I get a chance to ask him what that is, he cocks the trigger and shoots.

I scream as blood soaks through the right leg of Charles' slacks. Charles, however, doesn't make a sound. I can still see the faint rise and fall of his back while he takes labored breaths, but he's completely silent. He must've passed out.

"You're a goddamn psycho!" I yank on the ropes as hard as I possibly can, trying to get free. I cry out when it feels like I've just about dislocated my shoulder.

Preston trains the gun on me. "Don't make this more difficult than it needs to be."

"*Fuck you!*"

His eyes flash with rage. "You little slut. I think I need to teach you some fucking respect."

I pull at my restraints furiously as Preston gets closer and closer, but it's no use. When he reaches the bed, he tucks the gun into the back waistband of his pants and climbs onto the mattress, jabbing his knee into my chest, knocking the breath out of me. I plant my feet on the bed, making a pathetic attempt at a bridge pose as he fumbles with the button on my jeans. He's at the wrong angle for me to nail him in the balls, but that doesn't stop me from trying.

"Hold still, you bitch!" he growls.

"Eat shit!" I counter.

I turn my head as his fist comes flying toward my face. Preston's hand connects with my cheekbone, which hurts like a motherfucker, but at least it wasn't my eye, I suppose. I'm stunned just long enough for him to unfasten my jeans and start pulling them over my hips.

"Get your nasty fucking hands off of me!"

I twist and turn my lower body, trying to prevent the denim from sliding down my legs, but not being able to use my hands is really hindering any progress.

Preston gives me a sinister smile as he success-fully removes my pants and tosses them behind him. He grips my bare legs, digging his thumb into a nerve on my upper inner thigh. I cry out when he presses harder, and a sharp pain steals my breath. His hands are mere inches away from my panty line as he shoves my knees into my chest. Preston holds my knees in place as he stares down at the small scrap of cotton separating my bare pussy from his greedy eyes.

Preston leans forward, banding one arm over my legs. Then he drops his hips and moans.

"If you haven't figured it out yet, *my sweet flower*, I *like it* when you fight back. It makes my dick hard." He presses his erection into me, punctuating his statement.

I bare my teeth at him. "What did you just call me?"

"Oh? Did you like that? I remember your mother used to say that to you. At the time, I thought it was a silly term of endearment, but now, I'm curious if it's an accurate description of your sweet cunt. My son certainly seems to think it's worth throwing everything away for."

Preston circles my ankles again and pulls them around his waist as he proceeds to dry hump me. I'm about to start screaming when my toe butts up against the gun. I don't hesitate for a second. I tighten my thighs around Preston and bring my feet together just enough to pull the weapon out of his pants.

He figures out what I'm doing pretty fast and twists out of my grip, but not before I get the gun and kick it to the floor. Preston rewinds his hand, and bitch slaps me in the same spot he punched me earlier. My eyes fill with tears, quickly losing the battle to keep them at bay. Vomit climbs up my throat as he pins my legs to my chest again, and starts rubbing me through my underwear with a look of sheer ecstasy on his perverted face.

"You're a sick bastard!"

He laughs sardonically as he dips the tip of his thumb inside of me through the thin cotton barrier. "And you're a fucking cock tease. We make a good pair, don't we?"

I frantically scroll through my brain, struggling to find a way out of this. Panic overwhelms me as my mind refuses to produce anything viable. How many times do I have to be assaulted by these elitist pricks before enough is enough? Seriously, it's a fucking miracle my sanity is still intact. I don't know if that'll still be the case if this goes any further.

No, I *can't* think like that. I have to get out of this. There is no other option. If what Preston said is true —if my mom died because she was trying to do what she thought was best for me—then I owe this to her. I *refuse* to let her death be in vain. I will *not* let these sick fucks win. I steel my resolve when I figure out how I'm going to approach this.

Preston gives me a smarmy smile as he grips the straps of my underwear. "Now, I think we've had enough foreplay, don't you? Let's get these things off so we can have some *real* fun."

"Wait!"

To my surprise, he actually pauses. "What?"

"I'll do whatever you want." I muster all the sincerity I can manage into my tone. "I promise. I'll stop fighting... or... if you want me to pretend to fight, I can do that too."

Preston's forehead is unnaturally smooth as he frowns. "Do you think I'm stupid?"

"No." I shake my head. "Not at all; I swear. I just... I just need something from you first."

Preston sits back on his knees and assesses me

carefully. "All right, I'm curious enough to indulge you. What *exactly* do you need from me before I *take* what I want from you?"

"I want to be the one to kill him. Charles, I mean. I want the last thing he sees to be my face staring down the barrel of a gun."

His eyes narrow. "And why would you want to do that?"

"For what he did to my mom," I explain. "Where I grew up, if somebody takes something of value from you, you take back, no matter the cost. He had my mom shot to death, so it's only fair I do the same to him."

The crazy bastard likes this idea. I can tell. More importantly, he's starting to believe me.

"All you need to do is untie me. Then, I can shoot Charles, we can dump his body, then you can do whatever you want with me." When he still seems doubtful, I add, "You can even call me Mahalia if you'd like. I'll pretend to be her for as long as you want me to."

I swallow hard, waiting for him to make a decision. When his face lights up in a genuine—*albeit batshit*—smile, I know I've hooked him.

"Okay... I'll bite." His eyes narrow again. "But don't think I'm just going to hand you the gun and let you have a go at it. I'll be right behind you, *holding the gun*, while you pull the trigger."

Shit. Not exactly what I was hoping for, but I'll

have to take it and figure out the rest as I go. If I can get Preston to untie me, I'll be in a much better position to improvise.

I nod. "Okay."

"Then... I'm going to fuck every one of your holes while you scream for mercy." Preston's watching me carefully, gauging my reaction.

I gulp, allowing him to see the fear his words have summoned. "Whatever you want."

He nods, seemingly satisfied by my answer. Preston slides off the bed to retrieve the gun, placing it behind his back again.

"Don't get any funny ideas while I untie those ropes. If you go for the gun again, I'll fuck your pussy with the barrel while my dick is up your ass."

Jesus-fucking-Christ, this man is disturbed. Well and truly disturbed.

I hold my breath when he comes closer and reaches over me to begin the process of unknotting the restraints. Once my hands are free, I instinctively rub my wrists, breathing a sigh of relief.

"Get up." Preston makes a come hither motion with one hand while he uses the other to point the gun at me. "Let's get this over with."

I climb off the bed and slowly walk toward Preston with my hands raised in surrender. I tell myself to ignore the look he gives me as he eyes my bare legs, paying particular attention to the apex of my thighs.

"Good girl."

When I join him where he's standing over my unconscious father, he kicks Charles in the ribs, causing him to jolt awake. Preston flips the beaten man over with the toe of his tacky boat shoe, so he's on his back.

I look between my father, and the gun Preston has pointed at him. "What do I do? I've never shot a gun before."

His lips turn up in the corner. "Come here, sweet Jasmine. I'll show you what to do."

I tentatively take a few steps closer, gasping in surprise as he grabs my arm, pulling me into him. With my back at Preston's front, he wraps his arms around me from behind and nuzzles his nose into my hair.

"Mmm... you smell sweet too. I can't wait to get a taste of your pussy." Bile churns in my gut when he presses his hard-on into my lower back. Preston takes my arms, guiding them into position. He wraps his hands over mine as he curls my index finger over the trigger of the gun. "Now, I'm going to slide the safety off, just like this." He pauses for effect before doing just that. "Then we're going to aim for that bullseye right in the middle of his forehead." He lowers the gun until it's pointing at my father's head. "Wake up, Charles! You don't want to miss this."

My father's eyes open slightly, immediately honing in on me. My breath stutters when I see the resignation in his gaze—the hopelessness. No matter how much I hate this man, I don't want to actually kill him. I don't want that on my conscience. Besides, I'd much rather see him rot in a jail cell for the rest of his life.

"Any final words you'd like to say to your daughter?" Preston taunts. "Speak now or forever hold your peace."

"I-I'm s-sorry, Jasmine," Charles chokes out. "For... every... thing."

Tears start pouring out of my eyes with no warning. Preston has to catch me when my knees buckle.

He chuckles. "Oh, don't back out on me now, Jasmine. We're just getting to the good part."

I take a fortifying breath when he positions my finger back on the trigger. Shit. Think fast, Jasmine. How am I going to get out of this? Right as Preston's slowly putting pressure on my finger, an eerily calm voice stops him in his tracks.

"Let her go, or I'll put a bullet in *your* brain."

chapter twenty-six

KINGSTON

My father's eyes swing in my direction to find me pointing my gun directly at him. Jazz gasps when he bands an arm around her torso and points his gun to her temple. It takes every ounce of control I possess to remain calm.

"Now, now, Kingston. I would put the gun down if I were you. You wouldn't want poor Jasmine here to get hurt, would you?"

I briefly take inventory of my girl's appearance. My jaw tics when I notice a bruise blooming on her left cheek, but other than that, she seems relatively unchanged. Although considering her pants are gone, I have to ask.

"You okay, Jazz?" I want to stab myself in the eye the moment the words leave my mouth. Of course, she's not okay. Even if my dad hasn't had the chance to do any real damage yet, she still has a madman pressing a gun against her temple.

"I'm okay." She winces when my father tightens his grip.

"She won't be if you don't put the gun down," my asshole father promises.

"Step. The. Fuck. Away. From. Her." Each word that comes out of my mouth is laced with deadly intent. "I'm not afraid to kill you."

"Like father, like son," he snarls, pointing the gun directly at me now.

Unfortunately, he still has a tight hold on Jazz. I'm confident in my aim, but too many things can go wrong if I fired with her standing so close to him. It's not a risk I'm willing to take. I just hope the guys have successfully cleared the decks. The last thing I need is for someone else to come in here and add to my problem.

"I am *nothing* like you, old man."

"Really?" The arm that's holding Jazz moves until his hand is right over her breast. My trigger finger gets itchy when he squeezes it, taunting me. "We have the same taste in women."

I have to consciously avoid looking at Jazz's face right now because I don't think I can handle seeing the fear I know she must be feeling. "I'm not going to say it again, Dad. Let her go."

"Or what?" he scoffs. "I don't think you have the balls to shoot me."

I aim the gun to the right and pull the trigger. Jazz screams when the mirror above the dresser shatters. Out of the corner of my eye, I see Charles crawling on the floor, slowly inching toward them. I quickly glance his way and find him looking right back at me, silently trying to communicate his intentions. I don't trust that bastard as far as I can throw him, but I do believe his hatred for my father is strong enough to let this play out. I know I need to keep my father distracted long enough for that to happen, though.

"You don't think so?" A muscle in his cheek jumps as I goad him. "Why not? Because you've been such an exemplary father all these years?"

"You ungrateful little shit. I should've had someone kill you, just like I did with your bitch of a mother." My father's mouth forms into a malicious grin when he sees my lack of shock. "Ah, I can see that comes as no surprise to you. Maybe you *are* smarter than I've given you credit for. Does your sister know?"

"Know what an evil bastard you are?" I ask. "Yes. Does she know the details of what you and Callahan have done? She's about to find out. I'm sure it'll be all over every news channel soon enough."

His eyes narrow. "What's that supposed to mean?"

"It means exactly what I said. By the time you get off this boat, Ainsley—*and the rest of the world*—will know all your dirty deeds. The trafficking, the embezzlement, the cartel connections, bribery, and blackmail. *All of it.*" When his eyes widen, I continue. "You see, dear father, the FBI has been on to you two for a long time. And it just so happens that your jilted lover, Madeline, gave them the missing piece of the puzzle they needed to bust your ass. Your warehouse is being raided as we speak."

His eyes flash with rage, right before he points the gun at Charles and shoots him in the head. Blood splatters as Charles' lifeless body immediately falls to the floor. My father then swings the gun back to me, but Jazz uses the distraction to shove out of his hold before he gets the chance to pull the trigger. As his weapon drops to the floor, Jazz takes the opportunity to duck into a closet. With her out of the line of fire, I can now focus solely on taking this motherfucker down.

My father's nostrils flare, and his eyes are crazed as he lunges for me. I don't give him a chance to touch me, though. I aim the barrel of my gun and fire. My first shot hits him in the leg, causing him to fall to his knees. He doubles over when my second shot hits him in the shoulder.

"You shot me!" He scrambles for the gun he dropped when Jazz pushed him, but he's having trouble moving his arm.

I step forward and kick the gun away. "And I'll do it again if you don't give up. I'd rather let the feds deal with you so I can enjoy the thought of you rotting away getting raped in prison for the rest of your miserable life, but I'm not afraid to blow your brains out if you force my hand. Either way, you're no longer a problem."

"You'd murder your father for a piece of pussy?" he screams.

I scoff. "No. I'd kill you because you're a sadistic fuck who doesn't deserve to breathe. The world is a better place without you."

"When did you become such a goddamn vigilante?" My father's face pales and sweat beads his brow as the blood loss starts to affect him.

"Right around the time I found out you were responsible for my mother's death. But to be fair, I didn't like you very much before then."

"I wish you were never born, you little punk."

"And *I* wish you were the one who died that day instead of her."

I see the moment he decides to go for it. I suppose he thinks he has nothing to lose, which I can't exactly say I disagree. I fire my last shot the second my dad reaches for his gun. The bullet lands in the center of his forehead, the light instantly fading from the same hazel eyes I see in the mirror every morning. I feel strangely unaffected by the fact that I just killed my father as I tuck my gun in the back of my jeans and head straight for the closet where Jazz is seeking shelter.

"Jazz."

"Oh my God, are you okay?" Jazz frantically runs her hands over my face, inspecting me for damage.

"I'm fine." I lightly brush the bruise on her jaw. Her eyes are bloodshot from crying, and she's shaking, but she appears mostly okay. "Are you? Did he touch you?"

She shakes her head. "No. He didn't get the chance before you came. Is it... is he..."

I nod. "Dead. Both of them."

Jazz wraps her arms around my neck and pulls me into her, sobbing into my chest. I hold on tightly, never wanting to let go. I sink to the floor and pull her into my lap, giving her time to process everything.

"So, it's over? It's really over?" She sniffles.

I kiss the top of her head. "It's over."

"Kingston?" My PI, John, calls out. "It's clear, Bentley."

"Yo, dawg, you in here?"

Jazz lifts her head. "Bent? In here!"

A moment later, Bentley and John appear in the doorway to the closet.

"Hey, baby girl," Bentley says. "You okay?"

She sniffles. "Yeah."

John nods to me in acknowledgment. "Everything good? I heard shots."

"Yep," I confirm. "Everything okay up top?"

"It's clear. The only other person on the boat was the captain, and I took him down quickly. He's cuffed to one of the railings on the upper deck. Your friend Reed is watching him."

"How did you all get here so quickly?" Jazz questions.

I smooth some hair away from her face and finger the locket around her neck. "I was waiting at the driving school to pick you up. The second I saw your instructor returning without you, I checked the GPS. When I saw you were at the marina, I knew my father had gotten to you somehow. I called the guys right away and told them to meet me here."

"Aren't we offshore? Where'd you get a boat?"

I nod. "About two miles or so. I borrowed some guy's speedboat. He was just getting ready to go out."

Jazz raises her eyebrows. "And he willingly just let you have it, huh?"

I shrug. "I gave him the keys to my Agera as collateral."

She smiles softly. "Thank God you're such a stalkery stalker."

"Don't encourage him, Jazzy." Bent laughs. "What do you want to do now, bro?" He jerks his head over his shoulder, adopting a more serious expression when he gestures to the two dead bodies behind him. "What do we do with them?"

"I'll call it in. I need to check in anyway." John holds up his cell. "If you'll excuse me."

I nod. "Thanks, man."

I take a deep breath and help Jazz stand. Bentley averts his eyes when he notices she's not wearing any pants.

"I... uh... I'll meet you up top, yeah?"

Jazz blushes. "Yeah, Bent. Thanks."

I wait while Jazz gets dressed, then we both exit the master cabin, carefully avoiding the two bodies. Jazz stops at the threshold and turns around to survey the room. She takes a deep breath as her eyes land on Charles, before she grabs my hand and we head up to the bridge together. Right before we get there to meet up with the guys, I pull her to a stop.

Her delicate brows crease. "What's wrong?"

"Nothing," I assure her. "Just needed to say something before we have to deal with the inevitable shitstorm of explaining what happened here."

Jazz runs her finger along the length of my eyebrow, down the bridge of my nose. "What's that?"

I press my lips against hers. "I love you. You know that's never going to change, right?"

She smiles. "I know. Because I feel the same, even if you are an insufferable caveman at times."

I grab her ass as I'm pulling her into me. "You bet this sweet ass I am. Don't expect that to change where you're concerned."

Jazz laughs. "No worries, there, big guy. I'm under no delusions that will *ever* happen."

"As long as we're clear." I wink, before adopting a more serious expression. "You okay?"

"Yeah. I will be." Jazz nods then tugs on my hand. "C'mon, you Neanderthal. Let's get this over with so we can move on with the rest of our lives."

Sounds pretty fucking perfect to me.

chapter twenty-seven

JAZZ

"Jasmine, it's so nice to meet you finally."

I shake Sandra, my new attorney's hand. "You, too. Thanks for meeting with us. I'm sorry we had to keep rescheduling the appointment. It's been a crazy month."

She gives me a sympathetic smile. "No worries, whatsoever. Please, both of you have a seat."

Kingston pulls out a chair for me before taking a seat. It's been two weeks since our fathers' deaths, and those two weeks have been a nonstop whirlwind. When the news broke of the FBI bust, Kingston and I were bombarded with media attempts to book interviews. Once my boyfriend not-so-kindly told them all to fuck off and threatened to sue their asses if they didn't leave him, me, and Ainsley alone, they backed off.

The three of us just moved into the Malibu house, and I finally feel like I can breathe. Ainsley took the whole thing pretty hard, but as Kingston and I had predicted, Reed has been incredibly supportive. I think being in the new place will help all of us because we no longer have to face reminders of our demons on a daily basis.

Sandra opens a file and retrieves a few documents. She sets them in front of me with a pen. "As we discussed over the phone, Mr. Davenport was quite clear on what you were looking to achieve, but I wanted to hear it from you as well."

I bite back a smile as I see Kingston frowning out of the corner of my eye. The boy doesn't like it when someone questions him. When I take his hand and begin rubbing my thumb over his knuckles, his expression softens.

"Of course."

"So, the paperwork you have in front of you is for the legal name change. I just need your signature by each marker, and I'll file those with the court first thing in the morning. Since you're a legal adult, there should be no reason it isn't approved and processed in an expedited manner. Rivera will once again be your legal surname in no time."

"Thank you." I grab the pen and start signing my name by each tab. "And the other matter we discussed?"

"Yes, of course." Sandra removes some more paperwork. "As I was telling Mr. Davenport, we will file a petition for partial custody, but I can't make any promises, since there hasn't been any proven abuse or neglect. The first thing the court will do is appoint a minor's counsel. They serve as a neutral voice for the child, without compromising their rights, emotional well-being, or forcing the child to side with one parent or another. Or, in this case, parent over a sibling. Their mission is to find facts and keep the emotional component out of it. Whoever the court appoints to your sister's case will make sure Belle's health, safety, and welfare are a top priority when making their recommendations to the courts."

"Good," I tell her. "I wouldn't want it any other way."

"That's good to hear," she says. "Now, I like to be upfront with my clients and forewarn you that custody battles can get messy, take a lot of time, and the costs will undoubtedly add up. There are no promises that you'll be granted legal custody or visitation. You'll be fighting an uphill battle from the start considering you're still in high school and don't make enough money from your part-time job to support yourself financially. With that said, would you still like to proceed?"

"Absolutely." I nod. "I need to try."

Sandra smiles. "Okay, then. If—"

"I have a question," Kingston interrupts.

"Go ahead, Mr. Davenport."

"Would it help her case if we got married? California is a community property state, right? So, if we were married, she'd automatically be entitled to half my estate."

My jaw drops. "Kingston! I can't exp—"

Kingston raises his eyebrows expectantly at my attorney. "Well?"

She clears her throat. "Well, yes, that would certainly help. The courts like to see stability—both financial and within the family dynamic—when deciding whether to award custody. Although, community property only applies to assets you acquire *during* the marriage. Anything beforehand would be exempt."

"But if we open a joint bank account, those are considered Jazz's assets, correct?"

Sandra nods. "Correct."

"And if I put her name on the deed to the house, that counts too, right?"

"I'm sorry, *what?*" I interject. "Why would you put my name on the deed to the house?"

My boyfriend smiles. "Why *wouldn't* I? It's as much your house as it is mine. It doesn't matter who paid for it."

"Kingston!"

"Baby, let's not waste this nice lady's time by

talking about it right now, okay?" He winks. "We can fight about it—and make-up—later."

I cover my face with my hands. "Oh, my God. You're so embarrassing sometimes."

My attorney laughs. "You two remind me of my husband and me at your age."

"How long have you been married?" I ask.

"Thirty years next month." She covers the side of her mouth and stage whispers, "And the make-up sex is still as hot as it was in the beginning."

Kingston laughs while I can feel my face flushing.

I give him the stink eye. "I'll deal with you later."

"Anyway..." I jerk my thumb in Kingston's direction. "Before we were so rudely interrupted by this jackass... you were saying?"

"In a nutshell, it isn't going to be easy." She inclines her head in Kingston's direction. "But Mr. Davenport's *suggestions* would certainly help."

I sigh. "Okay. Well, I guess we will discuss this at home and get back to you."

She nods. "Sounds good. In the meantime, I'll file the petition to change your name."

"Thank you."

Kingston and I both stand and shake the attorney's hand before leaving her office.

I punch his arm as soon as we get in the car. "I can't believe you brought that up in there!"

He holds his hands up in surrender. "Whoa, there, Rocky. I was just trying to help."

"Kingston! You can't just suggest we get married to better the odds of winning a custody case."

"I didn't suggest we get married *just* to obtain custody. I did it because we're going to do it regardless, so if it'll help the case, why not get hitched earlier rather than later?"

I rub the bridge of my nose. "I'm sorry, did I miss the part where you *asked* me to marry your ass?"

He smirks. "Oh, baby, like I'd give you a choice."

My stink eye is back. "Bossy ass."

Kingston grabs the back of my head and pulls me into a kiss. "Don't pretend you don't love it."

I pull back and flip him off because he's right; I *can't* say I don't love it.

"Whatever," I mutter. "You're lucky I love you so much."

He laughs. "Not gonna argue with you on that one, babe."

∼

"Have you guys heard?" Ainsley asks.

She bombarded us as soon as Kingston and I got out of the car.

"Heard what?" Bentley asks, getting out of his Porsche from the spot next to ours.

"Headmaster Douche got fired over the weekend," Reed explains.

"What?" Kingston asks. "Why?"

348

Ainsley smiles. "He got caught banging Elinor Jackson in the auditorium."

"Whoa." Bentley whistles. "Wait. Who's Elinor Jackson?"

"A booster's wife." Ainsley's eyes widen. "One of the *biggest* booster's wives! Rumor has it he demanded Headmaster Davis' termination, or he would no longer write checks to the school, *and* he'd use his considerable influence with the other boosters to do the same."

"Damn. Can't say I'll miss that asshat one bit." I shrug.

"Me neither," Kingston agrees.

"Anyway..." Ainsley continues. "They're calling an assembly in the gym in place of first period today. They're going to introduce the new headmaster."

"Well, that didn't take long to find a replacement," Bentley remarks. "Any word on who it is?"

"Someone from another private school in the area, I think." Ainsley nods her head toward the building that houses the gym. Or *Athletic Center* as the Windsor snobs like to call it. "We should get in there so we can find seats together."

When we get to the gym, it's relatively full, so we wind up standing against the side wall instead of trying to find enough room on the bleachers. Mrs. Fuller, one of the administration ladies, walks up to the podium and waits for everyone to settle down before speaking.

"Good morning, students. As some of you may have heard, Headmaster Davis is no longer with us. He has... decided to pursue other opportunities."

"Yeah, other opportunities up Mrs. Jackson's vagina," Ainsley whispers.

Based on the laughter amongst the student body, I'd say similar comments are being passed around.

"Settle down, boys and girls!" Mrs. Fuller demands. Once the room quiets, she continues. "Now, as I was trying to say, we have a new head-master starting today, and I'd like you all to give him a warm Windsor welcome!" She motions to the middle-aged man sitting off to the side. "Please say hello to Headmaster Carrington."

The man joins Mrs. Fuller at the podium and waits for the lackluster applause to end. "Thank you, ladies and gentlemen. I'm very excited to be here. I've been headmaster at Cambridge Prep for the last fifteen years, and while I enjoyed my time there immensely, I couldn't be more excited about this opportunity. I was a Windsor wolf back in the day, and I've always wanted to return to the place where some of my fondest memories have occurred.

"It gives me great pleasure that my daughter will also be a Windsor wolf. I know it's not typical for a student to start so late into the school year, but I'm grateful the board was willing to make an exception so she can graduate from my alma mater." He searches the audience until his eyes lock on someone. "Go ahead, honey. Stand up."

Bentley snorts. "Nothing like being called out by your daddy in front of the whole school."

Ainsley smacks him with the back of her hand. "Be nice, Bentley."

"Honey, don't be shy," the headmaster insists. "Stand up so everyone can see you."

Everyone's gaze follows the headmaster's as his daughter rises from the bleachers. *Damn.* The girl legit looks like Zendaya's curvier little sister. She pushes her long, corkscrew curls to the side and stands tall while the entire room stares at her like an animal in the zoo. I can't exactly blame them—I'm staring too. She's stupid pretty.

"I wouldn't want to be in her shoes," I say. "Gotta give it to her though, she's holding her head high. That takes cojones in this crowd."

"What the fuck?" Bentley whispers.

I feel Kingston stiffen beside me right before he throws his arm out in front of Bentley. "Don't, man. Not here."

"Ladies and gentlemen," the headmaster continues. "I'd like you to meet my daughter, Sydney. She's a senior this year."

I look to my left and see Bentley's nostrils flare while Reed joins Kingston in flanking Bent like they think he's about to flip out or something.

"What is going on?" I whisper to Bentley. "Do you know her or something?"

"Oh, I fucking know her all right," Bentley hisses. "But what I *don't* know is how she's a senior in *high school* when she should be a senior in *college* right now."

I frown in confusion as I lean into Ainsley. "Do you have any idea what he's talking about?"

Ainsley's jaw is slack as she stares at the girl. "Uh..."

"What am I missing?" I'm asking anyone who will answer at this point. "Who is she?"

"She's a goddamn liar and a whore, that's who she is." I'm thrown back by the venom in Bentley's tone. "Fuck this shit. I'm out of here."

Kingston and Reed chase after Bentley as he rushes out of the gym.

"Ainsley? What the hell was that? Who is that girl?"

Ainsley swallows. "So, you know the story my brother told you about that frat party? The night Carissa was attacked?"

"Yeah... but what does that have to do with this?"

Ainsley nods to that Sydney girl. "Because *that* is the supposed sorority girl who had Bentley's dick in her mouth when Carissa walked into that party."

"What?!" My jaw drops. "I thought he hardly remembers anything from that party. How does he remember what she looks like? How do *you* know what she looks like when you weren't even there?"

"Because pictures were circulating *all over* Insta and Snap after it happened before they got flagged. I can't even tell you how many times someone texted Bentley a screenshot of him getting his dick sucked in front of the whole party. Those idiots thought he'd *appreciate* the memory, having no idea we were dealing with Carissa's trauma at the time."

I turn to her. "But why does Bentley seem so angry with the new girl? I don't get that part. She didn't force him to put his dick in her mouth, nor did she have any idea Carissa would show up at that party. Hell, she probably had no idea Carissa even existed."

Ainsley shrugs. "My best guess is because that girl is a walking, talking reminder of what Bentley considers his greatest mistake. He probably thought he'd never see her face again, and he was perfectly okay with that."

I cup a hand over my mouth. "Oh, God. Poor Bent."

Ainsley snorts. "If you're going to feel sorry for someone, don't leave out Sydney Carrington. Because I have a feeling, Bentley is *not* going to handle this very well."

Oh, fuck. I can just imagine. I've witnessed Bentley's mean streak on a few occasions now, and I would *not* want to be on the receiving end of it.

Based on his reaction just now, I'd say he's leaning in that direction.

"Shit," I mutter.

"Yeah..." Ainsley agrees. "As in a *shitshow* is about to begin. I suppose it was only a matter of time before the drama got stirred up again. This is Windsor, after all."

Lovely. Just what we all need: More drama.

epilogue

JAZZ

"Hello?"

"Hello. Is this Jasmine Callahan?"

"This is she." Until my name change is processed, anyway. "Who's calling?"

"My name is Bryant Jacoby. Your father hired me to manage the estate assets. He asked me to reach out to you in the event of his demise."

"Oh." I frown in confusion. I thought the feds seized all of Charles' assets. "What can I do for you, Mr. Jacoby?"

He clears his throat. "Yes... well, I need you to come into the office at your earliest convenience to sign some paperwork."

Now, I'm really baffled. "*What* paperwork?"

Kingston walks through the front door as I'm

pacing the living room. *Who are you talking to?* he mouths.

"I'm sorry, Mr. Jacoby, could you please hold on a moment?"

"Yes, of course."

I press the mute button on my phone to answer Kingston's question. "Charles' attorney. He says he needs me to sign some papers for the estate."

Kingston looks just as confused as I am. "Put him on speaker."

I take the call off mute and press the speaker button as Kingston and I sit on the couch. "Okay, I'm back. Now, what were you saying about some paperwork?"

"For the estate," he repeats. "To disburse funds to you, I need your signature on several documents."

I pinch the bridge of my nose. "Mr. Jacoby, I'm going to be frank. I have no clue what you're talking about. I'm assuming you heard about my father's *transgressions* prior to his death?"

"Well... yes, of course," he sputters.

"So, then perhaps you can understand my confusion. It's my understanding all of Charles Callahan's assets have been frozen until they can figure out which funds were acquired legally—if any—and restitution has been made."

"Yes, that's correct. But I'm not referring to his estate, Miss Callahan. I'm referring to your *mother's*. Mahalia Rivera was your mother, was she not?"

"Yes..." I stretch the word out. "But she didn't *have* any assets. I was a joint owner on her only bank account, and she had less than a hundred dollars to her name when she died."

Mr. Jacoby clears his throat, a little louder this time. "Miss Callahan, I believe you're mistaken. Your mother is the sole owner of several large investment accounts, and she listed you as the sole beneficiary of those accounts. Combined, her total estate is currently valued at two hundred and sixty-two million dollars, give or take."

"What?!" Now it's my turn to sputter. *"How is that possible?"*

Kingston's eyes widen. "Mr. Jacoby, my name is Kingston Davenport. I'm sitting here with Jazz... uh, Jasmine. May I ask you a few questions?"

"Miss Callahan, is it okay to speak freely in front of Mr. Davenport?" he asks.

"Yes, anything," I confirm.

"In that case... please proceed, Mr. Davenport."

"When were these investment accounts originally opened?"

It sounds like the attorney is flipping through some papers. "Throughout a two-year window, approximately sixteen to eighteen years ago. They were each opened with exactly ten million dollars and have grown substantially over the years since."

"Hold on again, please." Kingston presses the mute button and turns to me. "He was hiding assets in her name. If she did sign anything to open those accounts, it might have been under duress, or she didn't know what she was signing. If she didn't know those accounts existed, Charles would've still had full access to them to do anything he pleased, as long as he did it online." Kingston unmutes the call. "Can you tell us if any funds were added over the years?"

"Yes. There were many occurrences. I have quarterly statements from the last seven years. You're welcome to review them when you come in to sign the appropriate paperwork."

"Mr. Jacoby, I'll have to call you back."

"But—"

I end the call before he has a chance to finish his sentence.

"That's blood money, Kingston. I don't want anything to do with it. Why would he leave that money to me?"

"I think in his own fucked up way, he loved you and to Charles, money talks. Maybe this was his way of telling you that."

"I don't want his dirty money!"

"Now, hold up a sec," he says. "What else are you going to do? Hand it over to the feds?"

"That's *exactly* what I'm going to do!" I throw my hands up. "Do you have another suggestion?"

He smiles. "I do."

"What?"

"You can donate it to charities... victims of sex trafficking. Or we can start a new foundation. Think of what good all that money can do, Jazz. Plus, it'd be one helluva fuck you to Charles."

"I don't know..."

Kingston grabs my hand. "Just think about it, okay? If you take the money, you can ensure it goes directly to victims at the hands of people like our fathers. Hell, maybe even our fathers directly. Those women—and some men—can get therapy, have help transitioning back into society. It could even fund private organizations that hunt and dismantle trafficking rings. There's *a lot* that money can do. Will you at least consider it?"

I think about it for a moment. "Okay."

"Okay, you'll consider it?"

I shake my head. "No. Okay, I'll do it. But you have to help me find reputable places for it to go. I want to make sure every dime is given directly to victims in some way."

"I'll be with you every step of the way, Jazz."

"Well, I guess I should call him back and set an appointment to sign those papers, huh?"

Kingston picks up my phone and hands it to me. "And as soon as you're done, we'll start researching charities."

I nod. "Deal."

"What do you think, kiddo?" Kingston sets Belle down inside her new room and watches as she jumps onto her new bed.

"I love it!" she squeals. "It's all mine?"

I smile. "All yours, sweetheart. Anytime your daddy says you can have a sleepover, this is where you'll stay."

Belle runs around her room, checking everything out. "I wish I could live here forever!"

I tilt my head to the side. "But wouldn't you miss your daddy?"

Belle looks away and shrugs. "I dunno. Daddy isn't very nice, and now Monica's gone."

"What do you mean, Monica's *gone?* When did that happen?" I take a seat on the oversized pink chair in the corner of her room. "Come sit with me, sweetheart, and tell me what happened."

Belle climbs onto my lap. "I heard Monica yellin' at him about kissin' the neighbor lady. She never came home from work the other day, and Daddy says she's not comin' back ever."

I sigh. I knew it was only a matter of time before Jerome screwed up that relationship. "I'm sorry, honey. If you ever need to talk about it, we can Face-Time any time you want, day or night, okay?"

She frowns. "Do I hafta go back? Can't I just live with you and Kingston here at the beach?"

I give her a sad smile. "Oh, honey, I wish it were that easy."

"Hey, princess." Kingston kneels in front of us and takes Belle's hand. "If we could make it happen so you could live with us all the time, would you want that? You'd have to switch schools and everything."

I widen my eyes, giving Kingston a *what the hell are you doing?* look. The attorney told us *only a week ago* that it'll be a long, drawn-out process.

"Yes!" Belle nods. "My teacher is a meanie-butt anyway, so I don't care if I hafta get a new one."

Kingston laughs as he kisses Belle on the forehead and does the same to mine. "I'll be back in a little while, okay? I have to run an errand."

I eye him with suspicion. "What *kind* of errand?"

He winks. "It's a surprise."

When Kingston returns several hours later, Belle is sleeping on the couch, with Ainsley snoring lightly beside her. We built sandcastles and played on the beach with Ainsley for a while before the three of us came inside and had a princess movie marathon. Neither one of them made it halfway through the first movie before they crashed.

"Hey," I whisper, not wanting to wake the girls.

"Hey," he whispers back. "Come talk to me out on the back deck."

I carefully extricate myself from Belle's grip and meet Kingston outside.

"Come sit with me, baby." He pats the empty spot on the lounger.

I settle between Kingston's spread legs and lie back on his chest. The sun already set, so we listen to the waves crashing against the shore for a few moments before he speaks.

"So... I did a thing."

I twist around to face him. "What kind of thing?"

"I went to see Jerome."

"What? Why?"

"After what Belle said earlier... I thought about something. I'm surprised it didn't cross my mind earlier, but I had a hunch, and I wanted to see if I was right."

"About what?"

"To see if Belle's father was interested in a private custody negotiation."

"What do you mean?"

"We've been paying him for our weekly visits with her, right?"

"*You've* been paying him," I correct.

Kingston pinches my side. "As I said, *we've* been paying him for weekly visits, right? So it got me thinking. What if he took one lump sum payment, and we'd get to have her every day?"

"I'm not following, Kingston."

"I talked to Sandra on the drive. She confirmed that if Jerome forfeited his parental rights, as Belle's only remaining relative, you could petition to be her legal guardian. Now that you're a legal adult, and you have financial and home stability, there's no reason the court should deny your request. Sandra said she could file an emergency petition to have temporary custody awarded to us while all the legal stuff is processed."

"Are you serious?" I turn around, wrapping my legs around his back. "Did you talk to Jerome about it?"

"Yep." Kingston nods. "He told me if I write him a check, he'll sign whatever he needs to. The asshat felt the need to add that he never wanted a kid, so we were doing him a favor."

I scoff. "Yeah, 'cause *he's* the one we're so concerned about."

"Right." Kingston rolls his eyes. "Anyway... Sandra said she'll draw up the paperwork first thing in the morning. Jerome signs, I wire the money to him, and she's ours."

"Oh, my God." I frown when something comes to mind. "How much did he ask for? How much money does he think she's worth?"

"I told him to name a figure. He said a million. I think he wasn't expecting me to pay up, but when I agreed, the man literally jumped for joy."

"Kingston... I can't let you do that. I'd never be able to pay you back." I trace his eyebrow with my finger. "I love you so much for suggesting it, but..."

He pinches my lips together. "I love her, too, Jazz. I want Belle in our lives, too. I'm doing this just as much for me as I am for you and her. I would've given him my entire fortune if he asked. It's just money."

I laugh. "Only someone who's never struggled to keep food on the table would say something like that."

Kingston gives me a wry look. "Focus on what's important here, Jazz. Belle can be ours. Permanently. All you need to do is say yes."

I crawl onto his lap and pepper his jaw with kisses. "Yes. *All the yeses*."

He smiles. "Hopefully, you're this agreeable when I ask you another life-altering question down the road."

I smile back. "All you need to do is ask."

"Good to know." He winks.

"I wish my mom could see us now. See how happy we all are and that we're together."

I turn my face into Kingston's palm as he places it on my cheek. "I'd like to think both our moms can see us. Hell, they're probably hanging out in a fluffy cloud together, with their arms around each other like in that photo on the mantle, gushing about how their babies fell in love."

I smile because I can picture it perfectly. "You think so?"

"I really do." He nods slowly, searching my eyes. "I fucking love you so much, Jazz. I'm never going to stop telling you that, so if you have a problem with it, you'd better get over that shit right now."

I laugh because only this man could pull off throwing curse words into a romantic statement like that. "Don't worry, Caveman, I'm not going anywhere."

"If you try, I'll—"

I roll my eyes playfully. "Yeah, yeah, I know. You'll hunt my ass down."

His beautiful greenish-gold eyes twinkle with amusement. "You can bet on it, sweetheart."

～

NOTE FROM THE AUTHOR: Thank you for going on Jazz & Kingston's journey with me! While their story is complete, I wasn't quite ready to say goodbye to these characters, so Bentley has his own book called BROKEN PLAYBOY!

～

also available by laura lee

Standalone Novels

♥Beautifully Broken

♥Happy New You

♥Redemption

GO TO: https://www.subscribepage.com/LauraLeeBooks to sign up for Laura's newsletter and you'll be the first to know when she has a sale or new release!

about the author

Laura Lee is the *USA Today* bestselling author of steamy and sometimes ridiculously funny romance. She won her first writing contest at the ripe old age of nine, earning a trip to the state capital to showcase her manuscript. Thankfully for her, those early works will never see the light of day again!

Laura lives in the Pacific Northwest with her wonderful husband, two beautiful children, and three of the most poorly behaved cats in existence. She likes her fruit smoothies filled with rum, her cupboards stocked with Cadbury's chocolate, and her music turned up loud. When she's not chasing the kids around, writing, or watching HGTV, she's reading anything she can get her hands on. She's a sucker for spicy romances, especially those that can make her laugh!

For more information about the author, check out her website at: www.LauraLeeBooks.com

You can also find her "working" on social media quite frequently.
Facebook: @LauraLeeBooks1
Instagram: @LauraLeeBooks
Twitter: @LauraLeeBooks
Verve Romance: @LauraLeeBooks
Reader's Group: Laura Lee's Lounge
TikTok: @AuthorLauraLee

acknowledgments

To my husband, Tad: You are my rock. My soulmate. My ride or die. Thank you for being you.

To my beautiful children: You two are my world, even when you're driving me nuts.

To my friend and fellow author, Julia Wolf: Thank you for your brainstorming genius. Once again, this book wouldn't be out in the wild without you.

To my lovely betas Crystal, Julia, Alley & Heather: Thank you for being the first to read Fallen Heirs. Your feedback was invaluable.

To my author pals Julia, Heather, Sylvie, Stephanie, Alley, Molly, Elizabeth, Marika, Susannah, Krista, Kelsey, Brenda, Sara, Elle, Eva, Cassy, Tracy, Kristy, Lindsey, Samantha, Kristi, E.M., Dani, Carmel, Isabella, Cassie, Danielle, Jami, Brooke, Lauren, and anyone else I may have

missed. (Please don't take it personally—my brain is mush more often than not these days): Thank you for always being there when I need encouragement, someone to vent to, a brainstorming partner, a marketing partner, or just a good laugh or friendly face. You're all incredibly talented and awesome human beings. 2020 has been an absolute shitshow and you ladies have helped make it better.

To Christine and the Wildfire crew: Thank you for bringing me on board. I've learned so much in a short time and I can't wait to see what we can do together in the future!

To all the seriously awesome bloggers & bookstagrammers in the book world: I appreciate you so much, as a reader and a writer. We could all use a little escapism in the world right now, and you help with that tremendously.

To my incredible ARC team and Loungers: Thank you for always bringing a smile to my face. I love being able to interact with you on a regular basis.

To my editor, Ellie McLove of My Brother's Editor: Thank you for dealing with my inability to meet a deadline. No matter how late I am, you never fail to make it work. I appreciate everything you do.

Last but never least, to my readers: Thank you, thank you, thank you for sticking with me through the end of Jazz and Kingston's journey. I am honored and humbled by your enthusiasm for this series. In case you missed my note at the end of the story, Bentley is getting his own standalone book! I didn't originally plan to do that, but your love for him and this world got me thinking about all the different ways I can get that boy his own HEA. More details on that coming soon!

Whether you've been with me for a while, or you found me through this series, I appreciate your support more than words can say. I couldn't do what I love for a living without you. XOXO

Printed in Great Britain
by Amazon